BE FIRST OR BE DEAD

A hard-boiled, political, international thriller

I0461002

NIK KRASNO

Hosting guest - star contributor (author of the Chapter "**Insomnia**")
Best-selling author - **Alex Shaw**

Introducing his **guest star character** – the undefeatable **Aidan Snow**

NEPLOKHO PUBLISHING

Oligarch Series:

RISE OF AN OLIGARCH, The Way It Is: Book 1,
2014

MORTAL SHOWDOWN, Oligarch series: Book 1½,
2015

BE FIRST OR BE DEAD, Oligarch series: Book 2½,
2016

ISBN 978-0-9930827-8-8

If you are Quentin Tarantino, Guy Ritchie or an aspiring director interested in adapting this book into a movie, please, feel free to contact the author.

This is a work of fiction. Names, characters, businesses, organizations, countries, places, events and incidents either are the product of the author's imagination or are used fictitiously. Any resemblance to actual persons, living or dead, corporations, organizations, entities, events or locations is entirely

Map of Ukraine from The World Factbook:

*"Kyiv" is often spelled "Kiev" in the West and in this story

Oligarch - *a person who belongs to a small group of people who govern or control a country, business, etc.*

Summary of the Previous Book in the Series

Mikhail (Misha, Michael) Vorotavich is a Ukrainian oligarch, who's just triumphed over his nemesis, a former KGB chief, known as the Puppet Master. Not only is Michael victorious, but he has also secured the top spot on the *Forbes* Billionaires List — an ambition he's fostered for a long time.

Being the richest person on Earth, having dealt in his own harsh way with most of his enemies, and being only forty-something with just a slightly visible scar above his right eye and a bullet stuck in his brain after an assassination attempt, Misha has everything to enjoy a wealthy, worriless life, and his new status.

The final transaction that boosted his rise in the charts involved Ms Greenberg — an old, super-rich aristocrat. Misha suspects that she belongs to the clandestine clique of billionaire dynasties, which just might have a much larger influence on global economical and political dynamics than many known public political and economic figures.

Prologue

The brief mix of a dream with the reality was confusing. At first I didn't understand why my wife had elbowed me.

"It's your phone. Shut it down! It's 2 a.m.," she growled.

Another ring. *Fuck, why didn't I put it on silent?*

The screen read "David".

If my best friend was calling at this hour, something had happened.

"What is it, Dave?" I tried to restart my brain, which was still half asleep and wandering dreamland.

"Michael, turn on your TV and see whether you need to find shelter. I'm in the Bay Area on that IT conference you've sent me to and it's a fucking disaster here. A Russian ballistic missile just fell into the ocean near the beach. Some saw it approaching. There might be more. The entire city is in panic!" David's tone poured a verbal bucket of water on me.

While listening to him, I walked to the living room and switched the TV on. It occupied the entire wall in my London mansion.

I lowered the cell phone and watched a falling missile and its contrail, which was probably filmed by somebody on his cell phone, since the picture was shaky.

"Thanks, for the heads-up, man. What the fuck is going on? Stay somewhere safe. I'll check on London and get back to you later." I killed the connection.

My sleepiness was gone completely. I retrieved a bottle of tonic from the fridge, keeping my eyes on the TV, as the BBC news channel went into science fiction mode, broadcasting surrealistic stuff from several different places at once.

The BBC reporter from Kiev eagerly reported that,

"At 05:00, the Guards Tank Division of the Russian army crossed the Minsk treaty armistice lines from the unrecognized Donetsk People's Republic. They advanced into the territories under Ukrainian control, invaded Mariupol to the southwest, and attacked Ukrainian defense lines on other directions. Russian artillery and air-force have added heavy barrages and air strikes on the Southwest front."

Holy shit! I had business in Mariupol.

The camera moved and showed a crater behind the reporter, who explained,

"Concurrently with the ground attack in the Eastern Ukraine, two rockets fired from the territory of the Russian Federation hit Kiev, the capital of Ukraine."

BBC switched scenery and showed the Pentagon. This time, a female journalist spoke.

"A Squadron of MiG–35s crossed the Bering Strait, entered US airspace over Alaska, and left it after thirty-seven seconds. The US air-force, which scrambled an interception squadron, chose not to pursue.

The ballistic rocket fired from the Kamchatka air-space unit base of the Russian Armed Forces, fell into the ocean just two miles short of US territorial waters near San-Francisco. Its interception by a US military satellite failed.

The President of the United States was updated and a Pentagon spokesman is expected to go live with an announcement as consultations proceed."

Further reports showed grocery stores in the US and Russia flooded with people who snatched up canned food and other long-lasting supplies.

Just like on 9/11 in 2001, I stayed glued to the TV screen for hours, trying to grasp how the world I thought I'd known had suddenly changed so drastically.

Every now and then, the news tickers updated the unfolding chain of events. The security threat level in all NATO countries was immediately raised to an exceptional level, and emergency preparations ensued.

It looked like Armageddon. World War III seemed inevitable...

Chapter 1 - Ibiza

Several days earlier

It was a fat line. Third for this evening. *Damn, what a good feeling!* I enjoyed the instant numbness spreading through my face as a pleasant side-effect.

Am I getting close to an overdose? I thought, wiping my nose with the back of my hand.

I hadn't done coke for years. It would be a pity to die or fall into another coma just when I started to enjoy reaching the top of the economic heap. They say coke makes you a god. *That's true, I'm an alpha male, I'm a god! And I'm also too fucked up to be coming up with such ideas.* I smiled. If I wasn't high I would probably worry about my current state, but now I just enjoyed the evening. How could anyone not enjoy it? I was at *Pacha*—Ibiza's best nightclub—on coke, with good friends, and endless opportunities to lay a goddess or two as the night unfolded.

Whatever I was, I felt an energy surge spread through my body, and my mind became super-clear. The light trance music grew louder and neon lights brighter. Life was good. The VIP lounge formed half a balcony overlooking the dancing crowd.

I waved my hand for attention. "Hey, Emil, I'm going to dance it up a bit. Wanna come?"

Emil was a tall, smug, dark-haired guy, four years older than me, but unlike me, without grey hair yet

(*what a cunt!*), the only son of Juliette Greenberg—
my new partner in Gazdiesel. He was the ultimate
British playboy. Handsome, sybaritic, aristocratic, yet
powerful and enigmatic. His family's bank and I
shared equal amounts of stock in this Russian
carbonate monster, while I also shared my leisure
with the bank's proud, prospective heir. We hung out
a lot lately, as my usual bunch had shrunk
considerably: David being derailed by his marriage;
John—the American banker who used to work for
me—by early retirement; Denis—by lying at the
bottom of the Med near the French Riviera, and
Boris—by governing the embattled Luhansk district.
Arthur was around, but you can hardly rely on a
mean, silent guy as good company for debauchery.

"No, mate, you go bring us some birds. You're too
old for dancing; remember that. Don't do anything
obscene, otherwise it'll be all over the news even
before you zip your fly."

"Shit, man, I came here to feel unrestrained. Don't
spoil it for me. I don't wanna be a VIP tonight, just a
dancing junkie. It's dull in here; I'm going out."

"Bring some Russians over, I feel Slavic tonight," he
yelled at my back.

I regretted that David, my best friend, had invested
so much into his new family and hadn't come along.
If he was here, I would just need to change condoms
every hour or so, what with the assortment of chicks
he usually brought. I could bet that David equally

11

regretted his artificial abstinence because of this marriage disaster.

I should take some pics of the fabulous chicks around here to tease him later.

My trip onto the dance floor was quick. I lingered a bit by the bar, soaking up the atmosphere.

Then I spotted them.   Three blondes, no— goddesses really—almost my height, seemingly unsure what to order. *You wanted Russians, Emil?*

"Hey pretty ladies, order whatever you want. I'll treat you to a drink and then take you to the club's best lounge. The DJ will be joining us soon, and I have something much more interesting than the bar can offer." It wasn't a suggestion; it was an order.

They were used to it. More so, they *expected* it. They came here alone, not just to dance, but to find an alpha male who first and foremost should be rich. The good thing about Russians was they knew how to value luxury— and maybe it was the only thing they truly valued. And they probably figured out what I was hinting at that was more interesting than drinks.

But they needed to play it cool.

"Thanks, but we don't know you." The closest blonde reacted with phony disinterest, but took my drink offer.

"He *does* look familiar," the tallest girl chimed in with more excitement. "Aren't you that guy from oil, or football, or something?"

"Something of that sort. I play hockey and extract coal."

They giggled and, not that I expected otherwise, the ice between us had finally broken.

"Mikhail is the name. Come."

They exchanged glances, grabbed the drinks, and followed, still feigning reluctance.

Upstairs I introduced them to Emil, who welcomed them by smacking his lips. I also mentioned Arthur, lurking in the darkest corner of the prestigious VIP cabin, the only one in the club. Other VIP areas were being sold, but this one was never for sale, and was kept by the club owners for very special guests.

Knowing what a stunning impression Emil usually made on women, I suspected they would smack their lips, too.

I doubted Arthur would take any active part in chatting them up, but lucky for him, there were three, making an equal matchup, unless I decided to take a couple.

I unscrewed some fancy vodka, frowning at the club's choice of booze, and poured myself and Emil a shot. We clinked glasses with each of the girls.

"To you, ladies. I wish us all an unforgettable night."

Emil and I downed the shots while the ladies sipped. *Still playing shy, huh?*

"Wanna remain incognito or introduce yourself?" I asked, seeing that Emil was taking out the coke again.

"I'm Zhanna." The tallest smiled. I understood how a smile could light up a face, and at that very moment, I'd made my choice. She probably noticed a sparkle in my eyes, as her smile became broader.

The two others were Dina and Natasha. The last one obviously caught Emil's attention. He showed her the bag in a speechless question.

Not that fast.

"Hey ladies, my friend Emil here is a bit of a pervert — or an aesthete, as some may argue, and cannot sniff unless it's from a girl's nipple. Who's gonna sacrifice one for the greater good?"

"O-ho, he must be popular among women, your friend," Natasha said playfully. Maybe because she'd noticed how lustfully Emil looked at her.

"He is. And you know why?"

"Why?"

"Because he always has the latest model of vibrator in his pocket."

"Oh, that's so gross," she objected, but laughed anyway.

Obviously they were not appalled by an offer of tit sniffing, although at first they released some uneasy chuckles. We were just getting into the right mood. They wanted coke and cock as well. I took the bottle of vodka, filled Emil's glass and mine, and poured the rest into the bucket of ice. I spun the now-empty bottle on the table. It stopped on Dina. I expected her to protest, but instead she got up. First uneasily, but then harmoniously with the music, she started to unzip her dress from behind.

"Hey Emil, help her. You see she needs some help, man."

Emil helped her all right, also unfastening her bra once her arms were out of the dress. Her dance became more ecstatic, yet she swayed to the rhythm with all its variations. The coke kicked in, and I felt mesmerized by her elegant, voluptuous shadow in the twilight and all the neon lights sparkling from behind it. After the music reached a crescendo, she turned to us slowly, hands raised above her head, still dancing and wriggling to the music. Wow, what a great set she had. I started to reconsider my choice of Zhanna.

Her long, erect nipples were firm as bullets. Emil poured some powder on each, spilling some on the floor as if it was nothing. He sniffed from one and wiped his nose afterwards. I was already up for the second tit.

It was the girls' turn now, so Emil arranged a fat row for each on the table and rolled a 500-euro banknote for them. They inhaled the lines eagerly and I assumed that we'd tuned up.

Spotting Dina trying to put her bra back on, I held my hand up.

"No, darling, that won't be necessary. You can't hide them as they are now an instrument...er, a launching pad for our highness and horniness as well."

Zhanna interrupted. "Hey, I remember who you are. You're Mikhail Vorotavich — an oil magnate living in London. You look younger than in the photos. I read about you, though you're not portrayed well in the Russian press."

"Well, I guess you can rebuff that when you return to Russia and share your own experiences. Interested in oil magnates, Zhanna?"

"No, it's just that I'm working as a head of department with your biggest competitor." She smiled again and I melted—hypnotized.

"Head of department? If I was your boss, you'd have been a president of the company a long time ago."

"Maybe I'll be the president of yours?" She smiled slyly and somehow erotically.

"A smile or two like this one and that's the most plausible scenario." I half-hugged her from behind and sat closer.

Seeing that Emil was engaged with the two others, we drank with our arms crossed, followed by a long, sweet kiss. Damn, she was tasty.

A friend of mine from New York who told me about nipple sniffing in the first place claimed coke made them wet. I hoped to check that out.

Emil left for the bathroom with Dina and returned with a broad smile some twenty or thirty minutes later. I thought I would follow his example with Zhanna, but although she kissed me eagerly, she thwarted my attempt to get into her panties and scorned my offer to get some solitude in the bathroom.

"You are mistaken about us, Misha. Although my friends are in a mischievous mood, don't expect sex from me here."

Fair enough. I had few more venues for later, so I switched my attention to the group again, as I was not at the age where just kissing without the natural follow-up was that enjoyable.

***

After hanging out for a couple of more hours, going back and forth to the dance floor, downing drinks, doing coke, occasional kisses and a quick chat and sniff with Eclectico, the resident DJ, I noticed Arthur's growing disinterest and dragged the entire group to Emil's yacht, which served as our common residence in Ibiza.

The yacht was anchored within walking distance. We heard a huge "wow" from each of them when we approached—it was impossible to miss the yacht's size and opulence. If they had any doubts, the yacht and Emil's trained staff dispelled them.

At 3 a.m., we still had a couple of hours before the after-party at Space—the most famous after-party club in Ibiza. I didn't know why anyone bothered searching for youth elixir when it had already been found, and it was coke. I felt light-headed in horny anticipation. Emil took Dina to his president's compartment and asked Natasha to join them, but Zhanna insisted Natasha would be coming with me and her instead.

At first spooked by that idea, I was speechless when I came out of the bathroom in my suite and found them both naked, arranging another line on the bar stand of my cabin. The blonde, identical lower haircuts turned me on immediately. *You probably use the same barber, huh?*

Seeing those sweeties, I could understand why cunnilingus was popular with some folks. Not something I liked to do, though. I almost tore my own clothes off and rejected another line—it might've killed my erection. My nose was already running anyway.

Not ready to get in yet, I pulled them both to the shower and turned the water on. Natasha went down on me, while I caressed Zhanna with my hand and her gorgeous nipples with my lips, causing her to pant from pleasure and anticipation. On coke it would be hard to get it on, and harder to come, but I was eager to try, and Natasha seemed eager to beat the side effects. I hoped Emil didn't have cameras in this compartment, as I would prefer that this session never be recorded except in my memory, where I knew it would be ensconced forever.

It felt never-ending. What an orgy that was! Actually, maybe I'd have liked a recording.

After a long, enjoyable time and a shower, we were ready to head out again. We knocked on Emil's door, which disgorged a fucked-up Emil with Dina hanging onto his arm. Nevertheless, they were in good spirits, so Space, where a table for us should've been already arranged, was our next stop.

In Ibiza, it doesn't matter if you are fifteen or one hundred and fifteen, if you've already made the mistake of going in the first place, you don't sleep. Well, maybe drunken Brits hanging out in San Antonio—a booze town on the other end of the island—do.

Once settled around our table, and anticipating the imminent sunrise, I leaned back in my chair and closed my eyes, moving my head in rhythm to the house music. This was a fabulous night and we'd just anchored few hours ago. We still had Amnesia and Privilege —the biggest Ibiza venues ahead.

I felt like talking, so I opened one eye to check whether Emil was in a condition to chat. It seemed so, as he was pouring martinis. The girls had left the table and joined the dancing crowd.

Emil felt like sharing experiences. "Hey man, you've got my respect. In just the couple of hours since we docked, you already procured some gorgeous babes. You're my man! This Dina is something else. I might even keep her around for a while. Twenty-two years old. Fresh, tight, a real gazelle. The things she does, not everyone can even think of. Did you do both the others?"

"Yep—more precisely, they did me. Although only Zhanna is to my taste, but this Natasha would be so unhappy if I didn't, since Arthur cold-shouldered her."

"What a considerate guy, you are, Misha. Gonna arrange her a job, buy her a flat, finance her abortion?" Emil was a caustic motherfucker. Worse even than me.

"I hope that it never comes to the last bit, as I always use a rubber, but I do feel some pity for those poor ladies. Rich or not, I remained a simple proletarian."

"Ha-ha-ha. Don't ski tonight any more. Don't pretend to be a miner while wearing fancy clothes and a watch that probably costs ten miners' annual salaries!"

"And this bothers me. What do you think? You know I had a little argument about communism versus capitalism with your former partner, the Puppet Master, before he perished in that unfortunate accident. He was a fervent adept of the former. And you know what? I'm not sure he's completely wrong, now that I'm thinking about it." I loved coke for the clarity of mind.

"Interesting. What's on your mind? If anyone overhears the crap we're talking about at five-thirty in the morning at Space, he'd freak out." He burst out laughing again.

20

"Sometimes you just need some good house music for a good talk." I drummed with my fingers on the table. "Anyways, what I was thinking is that the wealth distribution is not fair. Maybe communists also start from this thought. Think about it, I can't sail fifteen yachts or fly fifteen private jets simultaneously. I can barely do two chicks in your shower at my age."

Emil liked that one. As he nodded respectfully, I continued.

"You know, maybe ninety percent of the accumulated wealth of the super-rich sits somewhere hidden, often untaxed in the bank or in investment funds, searching for this or that investment, in order to bring more money. The only thing they care about is that their wealth would accrue few percent a year. They would never use it for something that matters and it'll just pass on to their descendants and they would do the same and so on."

"So, what's wrong with that?" Emil frowned. "Why can't I inherit from my family?"

"I'm not talking about you specifically, but a few things are wrong. Imagine how many people are in need of a loan, of a helping hand, of cash which they need like a breath of fresh air. How can I sit in the same car with my driver and exchange jokes, knowing that although he gets a good salary from me, he sometimes struggles to pay his mortgage? Maybe it's just me, but I can't. I tend to help him and others in my circle. You see, it doesn't seem logical to keep all this money tucked away, never to be used for something special, while many are so short of much smaller amounts. Think of the trillions of dollars—tantamount to the collective budget of half of the world—stashed away somewhere that don't do anything. That's inefficient on a huge scale. It's infuriating, if you think about it. One of the functions of society or the state is to redistribute wealth more fairly and that doesn't happen. In Reagan's time, they said that it was necessary to help businessmen and then something would trickle down to the laymen. But it's not happening. Each penny gets stashed in those hidden, unidentified, non-reported accounts. Something must be changed, and on the highest level. The few who understand it donate most of their wealth, and it's a good starter. Maybe we need to make it mandatory."

"Misha, I start to see Lenin in you. Don't expropriate my yacht, please. We might get lucky there a couple of more times while in Ibiza."

"You'd be the last one, don't worry, Emil. I also fuck there. Let me finish. So what I was thinking is that we need to change the rules. The capital should be allowed to be accumulated, let's say to the maximum luxury level times three, so you can always buy three yachts, three planes, whatever. Let's say one hundred million dollars. The rest, unless you invest in production, industry or something helpful, you need to give away to the people of your choice that need the money. And I'm talking about considerable amounts, so you really help to change their lives. They, in their turn, should commit to pay you, let's say two percent of what they earn for the rest of their lives, so it won't be a totally free ride. Thus, each would have a 'family' of dependents, let it be fifteen, twenty, one hundred and fifty, or whatever, but you would know that you helped real people to make their lives better. Imagine, instead of so many people hating you for being rich and suspecting some foul play on your part while making your fortune, you'd have a devoted clan of your supporters, followers and dependents, which, if you are decent with them when giving them the money, may even die for you. What do you say?" I hadn't even noticed I'd become so high.

But Emil did. "I say drugs don't do you any good. This undermines the entire system we built and fostered for centuries. What about the sanctity of private property?"

"Just bullshit. Nothing else."

"Ha-ha, really? But that's capitalistic communism you're suggesting—to let people chase the dollar, but to redistribute evenly above a certain ceiling."

I laughed. "Nice definition, I see what you mean. Sort of. So what's wrong with that? You know, when I reminisce about my childhood before my father was taken away by the KGB, it wasn't that bad. For the

23

sake of argument: we were all equal; no one was rich. Although our life was quite modest, no one was starving. There were no beggars or homeless on the streets. There was no unemployment. The inherent competitiveness was not about money, but about sports, girls, audacity. You know what the main problem with communism was?"

"What?" Emil wasn't particularly interested.

"That it was tried in Russia. I'm from the same roots, and I can tell that Russians are cruel — savage even. Stalin is believed to have killed millions of people for the idea and because of his own paranoia. If communism was implemented in a subtler society, it could've been a resounding success."

"Misha, don't be nostalgic. We are not gonna let anything of the sort happen. Period. It's against our interests."

"But you do realize that the majority might support the idea?"

"Maybe. But do you think my driver, cook, and bodyguard should decide for me how much money I can have, and how much to give them?"

"No, but shouldn't the majority decide? Instead, what happens is that a small bunch of super-rich decide for all the rest. My theory sounds fair. We'll have a clear set of rules."

"Nonsense. Everybody would abuse them and you, Misha, I'm sure, would be the first."

I laughed again. "True, but that's because I hate rules—"

"But why would anyone care to create a large business to compete and dethrone your arse from *Forbes*, if you have a cap?"

"I'll tell you why. For the sport. To win. And also to help those people. You know, it's fun to help real people. Not to donate to charities for tax benefits where half of the money is stolen or wasted on fat managers' salaries. I'm talking about real people from your day-to-day circle. Think about it, Emil, it's even disastrous for the economy and business that so much money sits somewhere frozen, doing nothing, when so many people need it. If you don't offer a fair solution, they would come and take it without asking us, because they know where to take, and from whom."

"Ah, you are afraid, my friend, that's why you think this way. Don't you worry about that, Misha. Unlike Russia, we haven't had revolutions in the West for at least two hundred years. We've had this system running for centuries and we know how to steer it. Who's gonna promote silly ideas? You won't. I'm sure of that. Peoples' incumbents'? Just a fallacy. When's the last time you saw a poor or working class lawmaker or parliament member anywhere after the USSR dissolved? Exactly, nowhere. Do you think a millionaire can truly represent steel workers? Only for pretence."

"That's a sad truth of our world." I sighed. "Anyway, what's *your* vision and plans, Mr. Russian-loving aristocrat?"

"Us? Oh, we plan to expand, Misha. Big time—"

The girls returned from the dance floor, and Zhanna jumped on my knees, trying to grab my martini.

"Hey easy, hen, there's plenty for everyone. You don't need to drink from my glass. Natasha, pass over some glasses."

What a night, I thought for umpteenth time. *Ibiza is a magic island.*

On top of my high rapidly turning into an unpleasant comedown, something sat heavily on my heart. Maybe it was about Emil's expansion plans? I abandoned that thought, as it was hard to be worried about anything in Ibiza.

The girls, still high and having an entire, all-inclusive, paid-up table at their disposal, preferred to party on while Emil and I called it quits and headed back to the yacht. The first night had been extraordinary; what could the second possibly bring us?

Chapter 2 - Insomnia (courtesy of Alex Shaw)

I watched fingers of watery light feel their way into the darkness across the marble floor like an animal sniffing out its prey; I rolled out of bed without waking my guests, and padded to the balcony. I'd been unable to sleep a wink, and now dawn had arrived. The air was fresh and tainted with the scent of the sea. I breathed in deeply and yawned— then winced—my jaw still hurt. Outside, the town was asleep and the water was still, save for a pair of fishing boats silently heading for the horizon. I envied their simple, stress-free existence. Then and there, I vowed that when I retired, I'd get a large yacht, replacing the one destroyed by a Russian torpedo, and spend my time roaming from island to island. Who really needed money and power? I closed my eyes and listened to the sea lapping against the boats in the harbor and the rhythmic knocking of the pontoons. I felt the warmth of the sun on my face and sensed an orange vista through my eyelids. I slowly opened them again, content.

A noise came from the bed; a snore. I turned to look back into the room. Both ladies were out for the count. I envied their calm, seemingly hangoverless sleep. The coke had kept me wired and awake. They were beautiful, and the sunlight outlined their naked forms perfectly. Up until the fight, it had been another perfect night—almost *too* perfect.

Having two new, naked women in the room just like the night before was becoming a habit.

My mind wandered back to a few hours before, when I'd been sitting at our private table in Amnesia, one of the most awesome clubs on the island.

***

Two men, shirts stretched by their large physiques, were at the end of the bar, glaring at me. They had the shaven heads and flattened noses of hired muscle. I'd ignored them and remained in my seat, sipping champagne. Normally I was a vodka or cognac man, but the girls had wanted champagne, and who was I to refuse them? The nearer of the two men who had a livid scar on his left cheek approached me, his rolling gait betraying a level of self-belief rarely seen outside of a boxing ring.

"You want women? I have women, the best on the island." The words were in English, and the accent Russian.

"No thank you, I'm fine."

Unperturbed, he pointed at my bottle sitting in the ice bucket. "I see you are a man who loves expensive things, and believe me, my girls are better than the finest caviar you will have ever tasted."

"You mean they smell of fish?" I quipped and instantly regretted it.

His eyes narrowed. "So, you are a funny man? You want to make fun of Vladimir and his beautiful ladies is that it?"

"I'm sorry."

"You are sorry?" He nodded. "Sorry is good. Perhaps you are after boys? Is that what you prefer? It makes no difference to me. I can see that you look a little, how to say in English — 'blue'. You are blue boy? Gay man, yes?"

I looked him up and down and chuckled. "No."

Vladimir's face darkened. "You again make fun?"

"I'm having fun." I raised my glass.

Vladimir beckoned his colleague over. "This is Oleg. Together we run the fun on the island. You understand me?"

I was starting to, and I didn't like it. I'd sent my own bodyguards and Arthur away. I'd told them to take the night off since Arthur really hated club-hopping and we didn't expect any trouble. They could be trusted, but I hadn't wanted them to lie for me when my wife asked what we'd been doing. I was out with Emil and he'd found a few "party ladies", as he called them.

My eyes darted around. Where was Emil?

"You understand?" Vladimir moved closer, obviously agitated.

"I understand. You run the fun." I tried to remain calm, while realizing that time and again, problems tend to occur out of the blue.

"Correct." Vladimir smiled, and I thought he looked like a pig. "Fun costs money, and I know you are a rich man. If you pay us, we can provide you with some real fun, or we can ensure that your fun is not interrupted."

"That would be very bad," Oleg said, his voice sounding too high for such a large body. "Having your fun interrupted can be very painful."

Money, the cause for most of the world's violence, the rest being caused by religion. "How much?"

"Just one moment." Vladimir held up a meaty palm. The two men conferred in Russian. I of course understood, but pretended not to. "Five hundred euros would make your evening very memorable, for the right reasons."

"Happy fun, for you and your friends," Oleg clarified.

It wasn't the money that was the issue. I had enough in my pocket to buy a small country. Well, almost. It was the concept that I took exception to. I slipped my hand slowly into my pocket and felt the soft leather of my Italian wallet. I didn't want the fun interrupted by some pigs. *We can call it a loan.* A wicked smile played on my lips as I imagined how Arthur would force these clowns to pay me back a grand each and beg for forgiveness.

The two Russians advanced.

"Simon, is that you?" A friendly yet forceful voice called out in English.

Both Russians turned to come face to face with a dark-haired man who, although not as wide as they were, was taller and looked like he knew his way around a gym.

"No it is not Simon," Vladimir said.

The new arrival smiled and stepped around the Russians. His gaze locked onto mine, and he winked. "Simon, that *is* you. How are you, my friend?"

I took the hint. "Great, take a seat have a drink—"

"Don't tell me you've forgotten me already? We met at the British Consulate."

On hearing the words 'British Consulate' the pair of Russians recoiled like vampires exposed to sunlight. Harassing diplomats wasn't the wisest move.

The man sat next to me, gazing at Vladimir and Oleg. "Was there something you wanted?"

"No. We were mistaken." Vladimir nudged Oleg, and they returned to the bar.

"Thanks," I said, "but I had that covered."

"I could tell."

I poured a glass of champagne and handed it to my new friend. "I'm Mikhail, and you are?"

"Aidan Snow. You are from Ukraine. I know who you are."

"Irish?"

"English. My mother just liked the name. Cheers."
He drank.

"So those two are the local 'Krisha'?"

Snow smiled at my use of the Russian word for *roof* used as slang to mean 'protection racket'. "That and more. Look, if you want a quiet night I'd suggest you go elsewhere. That pair are seriously bad news."

"I'll bear that in mind."

"Fine." Snow emptied his glass and stood. "See you later."

I watched him walk away. The two Russians were back at the bar. They stepped back as he passed them en route to the other side of the club. Were they afraid? Something was wrong, and it annoyed me not knowing what, but I had better things to waste energy on. I shrugged and refilled my glass as Emil returned with a girl on each arm and a third carrying another bottle in an ice bucket. The girls draped themselves over the soft seating. One had white powder on her cleavage and the other, powder around her mouth. Emil sat heavily next to me. I noticed white powder around the crotch of his black linen suit.

He caught my gaze. "What? You've never heard of a snow-job, old boy?"

I almost spat out my champagne.

***

Booze and birds. Emil was a wild man trapped in the body of a British aristocrat. The proud torchbearer for the excesses of all who had gone before him. Last night had been fun, but I couldn't keep up. Perhaps I was getting old, or just restless? I looked back out to sea again. The color of the water had changed as the sun had risen higher. It was going to be another beautiful day, but unless I got some sleep, I'd be wiped out. Perhaps more booze would do the trick?

A bottle of Courvoisier XO stood on the glass balcony table, beckoning me like a siren onto the rocks. I couldn't resist. The cork made a slight *pop* as I pulled it out. A long slug caused a wave of warmth to wash over me. I instantly felt more relaxed. I padded back into the room, sat on the bed, and ran my hand across the round buttock of the nearest girl. Thoughts of her on top of me brought a grin to my face, which in turn made my jaw hurt. I held up the cognac bottle and silently toasted her skills. Lying on my back, I closed my eyes, willing my brain to give in to sleep, but a myriad of thoughts ran through my head. I tried to latch onto my memories, hoping they would help me to doze off, but sleep refused to come.

The last few months had been crazy, rewarding—in fact, the best ever. My rivals and my business enemies had been dealt with, and I'd made it. I'd fulfilled my ambition, my dream of becoming one of the mega-rich. I damn well deserved to celebrate. So I had. I put my hand on the girl's butt again. No, I wouldn't wake them, I'd sleep and then we'd celebrate more.

There was a buzzing. I opened my eyes and saw that it was coming from my cell phone. And then remorse hit me. It was Masha, my wife and the mother of my children. Sex and love were two separate ships sailing on the same sea. Sometimes they sailed together, and other times alone. Masha was proud of my achievements, but she hated my excesses. She loved me, and I her, but sometimes I couldn't stop myself. I was a bad husband, and I detested being so. My life had been threatened on more than one occasion, and she understood that I needed to party away the fear before I could return to her as the husband she loved. It was messed up, and if I was being truthful with myself, *I* was messed up. God, I loved Masha and our children more than life itself. This had to stop. Sometime? I made a vow. The irony of the word rolled around my head.

No, I can't answer now. It's real early, I shouldn't be awake anyway was my line of thought.

My behavior was not the only thing Masha didn't like; she disapproved of my new company even less. At the party to celebrate the closing of the 'Gazdiesel' transaction, I'd introduced her to Viscountess Greenberg.

***

"It's extremely nice to finally meet you Mrs. Vorotavich." Viscountess Greenberg's manners were flawless. She had no match in the etiquette arena, making high courtesy seem natural. She preferred to gloss over the fact that she despised her former partner, the Puppet Master, and that Masha and I hated him. "I was so saddened to learn about the death of your father."

"Thank you, Viscountess." Masha had paused, concealing the surge of hatred, and gave an appropriate somber nod. "My husband has said so many good things about you that I was eager to see if they were indeed true."

Greenberg smiled genteelly, ignoring the barbed comment and introduced Emil. "Please let me take this opportunity to present my son." Her eyes flicked to me. "Michael, I believe you and Emil will have a lot in common."

And that was when I first met Emil three months ago. We exchanged handshakes like a pair of feral lions sizing each other up. There had been a half-smile playing on his lips and his gaze gave off a snobbish air. But this was nothing new or unusual to me; many of my friends were either overtly self-confident or pompous. New money seemed to do that to people. But Emil was old money. I hadn't seen anything bad in him, but immediately afterwards, Masha had told me exactly what she had thought.

"He's a snake, Misha, a dangerous venomous snake. I felt it as soon as his eyes looked at me; he's cold behind them. Dead. Don't make the same mistake you made with Denis. You must not trust him."

"Don't worry, darling," I'd said glibly, kissing her on the forehead. "I'm not looking for a new friend. He's a business connection, nothing more."

Masha's warning, like most things she said to me, was soon forgotten. I found myself socializing with Emil more and more and, without my realizing it, we became inseparable. And then we ended up in Amnesia, the club he'd suggested.

***

I'd continued to sip my champagne, a girl on either side, as Emil flirted with the third and any passing waitress. I wasn't really listening to anything they said, just enjoying the warm hands on my crotch and the kisses on my neck. We drank four more bottles of ridiculously expensive Krug before Emil abruptly stood, our cue to leave. We'd stumbled towards the door, propping each other up and out into the night air. I looked for my G Wagon then remembered that it too had the night off.

"Did you have fun?"

I turned, and a heavy fist connected with my chin. Vladimir. I landed in a heap on the ground, as the women screamed. I looked up; Vladimir towered over me whilst Oleg pushed Emil away.

There was a blur of movement and something hit Vladimir, flinging him sideways. I dizzily scampered away and pulled myself back up to my feet. Emil lolled against a wall, the girls huddling around him. Vladimir lay on his back in the dirt as another figure got to its haunches and made for Oleg. I squinted, finding the Englishman I'd met earlier—Snow. Oleg swung his fists; Snow ducked and delivered a straight punch to the gut. Oleg doubled up, and a blow to the back of the neck floored him.

"You think you can take me?" Vladimir, back on his feet, roared in Russian. "I was Spetznas!"

"I heard Bolshoi Ballet."

Even in the half-darkness I could sense the hatred burning in Vladimir's eyes. He adopted a Sambo stance and edged towards Snow. The Englishman was clearly trained and assumed his own defensive position. For a moment the duo seemed to move in step, like a pair of ballroom dancers, before the Russian feinted and then lunged. Snow read the move and stepped into the punch. With both arms up, working simultaneously, his right forearm forced Vladimir's punch sideways while the back of his left fist slammed into the Russian's nose. It was a simple but effective move; no one throwing a punch expected to receive another back before his own had struck. Vladimir blinked and retreated a half step. As he did so, Snow reversed the momentum of his right fist and struck the man hard in the face. Vladimir's legs buckled and he landed on his backside. Snow threw a straight kick at Vladimir's head and the Russian was unconscious before his head hit the ground.

"Go." Snow said, still speaking in Russian.

"Who are you?" I asked, holding my jaw.

"I told you, my name's Aidan Snow, and I'm on holiday."

***

As I lay in my bed with my thoughts becoming ever fuzzier, I knew that I'd have to thank this Aidan Snow. But who was he? Why had he been in the club? And what, exactly, was his relationship with the Russians? He spoke Russian and had a definite connection to Ukraine. I should make some checks upon return. Perhaps someday I'd find out. I felt myself start to drift away and smiled. The cognac was working. I would finally sleep.

Chapter 3 - Strange Calls

I must've fallen asleep after all. My first call was from my wife. Again. This time I couldn't ignore it. Not a pleasant start to the day when you have two naked women in your bed. I looked at my watch—11 a.m. I'd slept only three hours. Drowsily, I went out to the deck and locked the door behind me so none of the girls would surprise me with 'good morning' or anything silly while I talked to my wife.

Barely able to master a stable voice, I answered, "Hi, Masha. What's up?"

"Not you, from what I hear. Had a night out with Emil?"

Masha knew me all too well, so any attempt to conceal the obvious would be futile.

"Yeah. I'm shattered. Way too much alcohol."

"I hope it was only that, and you didn't indulge in anything else."

"I'm an old, married man, Masha. What can I possibly 'indulge' in?"

"Go get some sleep, Misha, and get back to me when you are in better shape. Our son's graduation party is the day after tomorrow. Let me know if you plan to come."

"Of course, I —"

The line went dead.

I hope she understands. My wife used to say that nothing of what I was doing bothered her, as long as she didn't know. She probably meant my business, but I gave it a broader interpretation.

I like nights better. I hate mornings.

I reentered the cabin and saw used and unused condoms scattered around with cigarette butts and a few empty bottles. Women's clothing covered most of the floor, and I felt an immediate urge to vacate the room. My enthusiasm from last night was gone completely, along with the last drops of cocaine in my blood.

At least I remembered their names and how they got here. *So the drinks and drugs must've not been too excessive last night*, I praised myself, but nonetheless felt groggy.

"Hey, girls." I started to shake them. Seeing some blue, blank eyes starting to open, I urged, "We are about to set sail to Morocco. If you wanna stay at Ibiza, you better hurry. My driver will take you to your hotel."

Of course, it was a total fabrication, but I needed them out. Quickly.

I managed to get them out in less than half an hour, apologizing for such a speedy departure and giving them five hundred euros to have some breakfast. I protested when they didn't want to take it.

"Don't insult me, ladies. It's the least I could do to make up for not having breakfast with you. Next time you pay for breakfast."

Before passing them to Arthur to get them back into town, I let Inga (*was that really her name?*) kiss me on the cheek and gave her my business card, designed especially for that kind of occasions. It bore the number of my assistant who was privy to such calls and instructed to reply that I'm away on a business trip any time someone called — for the first two times. If any chick was obsessive enough to call a third time, she would receive an answer that I'm dead and the will was to be read on Feb 29, no matter if it was a leap year or not. If I wanted to contact any of them, I would do so at my own discretion.

Having them out somewhat alleviated my hangover. Emil was rid of his girl too, sipping on a cocktail through a straw and receiving a body massage from his masseur who accompanied him everywhere.

"Hey, let's switch harbors. I told them we were going to Morocco."

"You're an inventive dude, Misha. Sure. You brought the chicks the first night and I did the last; now we're even." He grinned like Cheshire cat, obviously pleased with our recent adventures. "Who's that bloke who came to our rescue and humiliated those Russian thugs?"

"Aidan Snow. I met him in the club. He said he knew me, or who I was, or whatever. I don't just have haters, it seems." I answered his grin with my own. "I'll have Arthur find him and express my gratitude and friendship. He deserves appreciation for what he did. And I will tell Arthur to find those Russian lowlifes to make sure they've learned not to mess with the good guys."

"Ha, I don't envy them. I suspect Arthur may not be very tender in his approach. By the way, I was thinking about our conversation in Space. Tell me, you weren't serious about what you told me there, were you?"

"The unfairness, cap on accumulation of wealth? Of course, not. I was fucked-up all the way. In fact, I'm with you on the expansion you started to tell me about, if you have a decent venue." I'd told that to him in confidence, but I wasn't so sure that my narcotic-induced theory was flawed.

"Ah, that. You'll hear about it very soon." Emil smiled mysteriously.

He beckoned someone, and soon enough, I heard the anchor being pulled up and we started to sail towards the nearest cape.

Relaxed again, I crashed in another cabin, figuring that someone would need to clean the one I'd used the previous nights. That would probably take at least two to three hours.

Up again at around 3:00 p.m., I came out in much better shape, sipping coffee and looking for Emil. I found him in a hammock on the deck, engaged in a telephone conversation.

"... must go forward—that's not enough. What you've achieved is laughable. Sergey, you need to do it openly in all directions. More force, more firepower. And you need to make it felt in the capital. Yes. You must achieve the passage—" Somebody was probably translating on the other end, as Emil took long pauses between sentences.

"Sergey, I told you, don't worry about oil prices. They will go up. It's temporary. That's just some stray Arabs. I'm working on it." Another pause.

"Oh, don't tell me about the economy plunging. I didn't see anything plunging in your account. You know this gambit should be very profitable for both of us. We've discussed it already. So far, it goes according to the plan. Come on, you're supposed to be a tough guy. Don't destroy that image for me. Go for it openly.

"Yeah, sure, see you soon. I'm crediting your account. You'll be very pleased."

Emil hung up and signaled to me that he needed to make one more call.

I didn't care. I slouched into a sunbathing chair and viewed the scenery of our new harbor. Not that different from the previous one. Just beautiful. I loved this crazy island.

After a while I reluctantly got up, and seeing no waiters around, staggered towards the bar to grab something small to chew on. I brought the plate back to the deck and assumed my former position in the chair. Somewhere in the background, Emil was busy giving orders.

"... Mykola, you listen to me attentively. There is not much time left. I'm telling you, this time it's one hundred percent right. They will push aggressively. Be ready to fend them off, otherwise it's all over."

Hearing no sound for few minutes I thought he was done, but Emil still held his cell phone.

"No, that's too much. I can arrange two within a month, not a penny more. Enough. Be economical with supplies. But don't wait for anything, be prepared."

As Mykola was a Ukrainian variant for Nikolay, I assumed this time it was some Ukrainian on the line.

When he was finally done, he looked so triumphant that I couldn't just pass over it.

"What's that, Emil? You brokered a cease fire between Ukrainian and Russian troops, stripped someone of assets, or ordered some fresh blondes? You look so happy."

"Yeah, sort of all of the above. I'm trying to save our assets there, you know. Not an easy task."

"If you need some help in Ukraine, just let me know. For a handsome reward I might save a blonde or an asset for you."

"Thanks, Misha. You are a kind Mafioso. I like it. So, what's today? Amnesia again or Privilege?"

"The trio from yesterday is gonna be at Privilege tonight, so if we show up there, it might somewhat undermine my Moroccan departure line. Let's do Amnesia again. This time Arthur and some of his guys come with us, so he can have a go at this Vladimir and his sidekick, in case they show up again."

"Yeah, yeah. Okay, we'll see. Hang on. Let me finish my phone calls, mate."

I overheard that this time it was Jamal, on the other end of the call.

"As-salamu alaikum, dear Jamal. You know it's again about oil. You need to increase production, Sir."

"That's not how you help to increase oil prices," I thought.

"So what if those Yuras, Dimas, and Sashas call you every day? Let me worry about it. You have to keep the oil cheap. It's in our mutual best interest, trust me."

It sounded like Emil was involved in some complex, multilateral combination, screwing at least some of the participants.

Steve, Emil's personal assistant, approached and whispered something into Emil's ear.

It must've been something upsetting, as Emil practically jumped to his feet and replied, "Fire the lousy bastard. What chutzpah! I don't pay him driver's wages, but the salary of a high-tech engineer, I think. And he wants a raise? So what if I haven't raised his wages for five years? Did I promise I would?"

Steve was very uneasy, but he didn't dare interrupt his boss at such a time.

"He can't even wait with that until I return from vacation?! Yeah, he told me in London that he wanted to talk to me about something, but I didn't have time. So? You fire him right away. I want to pass a message to everyone. No severance pay. He's not even that good a driver."

Steve bowed and left without saying a word.

I didn't like to witness such a humiliating scene, but I kept it to myself.

A driver is a position of trust. I always tried to keep those near me happy. And generally, retaining someone for five years without a raise did sound like a very stingy approach. *Well, Emil struck me as neither a generous nor a particularly nice guy.*

***

The last night at Ibiza was much like the first two, however I did cut down on blanco. *Drugs are shit,* I reminded myself. Phony pleasures and happiness couldn't replace real ones.

After Amnesia, I hugged Emil, who intended to stay on the island for at least a week, and headed to the airport for the trip back to London, where I had family business to take care of as well as my regular one. My family always came first. I had occasional 'encounters' with other women, but I never let any of them penetrate my heart.

Although I'd loosened my grip a little bit, I was still pretty much a hands-on manager of everything that happened in the group's business.

Despite an apparent lull in Russian-Ukrainian confrontation, I felt something was cooking and that a delicate equilibrium might be ruined.

I usually trusted my gut feeling, but what was coming exceeded my wildest imagination.

Chapter 4 - World War III

Present

"Misha, that's it. It's gonna be all out. They're using the air force for the first time. There are rockets! They've even targeted Kiev. And here it's hell. I'm taking a fucking dump in the bomb shelter, can you imagine that? We are on the brink of a new world war. It's a total mess!" Boris, his Excellency, the governor of Luhansk at my behest, yelled through my cell phone.

I'd already heard about two Russian rockets hitting Kiev. One of them fell near the small Zhuliany airport. Another hit a Botanic Garden on the Right Bank of the Dnieper River. No casualties, but this was a major escalation, no doubt about it.

"Boris, maybe! But stop yelling, I don't hear mortar explosions near you. You can speak calmly; I still get it."

" I admire your composure. But Russians occupied Mariupol! You know what that means? You can remain nonchalant if you want, but we have fifty-thousand Russian soldiers everywhere, trying to break through the fortifications that we've barely had time to reinforce."

"You must be joking or exaggerating—fifty fucking thousand?"

It was no joke this time. They were serious. I couldn't hang out in London while this was going on.

"Okay, shut up, calm down and meet me in Kiev. I'm heading out now." I hung up.

My reunion with my family was too short. On the way to the airport, I called David to come meet me.

***

The four-hour flight gave me a good opportunity to think the whole situation through, as well as to look at the most recent updates available in the media. One thing was obvious—if Ukraine folded, the Russians wouldn't be too nice to me. Ever since the Puppet Master perished under uncertain circumstances, Russia's enmity towards me had dwindled, but hadn't disappeared completely. However, it wasn't about sympathy or feelings. Russia had its own very full, but still very hungry, bunch of court oligarchs that wouldn't miss a chance to get their hands on whatever looked lucrative. Some had offered to buy a few of my businesses in the past. If Russia got the upper hand, they might well think that now they could just *take* what was mine instead of buying it.

Any way I looked at the situation, I didn't see any good. Despite my usual composure, I disembarked from the plane in a very agitated state, enhanced by my pilot's reports during approach about more and more no-fly zones, probably because there were air battles in them.

My hope that the Puppet Master's death would cool confrontation between Russia and Ukraine was futile. Maybe too many bureaucrats in Russia were already trapped in the illusion that the Puppet Master fed them—or maybe there were external factors supporting Russia's aggressive approach.

The worried faces of my friends coming to meet me at the dignitaries' terminal of Boryspil International Airport didn't offer any comfort.

"Misha, let's talk here in the airport. I've just gotten an hour to sit with you and if the air route would open, I'll borrow your plane to get back to our headquarters in Severodonetsk, where I'm most needed." Boris sounded serious and determined.

"No objections on my part," said David.

"All right. Arthur, ask someone to send us the waiter to the second floor. Here, give them my PM card." I turned to David and Boris. "Remember they have microphones in every room here."

"Those bastards had better attend to some other tasks right now, other than eavesdropping on patriots," Boris spat, referring to the security services that had wired the entire deputies' terminal.

I couldn't agree more.

That was probably the most depressive management meeting that we'd ever had. No jokes, no silly remarks, no brilliant ideas. Only anxiety and frustration. We were all too aware that these might be the last days of a young country called Ukraine. Even Arthur, a strong military expert, didn't offer any solid plan.

After a rather short exchange about known threats, options, and action items, I tried to summarize.

"Listen, guys, from what I'm hearing, there is nothing much we can do to stop the Russians, but there are still a few things we should try. The way I see it, they might not act rationally any more. What could stop them, or cause them hesitate, is direct American or NATO involvement, acute domestic unrest, heroic Ukrainian resistance taking too high a toll of Russian troops, and finally some clandestine influence some parties may still have with Russian leadership."

Both friends nodded, and David added with a grin, "Occupying the Kremlin could also help."

"Yeah, that too." I liked a lighter atmosphere better. "Listen though, since I sold our Russian social network, I don't think we could do much inside Russia. Besides, its current leadership enjoys fantastic popularity at the moment. If they keep capturing territory, their support may even surpass the one hundred percent level, for all I know."

Boris smiled nervously at my little joke, understanding that his support as a governor would plummet to below zero as soon as he didn't have a region to govern. "What are they trying to achieve? A

Slavic empire for Asian people? You walk the streets of Moscow or Saint Petersburg these days and you can't help noticing that every third face is of Asian ancestry. They want to bring Asia into Europe? Europe becomes 'Islamized', Russia 'Asianized', and we have to suffer. They try to sell some Pan-Slavic ideology, while courting Asian nations. If anything, the true Slavic empire is us, Ukrainians, descending straight from the Kievan Rus, and maybe few more Slavic countries. We can't succumb to those Asian barbarians. You know whom we capture the most, fighting for Russians and separatists?"

"Whom?"

"The Chechens. They are oppressed by the Russians, so some of them are probably very happy to have an opportunity to kill some Slavs. They kill Ukrainians, but they mean Slavs in general."

"Listen, Boris, your theory might be true or false, it doesn't matter. We need to think of a course of action. We do have some things to try. I'll tell you what, I'll try to convince my new friends who own a big chunk of foreign media and prolific political connections to deepen and accelerate the Western response to the latest hostility. By the way, we can present some new facts that you can prove, and maybe to air interviews with some Chechens that you have apprehended. And I will call a few American friends who are more directly responsible."

I meant Romeo, of course, the head of the Ukrainian desk at Langley, whom I'd met, but I didn't want to say anything that might be overheard by hidden microphones. David and Boris understood whom I was talking about.

"Also, Boris, I'm giving you access to my emergency account. It has this amount in it." Again I didn't want to say it aloud, so I wrote "100M $" on a piece of paper and showed it to him.

"Don't wait for the government if it takes too long, just acquire directly whatever you need to finance defenses."

"Arthur, would your presence at the front help us somehow?" I turned my brief attention to my veteran chief of security.

He shook his head. Rarely did Arthur react negatively when special operations were involved, but this time his healthy pragmatism took the upper hand over his opportunistic enthusiasm.

I recalled those phone calls that Emil had on the yacht. I never believed in coincidences. He must've known something. I decided to share some information.

"Finally, I'm invited to a very interesting gathering of people who supposedly have a lot of influence on world order. Maybe they could help somehow. It's called informally, the "Magnificent Seven". You probably won't have a lot of info about them, but whatever you are able to procure, I'd appreciate. Here are the names, too." I handed them the list.

Again they nodded, studying the names. Seeing that they didn't have much to add at the moment, I adjourned the meeting, advised David that I was going to stay in Kiev for a few days, and let Boris look for the fastest way to get back to Luhansk region, be it in my jet or by some other method.

I had to make a few phone calls to set things into motion.

First, I dialed Emil. He didn't answer. Then I called Huberman Real Estate—my CIA interface—but they told me not to expect any senior 'real estate agent' calling back any time soon. That was odd, but of course, their Ukrainian desk was too busy to answer me, unless, as David suggested, I called from the Kremlin, announcing its surrender to Washington.

Since nobody I needed was available, I headed, in Arthur's company, to my limousine which waited with its motor running, and switched the TV on as we drove slowly towards the city.

Although two rockets had hit the city, in these parts of Kiev, nothing reflected the tensions of war. The girls were barely dressed in tune with hot summer weather. Some drunken fishermen walked towards the river as we approached the South Bridge over the Dnieper, and bored teenagers typed on cellular devices, sipping illegally purchased beer.

The TV broadcasted a totally different picture. Over four hundred people dead or missing in action in the Eastern regions of Ukraine —during the course of the day, Russians advanced, capturing two more towns, emergency meetings around the world, and so on.

I switched to some foreign channels and heard an assortment of stories about the crisis' aftermath. Oil prices dropped to twenty dollars per barrel of BRENT (sweet, light crude). The U.S. promised to supply weapons to Ukraine and send ships of the sixth fleet into the Black sea, and finally, of paramount importance, was Russia's rejoinder that any American involvement would have very serious ramifications. The "ramifications" were explained on Russian TV, so no one would be left uninformed. When I switched to Russian Channel One, some general was giving a profound interview, explaining that the US intelligence had exploited social networks and search engines to gather intelligence and provoke innocent people into violence, mutiny, and resistance, thus exploiting the masses for their own narrow needs. Some cyber expert, sitting in the studio, was ready to explain exactly how it was done, according to the screen's crawl line. Finally, the general delivered his punch line that Russian rockets fired from Kamchatka could cross the Pacific Ocean and reach San Francisco, Palo Alto, Silicon Valley, and other areas of the West Coast in mere minutes.

Probably to prove his point, one of those rockets was fired towards US, but fell *near* the shore.

The chain reaction over global security deterioration was predictable and almost immediate. I switched to the financial news and instantly saw a preponderance of red numbers on NASDAQ and the other financial markets: shares falling overall, and hi-tech companies in particular often plummeted by double-digit numbers.

But the last news bit that made me reconsider the entire chain of events, was a small announcement—overshadowed by all of the other urgent news —that Greenberg Investment Bank, "using the market's turbulence," purchased ten percent of the stock of "Arsehook", a major global social network, after Arsehook shares lost twenty percent of their value just in two days, and closed a deal to seal the purchase of another five percent from some undisclosed owners.

They fucking knew what would happen and were prepared! I didn't have any doubt now.

Chapter 5 - Swiss Rout

After two days in Kiev, just when Russian progress came to a halt (*Temporary?*), I went on a short trip. I only took Arthur with me.

Emil had invited me to a gathering of the Magnificent Seven as an "observant." He told me that it was an absolutely informal secret gathering, which took place every once in a while. It included the shadowy heavyweights of the global economy.

After he gave me some info on these "heavyweights", I couldn't recover from shock for a few days. If what Emil said was correct, each representative dynasty of the Seven held stock (very often *controlling*) in hundreds of corporations, and on top of that they were the biggest lenders to many more companies and their shareholders.

I tried to add up their holdings and arrived at more than half of the *Fortune 500* corporations, and I was sure there were more, as I didn't trace them all.

Instead of the Gold Fix, Ms. Greenberg, it's now a Global *Fix, isn't it?* I mused, recalling that she'd quitted membership in the London Gold Fix not that long ago. If it wasn't control over the global economy, then what else could I call it?

And these people were barely known to the public, rarely in the news (they controlled the news), and didn't boast about their wealth. A perfect disguise for world rulers.

Emil instructed me to land in Innsbruck and rent a random car, not in my name, of course, so as not to attract any attention, and proceed from there to a small Swiss village near St. Gallen.

The entire route was breathtaking. Arthur drove, and we traveled long mountain roads through the Alps. It somewhat lightened my gloomy mood. Canyons, snow peaks, waterfalls, bright green valleys, and caves all mixed with occasional villages with humans nowhere in sight. It looked painted rather than real, and belonged more to a fantasy world than to the real one. If anyone looked for the most beautiful corner on the globe, the Swiss Alps would certainly have a good chance to claim the title.

As we approached the village, we were flagged down by some police officers and told to follow their car.

We turned around, and after a half-hour drive, reached some heavy metal gates, which completely barred the road. The gates opened, and the police stayed behind while we continued our trip.

Five or six kilometers from where we parted ways with the police, we reached another gate with a few cars parked nearby. As the gate didn't open, we assumed that we needed to park and walk.

As soon as we approached, a small door at the bottom of the gates opened and we were greeted by three armed security men in full gear, each holding a machine gun. They were backed up by another security post twenty meters away, manned by at least three more guards partially concealed by a concrete fortification.

In English, but with a heavy German accent, we were instructed to leave telephones, cameras, weapons, and such with them and then pass through a metal detector. We were finally received by a gorgeous hostess with a radiant smile wearing a blue dress, who, in perfect English, welcomed us and suggested we proceed to the main entrance of this "secluded runaway," as she put it.

I would rather have stayed with her than proceed any further, but she'd already turned away, probably to present the same knockout smile to other newcomers.

We walked a path, paved by decorative stones, which led upwards and took a turn to the right. Halfway through the short turn, part of the mansion came into view. It had been previously concealed by the slope that we rounded.

The cubic glass entrance was illuminated with blue lighting, which caused the entire entrance to glow, even in the daylight, and behind it was what looked like a medieval fortress built within the mountain cave. The castle was so miraculous, as if taken from a fairy tale where its analogues usually hosted evil characters. It vaguely reminded me of Predjamski Grad in Slovenia which was also one of the most beautiful castles I'd ever seen, and similarly combined architecture with a natural mountain layout.

I was already amazed both by the hostess and the castle, so when we finally entered and were taken to the terrace, which hung above an abyss of a few hundred meters and offered a magnificent view of a huge lake, probably Bodensee, I was simply overwhelmed. This was a masterpiece of a unique, one-of-a-kind dwelling.

On top of that, the mountain air was refreshing and intoxicating, like coke. Seeing only a few people, and no one I knew, I took some canapés offered by the waiters, got whiskey with ice at the bar, and moved over to the balcony, followed by Arthur.

"Arthur, you don't need to shadow me here. Come, relax, grab some food. We are at the highest peak around and I don't see any suspicious choppers approaching from anywhere."

Apparently agreeing with me, he left me and sat on a couch, no doubt chosen because of its location on a small podium, which allowed him a good view of the entire hall and terrace.

At least it wasn't a tuxedo party, because I hated looking like a penguin. Taking another sip from the highball and having another canapé with red caviar this time, I thought I might even enjoy this function.

More attendees trickled into the hall. There were already twenty to twenty-five people around. Very few ladies, mostly groups of elderly men and their heirs. There were supposed to be seven families, or 'dynasties,' which sounded more impressive.

Soon enough, Emil appeared with his mother, Viscountess Greenberg. I didn't hurry to meet them, allowing them to shake hands with others in their progress towards the center of the hall. After few minutes, Emil parted ways with his mother and came to me with a full glass.

"Na zdorovye." He shook my hand.

"Cheers. Congratulations on your last purchase. Well and cheaply done!"

I figured I wasn't the only one congratulating him, as he quickly nodded in appreciation. I needed to confront him about the events that followed our goodbyes in Ibiza, but anticipating the questions, he said, "We'll have a chance to catch up a bit later. Come, let me introduce you to my friends."

We hadn't even reached the first group of people when the main door at the farthest side of the hall opened and a tall, sixty-something, overweight guy entered, accompanied by a once-gorgeous, no doubt about that, aging lady who was a bit younger than him. He didn't look like he belonged. He resembled a retired boxer rather than nobility, with his shining bald head, broad heavy shoulders, and a heavy jaw. He was probably the host; I noticed that the waiters bowed slightly when he passed them.

Our courses crossed as we strolled toward the center, and Emil used the opportunity to introduce us to each other.

"Antonio, that's Mikhail Vorotavich, the rising star of global business. So rising that he's managed to overshadow all the others already." Emil was half sarcastic, half serious.

I nodded and extended my hand. Emil continued, "Misha, this is Antonio Millingeri. He's not that known." Emil smiled mysteriously. "But for those who do know who he is, it's for being behind Subliminal Investments S.R.L., which would probably ring a bell for you."

"Sure, it's a pleasure, Mr. Millingeri." Of course I'd heard about this monstrous conglomerate, which had majority holdings in many telecoms around the world and was a founder of a multi-billion investment fund on top of that.

Millingeri smiled coldly. "Nice to have you around, Mr. Vorotavich. Please, enjoy."

"Mrs. Millingeri." I nodded as her husband pulled her away with him.

I regretted not bringing Masha. It would've been interesting to hear her opinion and intuitions of this motley crew.

Emil kept introducing me to the families. Most of them greeted me very formally, until we ran into his mother—my partner in Gazdiesel.

"Ms. Juliette, so nice to see you here, and in such great shape." My flattery was sincere, because she did look very good for her age.

"Ah, Michael, how are you?" Ms. Greenberg's smile was a bit warmer than that of the others. "I insisted Emil invite you. I believe in our partnership, Michael, much more than when we had that formidable ex-KGB chief, the Puppet Master, let him rest in peace."

"Thank you, Madam. I'll try to live up to your expectations." What else could I say? "I've become quite good friends with your son, ma'am, which in our age isn't trivial. Will there be a formal part to this gathering, or just mingling?"

"A small one, Misha. It's about to start." She pointed to where some people were already heading.

I noticed a huge curtain moving aside, opening another hall of roughly the same size, where a big table for forty to fifty people was already arranged. The hall was decorated in a hunting theme with horns, mummified heads, hunting gear, furs, and paintings of hunting scenes spread around on the walls, ceiling, and floor. *Not that animal friendly.*

I put my empty glass on the waiter's tray and followed the Greenbergs into the main hall.

After everyone was seated and had a fair chance to nibble on something, Antonio stood to say a few words. "Dear friends, I'm very pleased that it's my turn to host our usual gathering in such fateful times. Our friend Emil has arranged for us a rare opportunity to gain a huge foothold in the high-tech industry. In this millennium, when companies' capitalization can reach dozens, if not hundreds, of billions in a relatively short period, we need to be proactive in order to remain at the front—and even more importantly—on top. Now the situation is ripe to change the odds sharply in our favor." Antonio paused for a second while I looked around.

So far, I didn't understand what he was talking about, but I was probably the only one, as everyone looked receptive and knowledgeable.

"I think it's a good chance to arrange everything between us, so we won't step onto each other's toes in our little 'shopping season' opened for us so neatly by the Greenberg family.

Let me make two announcements before we proceed. Even three," Antonio recalled something, frowned, and continued. "First of all, let's congratulate the Greenbergs on their recent acquisition, and wish them smooth closing on the additional shares." There was a smattering of clapping and few clinks of glasses. Emil bowed in a pretentiously modest manner.

"Secondly, I will pass a list among you, with thirty-two corporations, which my analysts have handpicked as strategic for you to indicate who's going for what. I'm not sure we'd want this list circulating for long, so you'll have to memorize it before it's destroyed. If any of you choose the same corporation, you'd better decide between yourselves how you want to do it: in partnership, or giving up in your colleagues' favor. Remember, the window of opportunity won't be large, so you'll have to act quickly and diligently."

Antonio sat, but then stood up again before the conversation erupted. "Finally, and forgive me, for I've almost forgot. Let me welcome Mr. Michael Vorotavich. It's only rarely that we let someone new join our circle, but Ms. Greenberg is absolutely positive that he's a worthy member, and his recent accomplishments may testify for his aptness as well."

It was my turn to bow and I smirked, as he'd caught me by surprise.

Now it was time for around-the-table discussions, and I was eager to try to understand what this was all about.

Something was unusual, even archaic, about the meeting and I tried to put my finger on what it was. Yes! That was it: No telephone rang during the entire time. It was so unusual, that I couldn't have missed it.

I asked the waiter to bring me another whiskey and took Emil's plate from under his nose, leaving him startled with a knife and a fork in his hands.

"My friend, before you devour those unequivocally delicious dishes, you must answer a couple of questions, so I won't sit here understanding shit about what's going on." I almost whispered the last part so his mother wouldn't overhear my vulgarity.

"Misha, with pleasure, you don't need to steal my plate for that." Emil tried to snatch it back from my hands.

"Here, here, all right." I let him have it back, so he wouldn't bite me instead. "What 'shopping season' are we talking about?"

"Straight to the core, huh? Well, you see this modest society has existed for a little over two hundred years in a slightly changing format. Nothing too unusual. We don't appoint American presidents, nor do we decide whether to uphold the independence of any former British colony, if that's what you think, but we do try to stay on the forefront of business, which became virtually global in the last thirty years."

You might not appoint, but how come two out of two former US presidents and two out of three former state secretaries work for the members of this group? I wondered about the intel I'd collected about the Magnificent Seven. I doubted that the connection was established only after their retirement.

Emil continued, "But nowadays it became a bit harder to stay on top, because the evaluation methods changed and these internet and high-tech companies are valued by active user numbers, traffic, clicks, and so on, and not by income generating methods. A company may not earn a dollar, but still be purchased for a few billions if the investors believe in the idea and figure out how to monetize the client base."

"So, you've decided to buy some of them out?"

"Simply put, yes. And you can grab your share too, that's why you are here. Misha, take a look around. Not here, I mean," Emil added, seeing me looking around the room. "More generally speaking. Did you notice, for example, how many photo studios are closed? Why? Because people store their photos on cell phones, computers, clouds for all I know. They are irrelevant now. I don't want us to follow their fate. You know, steel, shipyards, coal, petroleum is the old economy, not so sexy any more. It's social networks, big data, biotechnologies, and other modern stuff that attracts money. Not even space these days."

"Those are sound observations," I had to admit. "Indeed, you don't meet too many shoemakers or blacksmiths lately." I digested the info he'd given me. "But tell me, what's Ukraine and Russia got to do with all that? They didn't kill the photo shops, I hope."

"This, Misha, we'll discuss afterwards in private."

***

I cornered him after dessert, when the gathering returned to mingling.

I'd picked two companies on the list once it came to my hands. I wasn't sure I was really going to purchase them, but I marked them off anyway, hoping not to miss the opportunity since they were in line with my business. I hated missed opportunities, but I needed some more info from Emil first.

"Buying any companies, sir?" I approached him with another glass of whiskey, feeling good and relaxed, and maybe a bit drunk.

"On top what was announced? Yeah, I've picked a couple. You?"

"Me too. But we are buyers. What makes you think the owners would want to sell? And if they do, I don't even know how to finance the purchase. These companies are worth a shitload of money."

Emil gushed, "That's the best part, my friend. To buy something there is no need to talk too much about it. When you have to shoot, shoot. They are all public, their shares are traded on exchanges, and we reasonably expect these companies to depreciate to one-third or one-fourth of their current price in the nearest future."

"How's that? It's impossible." I started to sense the *real* opportunity; almost the same way I felt when I was offered stock in Gazdiesel.

"Ha-ha, with the help of Russia, mate. Simple. We will play some more war games. You see, Russian expansion is not the best news for stock exchanges, especially when the Russians will start to target these companies' headquarters. Didn't you hear Russia's remarks that these social networks were the CIA's invention to stir revolts? Or the Russian military strongmen threatening Palo Alto? You think those were random? The rocket falling near California's shore was an amazingly successful test case, don't you think? You know they can mention or approach other places too."

"You bastard! So *you* were behind the last moves? I had that thought after overhearing these telephone conversations, but it was too unbelievable to believe in and I simply dismissed it."

Emil looked pleased and pompous, as if he just came up with the most brilliant idea ever.

"Misha, why do you look upset? If I didn't invite you to enjoy the benefits, I could understand, but you are here and have a fair chance to enjoy the sell-out."

He thought I was worried about my slice of the pie, but surprisingly, even for me, I was actually worried about Ukraine being used as a prostitute in somebody's game: marked for invasion and her people for slaughter. It was sentimental on my part, but I couldn't let Ukraine sink or trade it so coldly for some stocks. My instinctive thought was that Emil's gambit was genius and monstrous at the same time, but I couldn't take part in it. Not on account of my country or my people, *any* people. I couldn't do that.

Emil picked up the conversation again. "There is another bird that we will kill with one throw. You know which?" I didn't answer, but he continued anyway. "Who do you think has the biggest slice in the defense business in the West?"

"Who?"

"We! And what happens when Russians flex their muscle?"

"NATO increases orders of different armaments by three—four times probably."

"Exactly, Misha! Ha-ha, you are an arms dealer, you should know."

I clenched my fists, but suppressed my urge to punch Emil in his handsome, yet evil and distorted, face. And then, by another titanic effort, I even produced a bleak smile of my own. I didn't want to share my emotions with someone who would scorn them.

But Emil was already too excited to stop or notice my emotional struggle. "There is also a third bird. Don't think it's only for our own benefit. You may forget, but there always was a recipe for jumpstarting an economy after depression. You know what it is?" It was a rhetoric question.

"A war! It's the best catalyst for an economy. A big war would be too tough. Everybody has weapons of mass destruction. But some tensions and increased military orders might help a country to get out of stagnation quickly. Everybody benefits from that! Even you would benefit from that, because your clients, in the wake of global tensions, would order more arms too. By the way, I know you have pretty good radars' manufacturer in Ukraine. I count on you and your connections, that when it goes out for bid, I will be the winner. I'll tell you what the winning price should be and we will hold it together—fifty-fifty. Don't tell me I'm a bad partner now!"

"True, Emil, you act like a real partner. Someone I can trust," I mumbled.

I didn't want to see any of these pretentiously aristocratic faces trading Ukraine and its people for more wealth and power like pawns in a chess game. Despite my sudden mood change and attitude, I needed to know more, so I exploited Emil's willingness to babble. This time it was really hard to keep my composure.

"But you won't really let Ukraine sink, will you? You don't really want these Russian bears to expand, right?" I wasn't sure at all, but I hoped that was correct.

"Pah, of course not. We don't need a super-strong Russia either. If they fly high, they become unruly. We just need them to wave their weapons in the air a bit, make the impression they are serious. Maybe even shoot another rocket in 'Frisco's direction, falling somewhere short in the Pacific. Nothing more."

"Are you sure you can control them?"

"I control their funds, if that means anything. Most of them are in my bank, ha-ha." Emil was full of himself. "What do you think? So far, they try to facilitate my humble requests. And I have another small leash in the form of oil prices." Emil produced a very shy smile, as if to downplay his role.

The Puppet Master is dead? Long live the new Puppet Master! I thought.

"My partnering with the Eastern bloc did bring some dividends after all, even if they are in the form of influence," Emil concluded.

"But most oil is in Arab hands, how do you, a Jew, control them?"

"Business is above religion, my friend, remember that. But you are right, Misha, I can control only to a certain degree. However, why do we have a club here? Arabs don't mind dealing with Italians for example and Mr. Millingeri's fund just happens to be very influential in oil spheres."

"I see, but take into account that when the parties come close to extremes, the rational behavior stops and erratic one takes over, so don't overplay it, Emil. That's a global scam you're pulling; and with all that Russian-Ukrainian confrontation, aren't you afraid the info would leak and of the possible repercussions then?" I was still awestruck and couldn't believe something of that scale was possible.

"Misha, you aren't as naive as you pretend. Do you really think someone who knows, and I'm sure some people do, cares about Russians killing Ukrainians or vice versa? For them the more the merrier. Would Don Corleone care if the Tattaglia family killed

Barzinis? He would be the first to give them the guns. You don't really believe that anyone cares about human casualties much, do you?"

"But people are DYING there!" I was so shocked, I couldn't control what I said.

Emil snorted. "There are people dying in Syria and in many places in Africa. Do *you* care, does anyone? Maybe you didn't notice, but there are seven or eight billion of them. I can't believe you are asking these questions. Don't get soft all of a sudden. You'll ruin your own image. How much blood do you have on your hands?"

"None of normal people. Maybe of few villains."

"Maybe *you are the villain* and they were normal people? Those you've wasted, I mean." Emil simmered from my last question.

I didn't care. "I'm a savage, Emil. But you? You are from generations of nobility, business shark, known philanthropist. Doesn't make sense to me."

"Misha, relax. It's something small, OK?! Don't turn from a cosmopolitan to a local. And I really don't care if some Russian men kick some Ukrainian ass, as long as their chicks come partying to Ibiza." Emil tried to wind the conversation down to a lighter level.

He wandered off and I, too, didn't have any more reason to linger. I found Arthur and told him we'd be leaving.

His devious and atrocious plan was too much for me. Without saying any goodbyes, I rushed out, scanning the surroundings for that gorgeous hostess. It was already twilight as I entered the car, opened the fridge that I'd ordered when I rented the car, and took a big gulp of whiskey right from the bottle. I felt like throwing up, but now there was another question that popped into my head. *These guys were not really a bunch of philanthropists, although I called Emil one, why would they want me in on their business, offering me a share, being nice?*

I remembered all too well the Russian proverb that free cheese could only be in a mouse trap.

Chapter 6 - To Plunder or Not To Plunder?

To say I was infuriated is to say nothing. We drove through a mountainous path, sometimes in complete darkness. Here and there, our headlights showed a glimpse of an abyss on the side of the road, just centimeters from the car.

With Arthur at the wheel, I had a chance to contemplate the spider's web Emil and his dear friends were trying to pull Ukraine, Russia, and the rest of the world into. I had a sense of being involved in some science fiction saga. Being a rather experienced conspirer myself, I never believed in conspiracy theories of such a global scale as this. If somebody told me anything like that was possible, I would be the first one to suggest that that somebody needed involuntary psychiatric hospitalization. Yet, the whole process seemed to have solid evidence of taking place. I started to view the sale of my Russian social network to Greenbergs in a totally different light now. It couldn't be only for business. They wanted to have yet another leverage on the Russian establishment.

It was just a game for them. A Monopoly game, where you throw dice and collect properties and assets. They didn't see the people behind it. They never saw people; now I understood that. Cause turmoil, get stock exchanges plunging, and then buy what you want for as much as you want. *Nice play, fuckers.* When I was perfecting card hustles as a student with wins of a few hundred rubles, these guys were probably dividing Yugoslavia for their pleasure with winning pots of billions.

If these were capitalists, I was with the commies. Maybe my late nemesis was right and capitalism, as a system, placed too much emphasis on individualism and undermined the common and the community values?

Conceptually, they were probably right in buying high-tech at this time, but did I want a chunk of what I was offered at the expense of my country?

Well, why not? Calm down, Misha.

On the one hand, Ukraine was a failure and she never lived up to her statehood. Independent for just over twenty years, she had already undergone two revolutions. No matter what the pretext was for each, at the bottom line, both were aimed at corrupt leadership and policies. Whoever came to power never benefited the country much.

On the other hand, did the above mean that she was to be conquered, subdued, and torn apart?

I didn't necessarily see one following from the other. I certainly wasn't the most righteous citizen, but I loved my country.

Still undecided, I pondered it. No doubt, what this "magnificent" club was doing was just ugly, but it offered a good reward. It wasn't *me* pulling the strings, after all. Should I grab those two companies that were being offered for peanuts? It wasn't much different from the rigged privatization in Ukraine that I'd profited from so handsomely.

But I still couldn't do that. I could buy the companies, but I couldn't stand aside when my country's fate was at stake. Maybe Emil was right and I'd become a sissy, or maybe I just wasn't hungry enough anymore. And Emil was certainly right about at least one thing—there was blood on my hands. But I never killed someone for material benefit, to get hold of any possessions; while these guys were starting a war to reduce prices. That's not my style.

But should I intervene? These guys had a huge advantage on me in aggregate accumulated wealth and their global political and economical influence, and could probably run me over easily. This sounded like an ultimate challenge.

I'd reached a decision.

"Arthur, stop the car."

He pulled over and looked at me.

"Listen, these guys are behind the recent surge of hostilities between Russia and Ukraine. We need to stop them. What gear do you have on you? They'll probably be leaving this way, too."

"I've a pistol and a knife, but what do you wanna do? Just meet them here, block their way and get rid of the fuckers?" Arthur was up to that idea; I could sense it in his voice.

"Probably not, because we need them to give the stop order. If they are killed, there will be nobody to tell Russians to stop. So, we probably need Emil alive." I didn't care to explain much of the background.

"This guy probably knows what he's into. I've noticed today, as opposed to previous times you'd met with him, his security was beefed up to five armed men. They came about half an hour after us. I'll tell you what, you hide here in the mountains, and I'll deal with it." Arthur was all business, probably figuring out how to deal with five presumably well-trained bodyguards.

"No, man, I'm not gonna send you on a suicide mission, like you did to me when you'd sent me to the Puppet Master's den in the past." I taunted him a little.

Arthur frowned.

"Come, keep driving, Arthur." I reconsidered my own emotional surge. "We shouldn't do anything impromptu. You should think it over and come up with a detailed, doable plan and then fill me in on it."

"Will do, boss."

As we were contemplating how to tackle this ugly bunch, it seemed they had their own plan for me, which appeared to be readymade and long-initiated. Unfortunately, I realized that after it was too late.

Chapter 7 - Run, Misha, Run

They didn't waste any time. The option for a full-blown showdown with Russia was craftily planned, especially with the media owned by my new "friends" fuelling the hysteria. Extraordinary meetings of everyone from NATO, EU, and OPEC, down to janitors on every street were held in a panic.

The stock exchanges kept plummeting and the redlines on the charts were constant for the last few days. Trading was stopped every once in a while to prevent a total collapse. An air of turmoil and Armageddon was clearly being felt everywhere.

The situation was ripe for a 'shopping season', as Emil and his friends tagged it.

Emil called me a week after our quarrel, all business and cold.

"Michael, are you still interested in those two companies?"

"Yep, I am." This time I was prepared not to betray my feelings. "It would be an inexcusable blunder not to grab something at one-fourth of its real price, wouldn't it? How should I proceed?"

"Well, you better get going then, because the Russians won't keep the pressure up forever just for you."

"What do you mean just for me? Are you joking?" I started to feel something was rotten.

"Of course, someone like you would want to use the rapid depreciation to make some purchases of strategic companies. Who wouldn't?"

He soothed my rising suspicions for a second.

"The stock exchanges are unbelievably low. Good time for making some purchases indeed." I cackled.

"Misha, unfortunately, your sponsorship of the Russian offensive through your Kremlin channels is about to be revealed. How can you do this just to buy something cheaply?"

"What's that? What is this bullshit, Emil?" I wasn't quick enough to think of just disconnecting the call.

"The editor-in-chief of *Financial Whiles,* which I own, called me and claimed that one of his reporters demanded to go on the air with irrefutable evidence that you'd instigated the recent escalation and that its probable reason was causing turmoil in financial markets."

I hung up, but it was too late. The bastard was obviously recording me. This very recording was probably the 'irrefutable proof.' *Shit! Thanks God, I didn't mouth off anything incriminating,* I thought, *or did I?* I wasn't sure, because it was so easy to manipulate words. I knew this game like no one else.

When you record someone, it's either to use it for offence or to hold it as leverage. I hoped it was the latter, as we were still sort of partners in Gazdiesel, despite our recent tiff.

After a few calls aimed at finding out what was going on to Emil's mother, which weren't answered, I switched to more pressing affairs, still angry with how easily Emil pulled it off on me.

With some hesitation now, I nonetheless ordered my securities traders to start buying the shares of the companies that interested me, and to establish contact with their shareholders to negotiate further buyouts after I'd accumulated a sizable amount of stock.

For the heck of it, I also ordered purchases of shares of the companies that were on the list, but chosen by the others. *I haven't received a club platinum card, have I? I'm not* that *bound by their non-competition pact.*

Seeing occasional green lines on the previously all-red charts probably reflected that these guys were buying big time. Nobody would notice that I was mirroring some of them. They were just tactical moves.

On a strategic level, I still had no idea how to save Ukraine from total destruction, so I considered a trip to Russia in an attempt to meet some decision makers there and fill them in on the plot cooked up by Americans—that was the best way to put it. My deliberations on how best to proceed were cut short when David, with what seemed like a roar, entered my office holding a copy of *Financial Whiles* bearing the headline: "The Richest Man on Earth Meddles with Human Life to Gain Extra Profits."

"Misha, the internet is blowing up with these. I've checked few sites already, and they duplicate this headline and some already generated bits with less subtle, anonymous comments like 'these filthy Jews want to have some Slavic flavor in the Arab blood they are drinking.' Nice people, huh?"

I glanced through the article. It contained extracts from my conversation with Emil.

"Motherfuckers! That's a fucking set up. They're framing me for what they're doing." I started to suspect that even my rise to the number one slot on *Forbes* had been planned in advance, so I'd be in a perfect position to smear with this shit. Sure as hell, it wasn't my last tiff with Emil that triggered this recent chain of events. I wiped the sweat from my forehead. "You see, David, it makes a lot of sense that I, a Ukrainian oligarch, which is the same as 'Russian' for many in the West, pull these strings. Who would believe that some English-Italian aristocrats are involved instead?"

That wasn't all.

The second news item was that my shares in Gazdiesel, held for my family's benefit by Greenberg Investment Bank, was foreclosed, and I saw on TV a court bailiff in front of the cameras, being handed a foreclosure writ from some English court regarding my shares.

After making a few phone calls, I found out that some bullshit company from the British Virgin Islands had filed a suit and paid a security for the foreclosure, claiming that the acquisition through inheritance was flawed, since the deceased perished in dubious circumstances, and the heirs might've been implicated. *Come on now, how can someone accuse me of wanting the Puppet Master dead, hee-hee?* I wondered how they'd managed to show personal interest so as to be admitted as a "due plaintiff".

So this is a well orchestrated, multi-layer attack, I thought, feeling very uneasy. The message was loud and clear, and I didn't need two warnings after surviving assassination attempts in the past. I needed to disappear as soon as possible, because it was war—not between Russia and Ukraine, but between the clandestine rulers of the world and old, rich me.

Damn, this started as such a beautiful summer morning, just to be spoiled by this disastrous news!

My role finally dawned on me—that of a scapegoat for all the recent mishaps: war, tensions, stock market turmoil, famine, absence of harvest somewhere, impotence of Western leaders, everything.

If you slander someone like this, you don't want him to have a chance to clear his name, and now my preferable condition for them would be dead.

How wrong was I in my belief in their friendship and partnership all along? They easily sacrificed the Puppet Master, who was their previous partner, so I shouldn't have expected a lot of loyalty from them.

To make the day just fucking completely perfect, Arthur came in, shut my protesting secretary behind my office door, closed the shades on my window although it was bullet-proof, and reported what I'd already deduced.

"Misha, we caught someone trying to fix this device to the bottom of your car." He held out an evil-looking device with some cut wires hanging loose. "It's a sophisticated plastic bomb with a remote mobile detonator. From a brief interrogation I've learned that the entire building is surrounded. They're just waiting for you to come out. I've spotted two snipers on the nearby roofs. Come, we need to get going."

Instinctively, I scanned the room for the dancing red dots of a sniper rifle. *Blyad, suka, I've read their cards, but was it too late?* I hoped not. I wasn't prepared for such a rapid turnabout. I didn't know their next move, but it seemed it was a direct assault with the intention to kill me. I opened my safe, where I always kept a million dollars' cash in a black, non-transparent bag, with untraceable banknote numbers. I left my cell, credit cards, belt, and jacket at the office, pulled Arthur after me, and led him down the fire stairwell into the men's toilet three floors down from my offices. My secretaries wouldn't think I was leaving, since I was only half-dressed and didn't say my usual goodbye and leave instructions.

Even if Arthur was bewildered, he didn't say anything.

"Listen, man, I just didn't wanna talk in my office, as it was probably wired or monitored from a distance. It's like this. The sweet guys you saw in Switzerland beat us to it and attacked first. These guys are no amateurs; they planned everything in advance and to the smallest detail. I'm very sure that what you've extracted from the guy you caught is true. What are we gonna do?" I started to panic. "The exits are watched; they have the necessary firepower for sure. We need to shake them and disappear from here. Even if I'm exaggerating, you know my rule: better be overzealous than lightheaded and fucked."

Arthur listened, took out his cell phone and shattered it with the butt of his pistol.

"*Now, go knock someone unconscious from behind and bring me some other clothes,*" I wrote on the mirror with a marker that I'd brought with me, then erased it after he'd read it.

With current technology, all my clothes could be wired with something tiny and untraceable. I was quickly turning paranoid, but I couldn't afford to make mistakes.

Arthur returned with some clothes in less than a minute. I hoped he wasn't overzealous with whoever 'lent' them to me.

After I'd changed, we went a few more floors down, where I believed we could talk without being intercepted or overheard.

"Now, how can we leave the building unnoticed, if the entrances are supposedly watched? You need to help me, as all I could think is to use the zip-line from this building to its neighbor or escape through a sewage system, but I probably watch too many actions films. What do you suggest?"

Arthur's face went blank as he thought it over. He would do a zip-line—something people like him could handle. But not me, I couldn't even think of getting out of the window on the tenth floor.

"Let's go, I have an idea."

Using the same emergency stairway, we went all the way down to the street floor and used the personnel entrance to the pizza restaurant which serviced mostly business center employees.

Arthur led me through the kitchen, quieting some cook who belligerently asked what we were doing in there with one swift punch to the jaw. He then checked the restaurant's customers from behind the counter, where nobody could see him.

Spotting a preteen boy going to the bathroom, he dashed in the same direction and beckoned me to follow.

He put his gun to the boy's head in the bathroom, causing me to open my mouth in awe, and then showed him a finger pressed to his lips, so the boy wouldn't think of screaming. The boy froze and was unlikely to recover from shock any time soon.

"What are you doing? Let the boy go!"

But he wouldn't listen, although he stopped pointing the gun at the boy. He tore a sheet of paper from the notepad on a waiter's tray by the entrance, scribbled a few words, told the boy to stay put, showed him the gun again, and left. He came back within a few seconds, and in few more seconds, the boy's frightened mom came running to the toilet's door. He'd probably passed her a note via some waiter.

This Arthur is a ruthless sadist. I had to remind myself of the obvious truth about my bodyguard and friend.

"Listen, mommy," Arthur said calmly, trying not to sound threatening. "You see, we are cornered here, but all we want is to get away. If you do exactly what I tell you, you and your boy will be safe in just a few minutes. If you don't, well, I'm not gonna kill your boy, but things would get complicated, you understand?"

She nodded, obviously on the verge of nervous breakdown.

"What you do now is this. You go out of the restaurant and at the opposite side of the road you'll see a few pizza delivery cars with the symbol of this restaurant. I'm pretty sure one at least one of them will be open with the keys inside. You take the car, go around the building, and come to the loading bay with its back as close to the restaurant's back door as possible. You can ram it into the wall if you want, but don't make a big crash, so not to attract attention. If all the cars are locked, you come back here. Understood?"

She nodded again.

"Go!"

She ran out.

I thought we only had a few minutes, no more, until security or the police or worse - the assailants would come looking to see what was going on as soon as someone found a knocked-out cook in the kitchen or paid attention to a hysterical woman running around stealing cars.

A little luck was still on our side, as we heard the screech of tires and a light BOOM at the back of the restaurant. I hoped the scene didn't look too suspicious to those watching the building from the outside. We opened the restaurant's doors inward, the car's outward, and got inside, together with the boy. Arthur yelled through the wall, which separated the cab from the back where we were.

"Drive out, turn left, follow the rules, so no one will pay attention, then turn right after three blocks and stop the car."

Apparently she didn't hear him, since we heard her muffled, "What, what, what and where is my boy?"

Arthur took his knife out, slammed it into the partition, and pried open a small gap. He repeated his instructions. We'd barely closed the back doors when the car jerked and went into motion. She turned after only two blocks, but that was good enough.

Arthur jumped out of the car, helped the boy out and yelled, "You can go now. I'm very sorry, ma'am."

If she could have killed him, she would've. She glared and ran away with her son in tow. I didn't blame her. I would kill someone like Arthur too, if it were my son.

Now what?

The street wasn't too crowded, but Arthur led me into one of the inner yards, where he saw a pair of bicycles probably left by some youngsters for a few seconds.

"We'll use these. We need to get farther away. Oligarchs don't ride bikes, so no one will even look at you. Just keep your face down."

He mounted one and urged me to follow suit. After a ten minute ride, when I was practically breathless after a long stint of uphill pedaling, Arthur gave me a break when he noticed a slightly open driver's window of an old Volkswagen Passat. He forced it all the way down with his knife, got inside, connected some wires, and once the engine was running, called me in.

I figured we'd escaped after we'd driven a few kilometers without a noticeable tail. It would take time before the police started looking for the car, if at all. Nevertheless, Arthur used small streets to lower the chances of encountering patrols.

In forty-five minutes we were out of town, and on the Kiev-Zhytomyr highway. After a couple of kilometers, Arthur turned right onto a barely visible path. I thought he was driving us into the woods, but we reached a small, uninhabited, hunter's hut—exactly what Arthur seemed to expect.

"Listen Misha, that's what we're gonna do. You stay here. If I don't return by 17:00, please assume that something happened and act on your own. Here is your bag." He tossed me my million-dollar satchel. "I'll go get a phone from any fucker that gets in my way, check what's going on and come back with something decent to drive."

Arthur looked composed, so I didn't fidget too much.

"Okay, go. Try to come back, I don't really feel like walking through the woods."

Arthur left, giving me a knife. I had few hours to kill without a cell phone or any other connection with civilization, which was only few kilometers away, just behind the wall of pines.

It felt so ridiculous to have all this cash on me while I was hungry and thirsty in the forest. I wondered jokingly if I could use a few dollars to buy a can of soda or beer from any stray wild boar or squirrel. To my surprise, there were a few un-refrigerated cans inside the hut. It looked like Arthur had prepared for this kind of situation. A *few dollars saved*, I cheered to myself.

***

Arthur returned much earlier than 5 pm, in a pissed-off mood.

"Here, have a sandwich, if you didn't manage to kill and roast some rat with the knife."

"Thanks, for that, Mr. Sarcastic." I was already chewing on it, and added, in a muffled-by-food voice, "What have you found out?"

"You were at least partially right, they thought out almost everything thoroughly in advance. Your plane has an explosive device attached to its wheels. I've told Sergey, who, as my leading explosive expert, is handling that, to be very careful with dismantling it, because it might detonate. He sent me a picture. I know such devices. It looks like a modification of the devices I used to study at the officers' academy. They are using Russians, Misha. Who else would go on such a despicable mission privately? The guy that we got confirmed that."

"I see. So I do have at least *some* instincts."

"It's not all. The chopper will require some overhaul. Someone added three to four kilograms of sand into its fuel tank. Blyad-suka. I don't have reports regarding the apartment or your other belongings. Won't be surprised to find something there too. They fucking stormed our office about an hour ago. When they'd discovered you were gone, I was told they got really upset."

"So, we are under attack again, huh? Listen, this time I'm gonna handle it differently. Too bad they are using Russian Special Forces. If it was the Western wankers, it'd be easier. But we'll show those bastards what is what."

I was pissed off as much as Arthur was. What the fuck was this? The greedy fuckers wanted to grab some companies through an artificial stock crisis and blame me for that? I was almost sure the concurrent Greek crisis was also engineered, rather than being brought about naturally.

I couldn't do shit now. No going to Russia, no nothing. I was too busy with survival again.

"I had some time to think, Arthur." I wiped my mouth and regretted he hadn't brought a few more sandwiches. "I probably need to disappear from here for a while until the dust settles. You arrange an RV for me, a motor-home rented in someone else's name, and I'll take a short ride around continental Europe. That's something I've wanted to do anyway. No boundaries there, no passport control, almost no highway cops. And it's a little less accessible to infiltration by Russian special-ops. You just need to sneak me out of Ukraine, but that shouldn't be too complicated. I won't need to check into hotels, and I can change country almost daily. I'll be switching SIM cards every couple of days. You arrange my escort and prepare a safe compound somewhere in Ukraine, from which I can work when everything's arranged and I can safely return. Ukraine is too vulnerable now until we are ready. It will take them time to find me and come up with an alternative plan. We've got some time now that their trap has been blown. I was analyzing the situation, and except for the slander, there is nothing that can incriminate me. Our base must be in Ukraine though, because here, no one would dare to re-publish that bullshit about me and whoever will, would probably be not important enough to be believed. Here, I'm known as a patriot. They wouldn't believe anything they are trying to accuse me of."

"But Ukraine is heavily penetrated by Russian undercover cells," Arthur countered.

"So, you take a unit from our Lug battalion defending the Luhansk area, and station it where you'd be able to organize appropriate defenses."

"Okay, Misha, there's some logic in what you propose. But remember, they'll be looking for any sign of you. You go online or enter your usual haunts whether physical or virtual, you get busted. I'm not sure I can leave you with anyone else for protection."

"We don't have a choice. You need to prepare a defensible location for me here." I was resolute.

"Okay, come, let's move further from Kiev for the time being. For all I know, there might be hit squads roaming the city in search of your rich ass."

We boarded a Hummer with police license plates that Arthur had brought with him, and returned to the highway.

We stayed the night at a remote farm near Zhytomyr with some people who were barely connected to some of Arthur's subordinates. They didn't know who I was, and arranged for us to sleep in the barn on a straw heap—something that I hadn't done since childhood.

After a couple of hours, Arthur probably had enough time to think about my suggestion. Just when I'd managed to calm down a bit after all the traumatic events of the day and was about to fall asleep, he renewed the conversation.

"Listen, I have an idea for the base. We can probably use the unfinished air force underground command near Kiev for this purpose. It's a bunker, almost completed, but has remained idle for several years now. They don't have the money to finish it. Do you think you can buy it through your connections?"

"Interesting idea. Let me check into it. I think, yes. The guys in the Ministry of Defense are very susceptible to sound business ideas. Ha-ha. I think I can buy it rather cheaply, if those who sign papers are suitably well rewarded."

That was a perfect task for Boris, whose ties with the Ministry of Defense were close, because he was the Governor of the oblast where most military activity took place and where a lot of combat units were quartered.

"Arthur, give this job to Boris. Tell him I allocate twelve million US dollars for the unfinished bunker and the entire land plot it comes with. It's the total budget, and it includes what I pay officially and what I wire to their personal accounts. The people in the ministry must understand that it's hardly worth that much, as it's probably rotten after a few years in the ground, exposed to rain, snow, sun, whatever."

Later, I learned that Boris closed the deal easily and elegantly, the split being three million into the state's budget and nine into the pockets of the ministry's officials.

What thieves. They were just fucking pigs!

Its real price was probably around twenty million, so I couldn't really complain about overpaying.

***

The next day, Arthur pressed harder on the gas pedal and, after the arrangements at the border were finalized, so my departure hadn't been registered, we crossed over into Romania, where some local lady who looked forty-something waited with a shabby motor-home bearing Romanian plates, a full tank, and a fridge full of food and drinks.

"That's Andriana, and she'd be traveling with you, Misha. When you cross into Serbia tomorrow, I'll have a reinforcement waiting for you."

The woman opened the left part of her raincoat and showed me an assault rifle hanging there.

Furious, I took Arthur aside.

"What's wrong with you? As far as security goes, this is a joke, and if you want to provide me a girl companion for the trip, it's a joke too, because the bitch is hideous. Tell her to return to her village to feed cows; I'm not taking her with me."

"Listen, this girl is one of the deadliest combatants that I've ever encountered. Believe me, I trust her pretty much the same as I would trust an entire unit of Lug to guard you. Regarding female companionship—I wouldn't try anything funny, but if she does instead—you are doomed, my friend. "

It didn't make sense to continue arguing after hearing such superlatives, so I went back and smiled broadly at Ms. Andriana.

"Buna Siara, Seniora." I said something that I remembered meant "good evening" in Romanian.

"Nice. Good evening, Michael. You get yourself comfy at the back and I will start driving. I want to leave a couple of hundred kilometers behind us before it's completely dark."

96

"Fine with me."

I hugged Arthur and told him to get in touch with Masha and to tell David to be in Dubrovnik in two days, preferably without a tail.

"Misha, you must lie low. No direct calls, no access to your sites. Nothing." Arthur seemed unconvinced I'd be able to keep that low a profile.

At least Andriana brought a mobile router with her, so I could surf the net while crossing over Romania from north to south.

First, I checked the financial news. Damn! Emil must've felt pretty smug these days. Indeed, the media, in a rare moment of unity, still discussed the nouveau riche's responsibility towards society and criticized my greedy methods, although only a few believed that I was indeed behind the war tensions. But those who did took it seriously, and demanded probes, inquiries, and other bullshit.

I was portrayed as an ugly Jewish traitor, exploiting my motherland's darkest hour to stuff my pockets with more cash and other forms of wealth.

The massive purchases going on went practically unnoticed. More so, they were so dispersed and untraceable to the same sources, that not even one transaction required antitrust committee authorization—neither in the U.S. nor in Europe.

Well done, Greenbergs and Millingeris — just modestly rich people, controlling the global economy.

After an hour on uneven and run-down Romanian roads, my eyes were tired and I was bored from stewing and thinking sour thoughts. When the time came, I hoped to right a few wrongs.

In the meantime, I had to relax a bit.

"Hey Andriana," I didn't mind chatting with my driver/bodyguard/companion. "So, how did you get to know Arthur?"

"We were married a long time ago."

I almost choked from embarrassment. Hadn't I told Arthur she was hideous? *God damn*, I was so egocentric that I knew little about the people surrounding me. I saw now that it wasn't beauty Arthur valued in women. Now many things had become clearer to me.

After a long pause, I resumed the questioning. "How long were you a couple?"

"Five years, a little more."

Damn, she was exactly as word-stingy as Arthur.

"And what happened?"

"I started as a young officer at Stazi, but after the rebellion and Ceausescu's execution, we weren't exactly admired at home, so I had to go abroad for a long time. Arthur, who was stationed here, had to stay for a while undercover and then was ordered to return. When he left the service, we didn't have enough in common any more to get back together, although we do have some warm feelings towards each other still—"

Arthur? Warm feelings? I tried to imagine him with warm feelings, holding a gun to a little boy's head. She must be wrong.

Chapter 8 - Corporate Defense

From Serbia to Bosnia and then to Croatia, we reached the city of Dubrovnik in the afternoon of the next day. Another car with three intimidating Serbs inside, whom Arthur had arranged, accompanied us. They joined us as we crossed into Serbia. These guys were Yugoslavian war veterans, for sure. I didn't want to pry by asking how many poor souls they'd killed twenty-something years ago, and maybe after that, as well.

As always, I was surrounded by bad company, but that made me feel safe.

I placed four calls via intermediaries to David. We agreed that he would wait for me, or someone acting on my behalf, in Dubrovnik to fetch him from the closest cafe to the Pile gate of the Old town.

I showed his picture to the scariest looking Serb and asked him to frighten David a little first. His wry smile told me that he liked the idea.

In the meantime, I waited for David in a local restaurant on a small recreation island in the Adriatic Sea, opposite Dubrovnik's shore. The uninhabited island was utilized mostly for leisure by fishermen, as a picnic site by tourists taking a sailing trip, and for secluded sex in nature by youngsters.

David was angry and pissed when he entered the private cabin that I'd rented.

"Hey, Misha, now that Johnny is fired, you pull your stupid jokes on me? This time you've gone over the line. This guy that you sent just stuck a gun in my back!"

"Why, weren't you scared shitless when this Goran guy asked politely for your majesty to follow him?"

"I almost had a heart attack, you moron."

"Sorry, man. I'm bored out of my mind traveling around, locked up in a motor-home with some silent shrew. Okay, sorry. You happy now? Listen I've got grand plans for you, so I don't have time for your whimpering here. Were you followed by the way?"

"Apology accepted, but grand plans sound like something pretty worrisome to me. No, I didn't see anyone suspicious."

"You are a Jewish boy. Not a girl, David, in case you forgot. Stop whining and complaining and listen up. So far, these guys are one to two steps ahead of us at every turn, and that's because they caught us by surprise. But we can't just be on the defensive. First of all, what you gotta do, you must keep the prices of our publicly traded companies up, otherwise my companies' shares will slump together with all the others. You can even wire false announcements to the stock exchanges, for all I care, because I'm sure these guys will want to buy everything floating on the market that's connected with me and maybe even try a hostile takeover, if they can. Make them pay dearly for that."

David nodded.

"Second, you need to transfer everything worth saving from these companies to new entities, but in such a manner that no one would notice. No reports to be issued, even where required by stock exchange regulations. I'm sure someone might sit in jail for that, because we are talking about criminal offences here, but I don't care. Appoint some homeless front man for the sensitive positions that would be willing to take the risks. Because we are at war now. You have to design the transactions, so that whoever tries to reverse them will be stuck for years in court to undo what was done."

"Misha, you can't do that, you'll lose millions just on taxes."

"No taxes, please, my friend. I don't like that word. Of course, you are right. You have a budget of two percent of their value for taxes and overhead. Here, I can't really operate my accounts these days, not even through the internet." I gave David a new power of attorney, which gave him access to some of my accounts.

"Gotcha. What are you going to do, Misha?"

Now that we'd finished the official part we could have a friendly talk.

"I don't know how yet, but I'll try to survive and to fight back, of course. I'm in clear and immediate danger, and these fuckers from the Seven will look for me everywhere and try to intercept any calls I make. I hope I've disappeared from their radars for the time being. I'll probably circle around for few more days until Arthur is ready with a compound from where I'll be able to operate safely."

"Want a beer or something, mate?" I pressed a button to fetch a waiter.

It was a pretty cool evening. Although no chicks were present, we had a relaxing time. David complained about how unused to family life he was, and that he missed our frequent debauchery and stuff like that. I listened with half an ear, happy to spend a calm evening with my best friend, updating each other on recent happenings.

"Here, I brought something for your long travel." David passed a package neatly wrapped in gift paper to me.

I tore the wrappings off and uncovered a book, which judging by its cover and the name—*The Vagina Tales*—was clearly erotic.

"Thanks, man. Good stuff. Now I have something to further stimulate jerking off during my lonely travels. Did you write it?"

"Close call, Misha! My sister, Daria, did. It's fresh out on the market and sells pretty good."

"Yeah, she's your sister, mate. You are just two mega-erotic siblings."

When we'd finished up and I'd received the bill, I asked David to cover it, since I had only dollars on me and no credit card.

To my surprise, he didn't have one either.

"Jessica doesn't allow me to use it. She claims that I spend too much and have too many questionable entries on the credit card slip. I'm telling you, this girl seems to be Mussolini or Franko, but what can I do?" He opened his arms in frustration.

I couldn't possibly ignore his utter humiliation.

"David, from a stud, you've turned into a completely impotent imbecile. What do you mean you don't have a credit card to your own accounts? Are you nuts? I've just given you power of attorney with access to over eight hundred million dollars and your wife doesn't even let you manage a penny from a family budget? That's absurd. I'll tell Arthur to whip you or Jess or whoever, until you become normal." I was half-amused and half pissed-off.

"What can I do, Misha, slap her silly?" David shrugged.

"No, of course, not. Some consider us chauvinists, but to hit a woman? Not our style. But you have to do something about it, mate."

I imagined how all those wimpy chairmen of central banks, in charge of billions of public and sovereign funds, were unable to get permission from their wives to buy a couple of beers at the local store. How pathetic.

Andriana came in and told us that if David wanted to make it on time to the flight back to Kiev, he'd better leave. We hugged and he left, accompanied by Goran.

However, it turned out that David's assumption that he wasn't followed was incorrect.

Chapter 9 - Complication

After taking David to the airport, Goran was supposed to wait for us at the secluded cottage in Dubrovnik, which we'd rented on a daily basis. He wasn't there. A bad feeling crept up my spine when Arthur reported that Jessica called him. It was an extraordinary event. She never before called Arthur or me because her brother probably told her we were a bit rough. What slander!

It could've meant only one thing: David hadn't returned home. What the fuck? I hoped nothing bad happened to him or Goran, although it was starting to look like he might've been abducted.

We checked. He never left Croatia by plane. I hoped Goran's silly joke of poking David with a gun wasn't coming true this time.

I told Arthur to leave everything, even the preparations for my safe haven and look for David. I couldn't stand the thought that I might lose him.

I figured that David was probably under heavy pressure, when access to my accounts, which I'd permitted David to work with, was denied because someone tried to access them with an incorrect password. It meant that David hadn't told them shit or had given them false info on purpose. However, I was sure that the pressure on him would grow.

I needed to do something quick.

First, Arthur's men found Goran. More precisely, his lifeless body. Tires, debris, audio discs, and some half-burnt remnants were scattered over a wide area. He was in the wrecked car, embracing the wheel. The scene was designed to appear as if he'd slipped from the mountain road into the abyss. We doubted it. The car had been dumped, probably after Goran was already dead or knocked out, but there were no traces of David.

That was, literally, a dead end, as nothing was recovered from the car's wreckage except for Goran and David's fingerprints and hair samples.

My alternative quest was a little bit more successful. The bank's security team, together with Arthur's cyber experts, were able to trace the location from where the attempted account break-in was made.

It led to a Wi-Fi zone at Split Bay. Arthur got people on the ground quickly. It took time for intensive search and countercheck of IP addresses, but in two hours, the exact location had been established, and it looked like the source was from a small sailing yacht.

After watching it from afar for fifteen minutes, Arthur's men cautiously approached and, seeing no visible opposition, stormed it. Acting in unison, two men broke the side windows aligning the pier and stuck their Uzis into the cabin, while another fighter pried the door open and entered. No one was inside. Only a piece of torn ear stuck to a piece of paper with a knife. The paper contained the words *Ex ungve leonem*, which meant 'from the claw we may judge of the lion' in Latin.

At my request, one of Arthur's men broadcasted the entire operation to me using a cell phone camera. I jumped to my feet and dropped my cell when, all of a sudden, I saw a huge explosion, a fireball, and then a sinking yacht, after the fire and smoke cleared a little. Opening the door or a movement inside must've triggered some mechanism, because just as the commander of the assault unit relayed the information to Arthur, the bomb was activated. I was sure we lost the entire team, because the streaming stopped. Arthur somewhat alleviated my despair, reporting a couple of minutes later that two fighters were badly injured, and no one dead. Fortunately, or purposefully, the explosives were potent enough to ruin the boat's hull, but not much more.

The ear part was lost, so it was impossible to establish whose it was. I only hoped it wasn't David's, as he was particularly proud of the shape of his ears.

Whoever meddled with me was still a few steps ahead. I didn't have anyone else to complete the mission that I'd assigned to David, and I needed my friend released before he sustained any serious damage. And,I had to keep moving.

I couldn't use multi-layered communication buffers anymore, so as soon as we reached Venice, which was my next stop, I found an internet cafe, opened up a new Skype account, and dialed Arthur.

"David's lost, disappeared. What are we gonna do now?" I hoped Arthur had some additional leads, but he was just silent.

"Listen, they can keep him anywhere as a hostage to present as a trump card when needed. Unless he goes online somehow, we have no clues. We need to get one of theirs maybe. Greenberg or the Italian? What do you say? At least we know where they live."

"I can bet they are not there. As long as they know that you're at large somewhere, they'll be cautious. But you're right. Let me see who we can lay our hands on."

A second later he added, "Misha, his wife is driving everybody nuts. You are lucky she doesn't have your temporary number. She's calling a press conference for tonight, filing complaints everywhere, making things complicated."

"Let her be, Arthur. Who can blame her? If I thought a press conference would help, I'd be there already. The only way I can influence her is through her brother Johnny, but for some reason I believe David would rather I do not."

I hated being helpless.

I had my family and my brother's family secured, but I was still on the run, and David was missing. Having nothing particular to do about that, I ordered Andriana to head north. Hell, if they traced and abducted David so quickly and efficiently, they would find me eventually. I needed to hold out until Arthur was ready to ensure my safety in Ukraine.

***

After an overnight in a small camp-site in Austria, we reached Lichtenstein by noon the following day. This tiny principality was a huge financial hub, especially so for delicate and illicit transactions. I had bank accounts and wealth managers here, but I couldn't see anyone, lest I reveal where I was.

We parked near a hotel and, having left me under the guard of our escort car, Andriana went into the shower. It was supposed to be just a short stop on our way.

I was so bored and horny that I almost followed her into the shower cabin, but as Arthur's ex-wife, it was a no-go.

All of a sudden, inspired by a growing libido, I recalled Giselle—a young intern in the private equity department of KDP Bank here in Lichtenstein who was very helpful when I'd rearranged some of my funds there some years ago. She was really nice, beyond what was required for business, and now, for some reason, her image caught my imagination. I thought I knew what the reason was.

As my principle always was *if you want to fuck, better do something about it*, I looked up her name on my private cloud database and punched her number on my mobile, neglecting security concerns. It wasn't that I knew what to do or say if she answered, but I hoped I still had some flair for improvisation.

"Hello," she answered coldly.

"Hi. Giselle? It's you, I'm not mistaken, I hope?"

"Yes, who is this?" Her voice became a little warmer.

"It's Michael Vorotavich. Remember, you helped the bank's manager to arrange my accounts some years ago?"

"Oh, but of course, how can I possibly forget a client of such a caliber? How are you, sir, what can I do for you?"

I would rather she'd remembered me as a handsome man and would have told her exactly what help was required, but that would be a rude starter.

"I'm on a very brief visit here in Lichtenstein and I don't even have the time or opportunity to visit the bank during business hours, but I do need to pass on some discreet instructions and to consult with you about a thing or two. You still work for the bank, right?"

"Yes." She was much more receptive now.

"So, what I was thinking, if you could come meet me at my hotel for a short consultation, I would be very grateful." I looked out of the window and told her which one it was. "You call to this number from the lobby."

After a short pause, she agreed.

When she returned from her shower, I sent Andriana to get a president's suite or, if it wasn't free, the best room they had in the hotel without mentioning my name, and to arrange for a tray of all the refreshments they had, fruits, and two bottles of their most expensive vintage wine.

I changed into more formal clothes, sprayed a bit of au-de-cologne, and headed out ten minutes after Andriana left. I met her halfway. She was already returning. I took a key from her without saying a word, walked leisurely to the hotel, and then took an elevator up to the fifth floor. The impending 'date' somewhat mitigated my fears concerning any pursuit.

The suite was exactly what I wanted: on the one hand, executive and ostentatious, but on the other, cozy and quiet.

She called after half an hour and I told her that I was waiting for her in room 518.

When she entered, my memory of a young girl was shattered and replaced by a mature, albeit still very attractive, woman. She'd probably done the same as I did: changed into a formal dress and added perfume.

"Hey, Giselle, you look fabulous. I remembered you as a very young trainee, but now you are a gorgeous woman and probably an experienced banker to boot."

She blushed a little and stretched her hand for a handshake. "Thank you. Nice to see you, Mr. Vorotavich."

"Come." I showed her to the table by the window. "What are you going to drink?"

"Drink? Nothing, sir, thank you." She was too all-business for my liking.

"No, Giselle, I know that you have a lot of clients from Eastern Europe. That's not how you do business with them." I smiled, poured two glasses of white wine, and handed one to her.

She tried to protest, but I assumed a stern visage and shook my head so resolutely that she understood she'd better not.

We clinked glasses, took a few sips—more correctly I took few sips—while she barely touched it, so I had to mock her.

"Come on, Giselle, you don't want to insult me, right? It's just wine, not poison. Please, show some respect. It's like Russian guanxi, you know — personal connection."

Her second attempt was much better. I had to talk business, although I didn't have the slightest desire to do so, or any acute need to reshuffle my funds here.

I explained briefly that I was under attack by very powerful families, controlling much of the media, where I was demonized on almost a daily basis, and that I needed to care for my funds very meticulously now.

"First, I need to make sure that you don't have these people among your shareholders." I showed her the list containing all members of M7.

She studied it briskly and shook her head. "We are a private bank with very few shareholders. I would know."

"Fine, but I'm still a little worried, because it's certain that your owners have very close ties with them and if they find out that I have funds in your institution, I'm afraid they are going to use every lawful and unlawful tactic to block them."

"No, no, sir, you have nothing to worry about. We disclose no information to anyone about our clients, only to a few governments regarding their own citizens."

"Don't be so naive, Giselle, although I do hope you preserve the utmost confidentiality. Now what I want to do; I want all deposits cancelled and all the funds at my checking account liquid and ready for disposal. Any stock investments you've made according to my earlier instructions you should convert into cash. We'll discuss now how it should be done. Is it possible, that you'd be my point of contact for any further instructions?"

"I would need to ask my boss, but in principle there shouldn't be a problem."

"Do you need me to sign anything?" I smiled.

"No, as long as the money stays with the bank, I can write that it was a telephone instruction."

"Good, because I don't want my visit to Lichtenstein becomes known to anyone."

We then went over my portfolio to decide how best to convert it into cash without substantial losses given the stock markets were at a low. She actually gave me a couple of sound ideas.

It goes without saying that I continually refilled our glasses, so by the time the business part was over, we'd downed almost the entire bottle. She wasn't protesting any more. I also tried to alleviate the atmosphere of a business meeting by telling a joke here and there, which brought about an occasional smile from Giselle. The saying that if you make the girl laugh, you can get her laid, usually worked.

I needed to change the meeting to a more personal thing

"Ah, Giselle, it's really a breath of fresh air to have this conversation with you. I've been on the run for over a week, locked up in a car, surrounded by bodyguards, who might even be speechless for all I know, because they never talk." I exaggerated on purpose. "And here you are—all blossoming, intelligent, smiling. Such a contrast! How about you share the burden of extensive travel with me and see some interesting places on the way?"

"Tempting as it may sound, I'm not sure my husband would approve of that, although he himself is on vacation at Bali with his friends, and I don't think he cares much what's happening back here." Although she said it jokingly too, I couldn't miss a slight touch of sadness and anger in her voice.

"You had a fight before he left and never called. Huh?" He sounded like a nice guy to me.

I'd voiced her thoughts too bluntly. She stood up and turned to the window, perhaps to conceal the tears.

Wasn't it the perfect moment to offer some comfort?

I stood up and embraced her slightly from behind. She didn't resist, so I turned her around and, seeing the glitter of tears in her eyes, kissed her first on the forehead and then on the lips. She didn't play along at first, probably confused, but after a moment she started adding her own taste and tongue into a long French kiss.

While kissing, I'd touched her breast, hidden behind her business blouse. They were firm and inviting. I couldn't stand touching them through the silk, so I unbuttoned just one button in the middle and slipped my hand under her bra. Very soon my kisses were also directed lower than her lips, as soon as I got her half undressed.

After a short necking session, her red panties were on the floor, she on my bed, and I on her. *Red panties for a business meeting?* The brief thought crossed my mind. That might have been a lucky coincidence.

The sex itself wasn't long, but we both put all of our recent frustration and pain into it. I didn't know about her, but I felt like hanging out a little longer. I'd become too hungry for a girl's caress.

"Michael, that was absolutely unnecessary," she said with a shy smile, still blushing.

"What are you talking about? It was the best business meeting I've ever had. Come, let's go through the menu, I want a bite of something more than fruit and your delicious tits."

She turned completely red and wrapped her shirt tighter to conceal her breasts. *Too late for that, honey.*

If her husband was in Indonesia, I deduced that she wouldn't be in a hurry. She hid in the bathroom when room service brought my order. Lichtenstein was a small country. The chances that the service guy knew her were very high.

***

After supper, I had another proper fuck, and only then was I ready to release her.

I didn't know whether sex was good therapy for women with unhappy family lives, but she left my suite in a much better mood.

There was no sense in continuing my journey, as it had gotten late. Giselle didn't want to stay the night, but I thought I might invite her for breakfast the next day, so I reported to Andriana that we'd be staying the night.

Just as I was falling asleep in front of the TV screen and wondering whether Giselle's small belly, in contrast with a slim and fit body, could've meant that she was pregnant, someone knocked demandingly on my door.

Chapter 10 - Unfair Haggling

I'd barely pressed 'Send' on my phone, relaying to Andriana that I'd had visitors, when the door blasted open from a powerful kick.

The first thing I saw was Andriana, tied up and being pushed into the room, and then I heard my message arriving on her phone. *So much for help.* The intruders probably suspected that I was armed, so they held her as a human shield.

But seeing me in the bathrobe alleviated their concerns. They pushed her aside into the corner and trickled in one after another, each holding a gun and a resolute expression on his face. I didn't see the Serbs—there was some hope they hadn't noticed the escort car, just the motor-home. In such a tiny country, even if someone called the police, I wasn't sure they had as many cops as the number of my visitors.

"I was about to open it. What's the hurry?" If I was to die, I could do it with style. After a couple of good rounds with Giselle it wasn't the worst ending.

There were six of them. Each looked overweight, but that was probably because of bulletproof vests under their clothes. They dispersed around the room's perimeter and turned to the entrance.

A young man remotely familiar entered the room, grabbed a chair near the window, brought it to the center of the room, and sat, swinging one leg over the other.

Insolent brat. I didn't invite him to sit in *my* room. I retreated to my bed and lay on it, disdaining their atrocious manners. Even at gunpoint, I didn't want them to feel they had any advantage, though perfectly aware that these were probably my last moments.

The armed guys made a move in my direction, but the youngster stopped them with a swift upward wave of his arm.

"Let him play. I'll tell you when we need some coercive force." A grin spread across his young, Italian face. *That's Millingeri's nephew!*

"Mr. Malinesi Junior, right?" My mistake pronouncing his surname was intentional. "I've checked my smartphone's calendar just before you entered and didn't see any appointment..."

He said something in Italian, and the guy closest to the window picked up my phone. Not to add an appointment, of course, but rather check whether the recording app was on.

The security guy nodded after switching my mobile off, and Junior turned to me again.

"The name is Lucas, Mr. Vorotavich."

Pretty cordial, but I didn't feel like saying *"Nice to meet you."*

He apparently didn't expect any pleasantries. "Listen up, wise guy. You've done a good job hiding, but we tracked your ass the second you accessed the cloud, ha-ha. After the initial plan on your neutralization didn't work, we've reconsidered our further moves and your miserable fate. We don't want you dead any more, as you've already had time to prepare and launch a counter offensive and your death might trigger some chain reaction that might be detrimental rather than advantageous. David told us some things that you were planning. I don't need to deal with revealing our cover at the moment."

I didn't applaud my *merciful* parole. *What was that that David told them? He must've exaggerated enormously the scale of threat I posed to them.* That was my second thought.

"Here is the deal, as I see it." This youngster wasn't easily swayed from his course, was he?

"You get the fuck out and sit quiet until the current financial crisis is over. You may safely assume that we are talking of under a year's time. And then everything's fine, we release David, your share of Gazdiesel. All is normal again."

Releasing David after a year? Jessica would kill me much earlier than that.

"It's not that you have too many choices here, but I'm still gonna ask: does the deal look good to you?"

He was right, I wasn't exactly in the bargaining position, so my response was...

"No, you go fuck yourself. You can kill me, but my countermove is set into motion. You ruin me, you equally ruin yourself. I need David released immediately and then there is a deal."

He was obviously contemplating my reply. I didn't think they needed David that much, and for that long.

"I'll tell you what, you lay low for two more weeks, and I'll come again to say hello and we'll see then, if the terms could be amended."

They left, and it dawned on me that he probably wasn't empowered to make decisions on David's release. He would need to consult his uncle. *Little piece of shit.*

I didn't have an opportunity to miss his departure, as he returned after a minute with his bulldogs. "Now, Misha, one more thing. We know you too well and have a detailed dossier on you, your methods, and the crazy shit you sometimes do. If you even *think* of using these two weeks to stage something stupid or to otherwise change the balance in your favor, remember that the results would be devastating. Here." He tossed something over and left—for good, I hoped—even before I could answer with a *"Fuck you."*

His fucking uncle probably told him to return. I opened the small box, which contained a badge with the letters "CC" and a strange geometrical shape underneath it. *Whatever.*

What was that about blowing their cover? That might be just a brilliant idea. Why didn't I come up with it myself?

Chapter 11 - Change of Plans

Arthur rushed to the hotel when Andriana didn't check in on time. He arrived at 4 a.m. Despite his haste, he missed all the action.

To say he was furious would definitely be an understatement. He was upset with Andriana, but released his anger on the Serbs, when he found them snoring in the car.

They claimed they were sprayed with some gas, but Arthur didn't believe that. I didn't want to witness what he planned to do with them, but I never saw them again. I hoped they were just fired and not dumped, lifeless, into some local river.

I hadn't seen Arthur for few days, so his arrival made me feel much safer. I showed him the little present I'd received from Lucas.

"What is it, some Italian Boy Scout movement?" I was actually in a rather good mood. Knowing who my adversary was made it easier than groping in the dark. After all, they had only seven families, albeit with a lot of siblings and associates.

Arthur looked at the badge, twisted it, even tried it with his teeth. "I don't know, but I will soon."

"This contour below the letters reminds me a shape of an island. It might be Sicily or Sardinia or a similar one."

***

Arthur told me what it was after making few inquiries.

"It's a symbol of an Italian mafia clan, known for its home-trained assassins."

"Some kind of Italian ninjas? It even sounds grotesque. Is the Italian mafia still alive? I thought they were superseded by corporations after running some casinos in Vegas." I referred to *The Godfather* movie. "Well, you don't threaten a whore with a dick. I'm not afraid of this Lucas and his uncle."

I spat and threw the fucking badge away.

At six in the morning, I told everyone to leave and tried to get some sleep so I would wake with a clearer mind, because now I had to make big decisions and (desirably) correct ones.

But before making decisions, after just a couple of hours spent in light slumber, the first thing I did was call Giselle.

She joined me for breakfast (a pretext), but more for a morning romp in the hay (the real reason). We'd parted only twelve hours ago, but so many events had happened in between that it felt like half a year. I didn't tell her about the night's drama, and she didn't notice anything unusual.

After she left, my first decision was that I had to leave Lichtenstein immediately, otherwise I might get hooked by Giselle's charms. What a sweet girl. Not a single word about banking, accounts, convertible securities, or derivatives was mentioned.

I told Arthur to be ready to move out, but before that, we held a quick meeting.

"Arthur, why do you think they left me alive? I don't buy this shit that they are afraid of any retaliation, no matter what David told them."

"Then, it became more beneficial to have you alive now than dead." Arthur's logic was simplistic, but probably correct.

"That's more like it. Let's assume they have incomparably more access to western media than I would ever have, and they could succeed in solidifying the theory that they're trying to sell that it's a local power struggle between Ukrainian and Russian oligarchs, interlocked with the groups behind the military confrontation," I thought out loud. "But, of course, if somebody should suspect their involvement, their merchandise, banks, and businesses would be boycotted and they might be prosecuted — or at least probed regarding their foreign practices."

"Okay, so keeping me alive would be a good explanation for further escalation of violence, but I don't think it's a strong enough reason. They must think they have some leash on me beyond even David. That's what worries me. Or they think they would be able to come up with an offer that would make me forget our past misunderstanding and bury the hatchet."

"Could be." Arthur shrugged.

I grew confident that my adversaries might've simply assumed that I was only money-motivated and if they offered me a generous enough reward, I would drop hostilities. I'd felt this attitude all along from Emil and his mother. That was probably the best leash, in their eyes.

"Now, fuck all this. I know you've prepared a safe compound near Kiev, but I'm not going there. David would hate me if I retreated because he was a captive. You have three days to prepare an operation to get hold of the lovely Swiss castle we visited a couple of weeks ago. That's gonna be my new base for the time being."

Chapter 12 - Long Journey

Although my disguise had been revealed, we continued with the motorhome to give the pretence that we were fine with everything. I'd covered half of Europe on wheels in a few days. *How fast could Russian tanks cover the entire continent?* It shouldn't take that long. They thought they controlled the Russian bears, but it seemed that they didn't even control the Greek squirrels.

I was crossing the huge combination rail and road Oresund bridge between Copenhagen and Malmo, enjoying the magnificent view of the Turning Torso skyscraper when Arthur started the operation I'd assigned him, around a thousand kilometers to the South. We were on the way to the airport, and I prayed that the wind gusts wouldn't sweep our RV into the strait connecting the Baltic and North Seas. The rig shook every time the wind gusted.

The hardest part was to get all our people across the border into Switzerland, or first to the European Union, and then to their final destination. It was a good thing that we maintained very close relations with a few border-control posts on the Ukrainian western frontier. Once inside Romania and Poland, it wasn't hard to get the necessary manpower into neutral, yet defenseless, Switzerland.

I insisted I be present, so we took a flight from Malmo and arrived when everything was ready. After a quick check, Arthur gave the go-ahead.

I didn't want to make a bloodbath out of my little gambit, because I didn't want the army or anything formidable to take note of what was going on in the mountains. However, I had a feeling that we could fend off the Swiss army or Special Forces, if needed.

I don't know where from, but Arthur somehow acquired all the utility line designs and determined which to cut and where to cut them. To start, Arthur's experts cut off the power supply and communications cables, making sure we got both the prime and secondaries. Then, he switched on a powerful radio jammer, using some Israeli military gadgets. After verifying that there was no 'noise' on the spectrum, except for our own communication, we were ready for the active stage.

Arthur's men bombarded the compound with thirty rounds of gas grenades, put on masks, and boarded choppers which were kept ready, just far enough away to be unnoticeable. I watched with pleasure as the heavy, fog-like smoke from the gas grenades drifted upwards, concealing everything underneath it.

Encountering no immediate fire on approach didn't mean anything, and for all we knew, there might be resistance from guards hiding in some gas-protected emergency room.

Once the fog thinned a bit and the choppers landed, we had thirty combatants on the ground who split into three teams to search the castle and the area. A fourth team had been stationed around the perimeter, near the gates and by the choppers, which were parked some distance from each other so that if one got hit and exploded, it wouldn't damage the others.

The first unconscious bodies were uncovered in the service dwelling wing and administrative quarters. After all were carefully tied up, they were moved outside while the gas cloud dispersed.

Our teams continued searching deeper inside the building. Soon, machine-gun fire erupted. Judging from the direction, the sound was coming from the inner part that was against the rock. Arthur ordered another team to approach that area and rushed in that direction himself.

He'd just entered the building when we all heard a blast and the building shook, causing some dust and plaster to fall off.

After a short while, I heard Arthur giving orders via my earpiece, which had been connected to the team's communication devices. He ordered a third team to assume positions on the nearby mountain slope and intercept an armed group when they emerged from a hidden exit.

Bewildered and unable to wait any more, I headed towards the entrance, despite Arthur's people's pleas for me to stay put. But Arthur beat me to it, appearing at the front door with more tied-up soldiers, some apparently wounded. He dumped them unceremoniously near those who had fainted, and ordered some combatants to return inside to finish the search. He scrutinized suitable candidates for interrogation.

He could use my help with that. Arthur walked beside me and updated me on what had happened inside. One of the teams, armed with a special detector for finding hollow spaces, found a hidden, locked door. When they tried to pry it open, those inside sprayed everyone with MP5 submachine guns. But once they realized they were outnumbered and faced with superior firepower, they tried to escape through a mountain tunnel. The blast we'd heard outside designed to open the door must've damaged the tunnel and blocked their way, because the pursuit team soon found them trapped. They agreed to surrender— but not before Arthur's team commander blasted the head off one who'd said something stupid and then tore the safety pin off an assault grenade.

I moved slowly alongside the row of prisoners to check what kind of captives we had. Most were still unconscious with peaceful, worriless expressions, but the ones wearing full combat gear seemed fully alert. They were security or military for sure, except for one guy who looked like a civilian and was obviously pissed off.

I was also pissed that we had neither Antonio nor Lucas among those taken captive, but if I were being honest with myself, I didn't really expect them to be at any location known to me.

Having no bigger fish, I ordered Arthur to question the civilian first, as he obviously wasn't service personnel, and if he was with an armed entourage, they might have been his bodyguards.

To my surprise, after a short while Arthur returned with only a little of somebody's blood on his fists and a satisfied grin on his face.

"This kid's surname is Millingeri. He's Antonio's son."

"Boy, that's great news. Our fishnet returns with a decent catch! David's chances of coming out alive have become much better. We can organize a prisoner swap now, can't we?" I was so glad that we'd undertaken this venture that I opened a flask filled with my favorite single malt, proclaimed, "to David!", and took a generous gulp. That was my first success after a series of setbacks sustained from the M7 fuckers.

Too bad my joy was short lived.

Chapter 13 - Boris

I felt tipsy almost immediately as my adrenaline-galvanized system started to absorb the alcohol. Then my phone rang.

Not too many people knew my recently changed mobile number, so seeing an unfamiliar number displayed on the screen was a surprise. Could it be that the Italians were already aware about what had happened in the Alps?

Could be. Undecided what I would say, I answered. But instead of Italians, I heard a trembling female voice, which after a short exchange I recognized as Tanya—Boris' personal assistant and probably mistress by now.

"He's wounded. It's very bad."

"I'll be right over." My voice started to tremble. I had a strange feeling of déjà-vu, as if reliving the situation when I was wounded in an assassination attempt, only then Boris had been me hearing the news, and I was Boris lying somewhere wounded.

It was bad, I knew it. It wasn't because of Tanya's voice. It was my intuition. I ran inside to look for Arthur, who was probably interrogating people, usually in an excessively cruel manner.

"Arthur, come we gotta get going. Boris is wounded."

Arthur was on his feet immediately, ready to act, infuriated by what I'd said.

Most people loved Boris for his sense of humor and for being the elder of the tribe, among many other things. Even Arthur—who didn't have any warm feelings for anyone, I was sure—had some for him.

I caught myself already mourning Boris. No, as long as there was a chance, there was a chance.

"Call David, he must know. We are flying to Ukraine."

Seeing a startled expression on Arthur's face, which was extremely rare, I didn't understand what was wrong.

"David is still missing, Misha."

"Right — "

The gravity of the situation dawned on me: my best friend missing and another wounded and almost dead. Everything was crumbling... I couldn't imagine the world without Boris or David, certainly not without both.

My faux coolness vanished, replaced by despair and grief, feelings I hadn't felt since my adolescence.

***

I saw him on the hospital bed, intubated, his entire chest bandaged. He was unconscious, his face white as marble. I didn't need to ask the doctor a thing, he just looked at me and shook his head. The best doctors from Kiev were here at my request in this provincial hospital, prompted by the generous amount of money I'd promised them. Another doctor was on my personal plane, coming from Israel.

I'd heard the story three times already from three different sources, two of which were eyewitnesses, and it was still beyond me as to how it all transpired.

As Luhansk was out of Ukrainian control, Boris's Governor's office moved to Severodontesk, neighboring the army field command headquarters. The entire area was well guarded by the Governor's own security and, naturally, by being adjacent to a military headquarters, which was always full of soldiers coming and going.

Nevertheless, in broad daylight, the headquarters were razed to the ground by the powerful blast of a planted explosive, detonated from afar, which caused havoc and panic through the entire district. Just when the dust settled and people started running in all direction trying to escape and looking for shelter, three armored military vehicles charged out of each of the three streets leading to the area, blocking the way, and began spraying everyone with heavy machine guns fixed to their roofs. This was accompanied by occasional AK-47 fire from the vehicles' windows. It was a massacre, a slaughter without mercy. On top of the twenty-seven killed by the blast, another ninety-five were riddled with bullets. The only survivors were those who were 'luckily' stuck under the debris of the collapsed building and didn't think of running when the second phase of the attack commenced.

Boris had been on the street after the explosion, trying to evacuate Tanya's boy, who'd come to visit his mother during her lunch break. Hit by three bullets to the chest, Boris fell, covering the boy with his body, thus saving him. When I heard that, I turned and surreptitiously wiped a tear. A cynical guy like Boris, he still had a big heart, however hardened by his tough surroundings.

After visiting the hospital, I walked through the square, where bloodstains were still very visible, even though the bodies had gone. There were so many red puddles turning brown, it felt like a mass grave and gave me the shivers.

Whoever staged the raid was deliberately going for the utmost number of casualties. Boris and many others were just civilians.

I couldn't ignore the natural question: did it also have something to do with me? This operation wasn't designated just to liquidate Ukrainian military forces hostile to the separatists, but to intimidate, to outrage, to demoralize. I didn't know the answer.

Those responsible should be held accountable. And I didn't mean the Hague Court for crimes against humanity. I had my own court of justice.

I hoped to have a chance to even some scores with the motherfuckers.

These thoughts were running through my head while I sat beside Boris's bed. I'd returned to the hospital after a short survey of the place where he'd been wounded. He couldn't talk; he hardly breathed, probably dreaming of better worlds, slowly leaving this one. After seeing him again, deteriorating, I didn't have any more doubts.

I hugged him, and I hugged Tanya and her boy before they left Boris's room to allow me some privacy. I thought Boris would have cared for this girl and her boy, and so I would too.

"What's your name, boy?"

"Artyom." He had a sad but firm voice.

"If you ever need something, you can always call or look for me and I'll be there."

I told Arthur I wanted this family provided with whatever they needed, ever. And also Boris's nephew—his only living relative. He would inherit Boris's fortune, and though Boris was a rich man, I thought he could use my help until the formalities had been taken care of.

I couldn't call it even a setback. It was a disaster, one of the most tragic moments I'd experienced.

The way the things looked, it might not be the last.

Chapter 14 - New Governor

Boris died at around 3 am. Arthur woke me. He didn't need to talk; I knew what it was about.

His funeral was national. It wasn't every day that a governor and a true patriot died under such tragic circumstances. Most high-level officials attended, as well as a few foreign dignitaries. Since Boris had no close family, I, as his closest associate, naturally assumed the role of organizer for the entire ceremony and the logistics.

I didn't want it to compete with other funerals being held around the same time for those who also perished in the same tragedy, so the ceremonial part was relatively modest. I pointedly stressed that Boris was a great man and leader, but no different from any other person.

I didn't need to write any notes, since I knew exactly what kind of post-mortem speech I would deliver, and I knew it would be broadcast.

Despite the risk, I wasn't afraid to stand by his grave in the open. No sniper would dare.

Autumn was in the air, driving out the weakening summer and turning previously warm gusts into a steady, chilly breezes. Despite the weather, the crowd attending the funeral was so huge, I couldn't see where it ended, even when I climbed few stairs on the improvised stage.

I cleared my throat and picked up the mike, protecting it from the wind with the fold of my raincoat.

"Dear friends, relatives, compatriots, and colleagues, all of you know what kind of person Boris was. There is no one in the region, and maybe in all of Ukraine, who doesn't know him. And deservedly so, because of his outstanding achievements in any position that he occupied over the years, be it a director of a factory, businessman, or political figure. But he was also known for his modest personality. A rich man, who was at the top, he had it all, yet he chose to continue serving his people, the region, the nation. He died, protecting this boy—" I swallowed a tear and pointed at Artyom, whom I'd told to stand near "— with his body. This characterizes him the most. Never for himself, always for others. But his death will be futile, if we lose the battle for which he sacrificed his life. We don't want to die, but there are things that we are ready to risk our lives for and stand till the end, till the victory — and it's Ukraine! Our motherland. Whoever thinks they can frighten us, make us retreat, give up, is very wrong. I hope we will find those responsible for this atrocity, as it wasn't a military operation, it was a massacre, ISIS-esque, and those who did it should be well aware that the retribution will reach them one day. This is a very sad occasion, but I want to appeal to those from abroad that pour oil on our local fires. Your games will not pass unnoticed. You should remember that each act has consequences, a toll that will be collected. Lastly, I want us all to remember Boris Uralski as a true hero, as a distinguished native son, fallen in battle for his region, for his people, for Ukraine."

When I'd approved the protocol for the ceremony, I let three more speakers say a few words. I didn't want it to become a lengthy, never-ending process where eulogies would melt into meaningless words.

While the second speaker concluded, Arthur reported in a whisper that some woman wanted to pass me something. He pointed to the right where, a few meters away, my security had stopped her. I spotted a tall blonde wearing a veil and dressed in black. As blondes wearing black or red were always my weakness, I nodded to make sure she noticed, and asked Arthur to take whatever she had for me, preferably unnoticed by the TV cameras, and to find out who she was.

TV cameras might have missed the episode, but Masha, who'd come from London to pay her last tribute to Boris, didn't, and hissed at me in jealous anger. I just shrugged and whispered that I didn't know her, and there was nothing to worry about. She was doubtful and probably dissatisfied with my answer, but I put the piece of paper that Arthur brought back into my shirt pocket and promised Masha I'd share with her what it was about. I couldn't deal with it at the cemetery.

I offered to build a memorial in Severodonetsk to all those who'd died in the incident, and I agreed with the Mayor of Kiev, that one of the streets in the capital would be named after Boris. I hoped Luhansk would one day return to Ukrainian rule, where it belonged, and we'd have something grandiose there in Boris' memory as well.

Once he was buried, I felt businesslike again. There were too many things to handle for a long period of grieving.

During the traditional meal and drinking devoted to the memory of the deceased, as the entire establishment was present, I told them that the governor's post would remain mine to man. Under the current circumstances, there weren't many volunteers willing to jump into the once-lucrative, but now too risky to be coveted, chair.

"Misha, do you want me to appoint you governor?" The newly-elected president, Dmitry Yaremchuk, asked when we stepped aside for a few private words.

We raised glasses full of vodka but didn't clink them together, as the tradition banned that at post-funeral receptions. Knowing Boris, I was somehow sure that even for this sad occasion, he would've preferred if I'd invited a few models in something close to bikinis to mingle with all the dignitaries. But I just couldn't do it.

"To Boris's memory, may he rest in peace." We downed the drinks and backed them up with a pickle—just like any others would do. Nothing fancy.

"Hardly, Dima." I returned to his earlier question. I was on a friendly footing with the President, so I could address him informally. He was a peer oligarch before he ran for the presidency. "I can't free myself for this, and I have a lot on my hands. By the way, we should have a meeting when I'm in Kiev, since I now know much more about the reasons for the latest rise in tensions with the Russians. We should see how to address that on your level."

"Fine, sure, but let's get back to the issue of the candidate for a governor. Who do you have in mind then, as it's a pivotal position and I wouldn't want to appoint just anyone?"

"Of course." I had a sudden idea. "You know what? Recently you granted Ukrainian citizenship and allowed foreigners to take senior positions. Let me toy a little bit with one candidate that might fit, and by the end of the meal, I'll tell you who I was thinking about."

"No problem, Misha, but nothing bizarre, please. We all know your inclination for showmanship." He cackled. "And no leftists or liberals, please. Not for this district."

"You know my theory, Dima? There is no right or left, liberal or conservative. There are people for whom the most important is 'who' and those

141

primarily interested in 'what'. Rightist, conservative, or whatever, they support anything that's done by 'theirs', and it doesn't matter what. While leftists or liberals judge whether something is right or wrong and pretend to be oblivious as to who's behind it. You see what I mean? I agree with you that in our case, we need someone of 'ours', who won't make too many evaluations, but will do anything to protect our cause."

I wasn't sure he understood my philosophic generalizations, but as his assistants approached with something urgent, I had to let him attend to his other affairs.

"Mr. President." I shook his hand ceremoniously.

I left him bewildered and went looking for Arthur. I needed him to consult on my last idea.

"This lady, she disappeared," he told me on approach.

I didn't understand what he was talking about.

"The one who gave you a note."

I'd completely forgotten about her.

"Well, fuck her for the moment. Not that important. I want to talk to you about another lady. I want to appoint Andriana to the position of Governor of Luhansk oblast."

No matter how well he'd been trained to conceal emotions, I managed to surprise him. I could tell that much.

"She's a Romanian."

"Come on, Arthur, what a lame excuse. I've got that sorted out with the President. What do you think of her as a candidate?"

"She's loyal."

"That's one." I started to count.

"She's trained to command and to manage people, and has experience in it."

"That's two."

"She's schooled in strategy, tactics, combat, and military theory."

"That's three, and I don't need more than that. For this war-torn region, we need someone with exactly that set of skills. Now that the advance command post has been bombed and the general and his subordinates are dead, it will take time to bring or train someone able to guide defense, because the Ukrainian army is so depleted and its commanding officers have so little live combat experience. I know the governor isn't directly responsible for the army, but I can talk to the President about promoting the commander of Lug, our battalion that I finance, to the position of commander for this theater and then they could work in conjunction. What do you say?"

"It could work." Arthur was still dumbfounded.

"Then I'll try to promote it."

My assumption had been right. The President didn't have that many options for the governor's position, nor for military command. After few questions, drinks, and even a laugh or two (as Dima, knowing me, was utterly surprised that I'd picked a woman), we shook hands on a done deal. But before that, he took a personal glance at her and was relieved to see that she was definitely not someone I'd fucked.

I recalled that I hadn't asked Andriana's opinion of my impromptu decision. Taking into account that she was an opinionated woman, I hoped I'd be able to convince her to pick up the gauntlet.

The conversation wasn't easy. What convinced her after all wasn't the opportunity to occupy a high-level government position, but more the peril it entailed and its military touch. Arthur and his ex-wife were nuts, but I couldn't care less as long as they were *my* nuts.

I waited impatiently for the feast to end, as I had pressing affairs in Switzerland, where I'd left my newly occupied castle full of my troops and hostages totally idle—although Arthur's people hadn't reported anything extraordinary.

But it turned out that his people were just unable to discern "extraordinary" from "regular".

Chapter 15 - Back to the Alps

I needed to evaluate the loot. We returned to Millingeri's Alpine nest two days after I'd left in haste to see Boris. It was the third time I'd arrived at their castle in a few weeks. My enchantment with it was long gone, and I almost hated this austere and exalted place—my enemy's den.

The immediate signs of the operation had already been removed and the power supply restored, however no communication or cellular coverage were allowed yet.

Arthur ordered his men to put a "no entry" road sign and a physical barrier in front of the existing metal gates six kilometers down the pathway, where the side road branched out from the main intercity route. A little behind all these, Arthur stationed a police car, clearly visible, so no one would try to pass. *Good thinking*.

So far, no one had attempted to wrest the castle back, but it didn't mean that our move would continue without a counter-thrust.

I should be ready for the worst. In the meantime, I was eager to see Mr. Millingeri Junior and to award him a slap or two of my own. In his case, I could understand Arthur's pleasure in beating people.

The smug motherfucker was venomous.

"So now you come? Too late now." He smiled viciously. "We agreed between each other that if anyone disappears without establishing contact within forty-eight hours, your friend David would be executed."

"Ah, yeah? Well, that's a bit unfortunate for you too, because if David's dead, you have no more than few more minutes to live, you stupid fuck."

I looked angrily at Arthur. His men should have reported this information, since it was obvious I wasn't the first one he'd told this to. They probably decided they were just hollow threats. I couldn't believe we might've lost David because of these idiots.

We were probably a few hours beyond the forty-eight-hour deadline! My only hope was that they might be uncertain as to when they had had the last contact with this guy. Examining the terrified face of Salvatore (someone had told me his name), I believed him, though there would be no salvation for him if David was dead.

With my hands noticeably trembling, I took my phone out, asked Arthur to allow cellular coverage for a few minutes, and dialed Emil. We hadn't spoken since our little private war erupted, but this wasn't a good time for foreplay and beating around the bush.

There were few very long beeps before he answered, probably contemplating why the fuck I was calling.

He didn't say a word, but I saw the call was on.

"Emil?"

"What the fuck do you want, Misha?"

"I want David, and I want him now, otherwise some whining motherfucker named Salvatore is gonna be twenty centimeters shorter, because his head will be traveling separately from his body to Sicily, or wherever the fuck all those Millingeris live."

I might've been recorded, eavesdropped, whatever. I couldn't care less. My best friend could die if I procrastinated.

"I'm pretty sure it's not you who's holding him, but you call me back to confirm that he's alive in ten minutes. If there is no call, you know what happens." I hung up, looked at my watch, and prayed silently for David to be alive. I wiped the sweat from my forehead.

My attention stayed on my watch, each minute of uncertainty causing anguish. He called back in six minutes.

"We want Salvatore back in exchange for this guy, who fucks our brains out anyway with his babble. Here —" I heard a weak "Misha—" in the background. David's voice, without doubt.

"Now we're talking." Thank God, he was still alive!

"And the castle."

"Fuck you, no castle. You want it back, you release my shares in Gazdiesel." Hearing no reaction on his part, I continued."The exchange will be tomorrow at 16:00 at the 27th kilometer marker on 7th highway from St. Gallen to Gossau's direction. You can bring the entire tribe of Italian assassins if you want; I'm not afraid of those wankers."

The location I (more precisely, Arthur) chose was a secluded, on-the-highway parking spot not far from the castle. I was bluffing, but he might've interpreted it literally, because when we came, the tribe of assassins were indeed there.

Chapter 16 - Interrogation

The reason I'd set the exchange for the next day was because I wanted to interrogate Salvatore properly. Arthur's crew could beat out information from anyone, but they didn't have enough intelligence to understand what information was needed or valuable, as they'd just proven by withholding vital facts from their commander.

That's where I could help.

I wouldn't torture him myself. For that purpose, I brought Arthur.

"Salvatore, my boy, I'm told that you're twenty-four years old. Why don't you screw girls, go jet-skiing in Rimini, or have an orgy at some private resort in Sardinia? How come you're at this secluded place in the beginning of the autumn? Reading books? Rehearsing for your bar exams?" I had a dossier on him, but it had a few missing pieces. I'd learned from it that he was studying to become a lawyer.

He didn't answer. Probably because he thought that I was only mocking him and trying to cause him to lose his composure (*bright boy*). I switched to more direct questions.

"Why was I chosen as the scapegoat?"

Since I was not upset over his silence after my first question, he must've assumed I would tolerate it further. I looked at Arthur, giving him a silent 'go ahead' and Salvatore received a full-strength kick to his balls.

I thought my ears would explode from his screaming and shrieking.

"Listen, Salvatore, I might sound like I'm joking, but I'm not here for fun. You either answer my question or you'll need to undergo a change of gender after our little talk, because your dick will become dysfunctional. Do you understand, or should I ask for another therapeutic intervention from my friend here?"

I didn't look at Arthur, so he wouldn't kick him again. I waited patiently for five to six seconds, after which he finally nodded.

"Okay, then, let me ask again: why was I chosen to be framed for the recent economic plunge?"

"Who else?" He groaned through gritted teeth. "You are number one now on the list, you are an outsider and from the geographic location where the trouble is. It's logical. You were an ideal candidate. Do you think that if our factory pollutes somebody's river, we're gonna run around and proclaim, 'We are the bad guys; we dumped junk into the river?' Besides, in a sense, you are responsible."

"How so?"

"Your fund was supporting, and paying for campaigns and soliciting the EU to send emissaries to broker an association agreement between Ukraine and Europe. Now those clowns misled everyone by reporting the deal would be struck, didn't they? And then it was spurned, a very likely eventuality that they failed to foresee. You paid for this and now there is a penalty."

Hmm, interesting. The Russians hated me for trying, while Europeans or Westerners as a whole hated me for failing to bring about the association. Was I the embodiment of all evil on the planet, for Christ's sake?

So far his answers sounded sincere, but when I stopped asking about me and directed my questions towards him, his family, and the Magnificent Seven, I suspected he'd begun to dodge again.

"Hey, Arthur, do you have that lie detector with you?"

Arthur nodded.

"Unpack it, man."

We attached the wires to Salvatore and I told Arthur, "Whenever the detector shows he's lying or the device is unable to decide, you have a free hand with this boy."

Salvatore eyed us warily.

After the first question I asked, the graph slightly peaked, and Arthur instantly knocked Salvatore out with a powerful right hook to the jaw.

"Arthur, are you mad? Now we need to wait until he comes to his senses and reconnect him. We haven't even calibrated the damn machine!"

But maybe it was a good lesson after all. Not for Salvatore's jaw, of course, which seemed to be broken, but for his overall understanding of our tolerance level. His lovely daddy might even thank me for the lesson in respecting his elders, at which his insolent son was failing.

"OK. Take three now." I closed an imaginary clapboard. "Now, my dear boy, to save some time, I'm not gonna ask questions, because your broken jaw is swelling, and I'm not sure you'll be able to speak for very long. For that reason, you're gonna tell me why you wanted me whacked, and why you decided against it later, the entire layout of your organization, your next moves, who killed Boris Uralski and why, and any pertinent information. If you are a good boy, my paramedics might save your jaw. If you aren't, the chances are not good. You can fire away."

And he did. He didn't know all the answers—it seemed he wasn't privy to all the intimate nuances, and I believed him. What he *did* know, together with my own intel, I summarized in a nutshell.

I was dealing with an all-powerful, informal organization with its own military wing, or "internal security," as Salvatore put it, steering committee, agenda, execution branch, and endless resources, which amounted to two-thirds of the entire global economy. Only seven families! *Who would believe it?* I had trouble believing it myself. However, when the high-tech market boomed, as well as the Asian markets, their share of the global pie, being mostly in traditional industry such as banking, investment funds, and natural resources, started to shrink and they didn't like that. So they conceived a plan, and I just came in handy on occasion. I was so controversial a figure that anyone would believe I could fuck with the global economy, prompt presidents to start wars (*that's what oligarchs do, don't they?*), and other nasty stuff.

Salvatore knew the general layout but didn't have information on his colleagues' next moves. He was sure that the planned takeovers of high-tech companies were fully underway, and some might've even been accomplished. I'd hoped to know more about that particular issue.

And I knew who was responsible for the Severodonetsk massacre. It was a Chechen unit made up of ruthless killers let loose on Ukraine and barely controlled even by the Russian command that just provided them new targets for their mayhem. The way he tried to talk around it led me to think that his family was somehow implicated, and that the Chechens outdid what they were asked. Fuck, these and other Chechens kept haunting me.

On the other hand, he knew a lot about those "Sicilian ninjas," as I'd tagged them, and I left Arthur alone to gather the intel he needed to be prepared to confront them.

The new knowledge aligned well with the information I'd procured following the note from the mysterious blonde.

Chapter 17 - Not Alone

Before returning to check on my loot in Switzerland, I'd deliberately opened the blonde's note when Masha and I were in the hotel following the funeral.

It contained an American cell number and a name—Patrick Galigan. At least it wasn't a woman's name, which would make Masha even more upset.

She took Boris's death hard, and couldn't stop crying. She always saw something fatherly in his attitude towards fatherless me. And she was probably right. She could also do the math of Boris dead and David missing and implored me and even Arthur, although it was futile, to put an end to the war that we were waging. I wished I could, but it wasn't up to us. We were the prey, not the hunters.

I hugged Masha and took out my cell phone. No one could kill me through a phone, unless it detonated, so I just punched the digits from the note onto my screen. It was still within business hours even on the American West Coast.

"Patrick Galigan."

It was a confident, masculine voice. I put my phone on speaker, so Masha would hear that it was not about women, although it always could be.

"Hi, this is Michael calling." I didn't know much more to say, so I hoped he—or they—who initiated the contact would care to explain.

It took him few seconds to react. "You're calling from Ukraine, right?" He sounded agitated now.

"That's right."

"Well, thank you for that. I hoped you'd call. I know who you are. You see, I can't be too detailed on the phone, but in a nutshell, my boss is in a very similar situation to yours." If I'd known this guy wasn't the boss, I would've told someone else to call him.

"Okay." I could only imagine what similarities our situations might have.

"The reason you're speaking with me and not with him—and he asked me to apologize for that on his behalf—is that he's in danger and doesn't use phones and the internet that much."

At least they had enough tact to understand that it was improper to solicit me through some subordinate. "I see, but who's your boss?"

"Well, sir, let him present himself when he meets you, if you would agree, of course."

"Is he in the States? I'm not sure I'll have time to travel that far any time soon."

"He will come to wherever you say, sir."

This Patrick was all courtesy.

"All right. How about Amsterdam? It'll be roughly halfway between here and the US, as there are not many landing fields in the Atlantic."

"It would be perfect."

We set the date but not the exact location, which we agreed to coordinate through Patrick a half hour before the meeting time.

Hopefully, if everything went well with exchange of 'prisoners of war', I could head for Amsterdam within a day or two.

Chapter 18 - Exchange

Most of the staff were released right after they were captured, following some brief questioning. I didn't want the authorities to stage a search or pursuit for absent or lost personnel. Only Salvatore and his bodyguards were held at the castle to prevent reporting the details about who and how many of my men were defending Mr. Millingeri's mountain residence. They were ready for release right after the 'main dish'.

In the meantime, we made our last preparations.

I didn't expect anything stupid on the part of my enemies until after the exchange, but we needed to prepare for any eventuality. As we controlled the slope, we had the height advantage, and it wasn't that hard to position snipers to cover the entire road section where we'd planned the meeting.

So far, our scouts hadn't reported anything funny going on near the location of the rendezvous.

I would arrive at least a quarter-hour after they did. *Let them fucking sweat*, although I was well aware that David was probably sweating, too.

Finally, Arthur, at the scene supervising the meeting, reported they had come.

"Come, daddy's waiting." I pulled Salvatore by a metal chain that we'd attached to him as a leash to make it more melodramatic and stress our disrespect. We'd cleaned him up and fixed his jaw, so he didn't look that damaged. His eyes, though, showed a lot less insubordination than when I'd first met him.

No matter how tense I was, the layout gave me an occasional laugh, as I thought of it as some kind of Hollywood drugs/diamonds versus money brief cases exchange, with armed men on my side and theirs.

I was pretty close in my estimate of how it would look. They came in three cars and arranged a line of five heavily-armed men holding machine and shot guns in front of them. I watched each ugly face closely. Yeah, I probably wouldn't stand a chance against any of them, but having Arthur by my side, I wasn't too worried. I was sure they'd spotted my snipers, so they deliberately pointed their weapons up, posing no immediate threat.

Neither David nor Millingeri Senior were visible, probably still inside one of the cars.

Despite the tension, I enjoyed those moments of pure adrenaline. As we walked towards them, I pulled Salvatore by the leash with Arthur and seven of his men following just two steps behind. The doors of the cars started to open and more of Millingeri's armed "soldiers" climbed out.

And then I saw David and that Antonio fucker. Something wasn't right about David's appearance.

When we got closer, my heart jumped, because David's face was a total mess. Not only was half his ear missing, there were a few fresh scars and bruises all over it. His left eye was practically concealed by swelling.

The motherfuckers had brutally beat him and cut him up! I couldn't restrain myself. I lost my temper and went straight for Millingeri's throat, dropping the chain by which I pulled Salvatore. Arthur intercepted me before Millingeri's thugs lowered their guns.

"You fucking sadist, what did you do?" I yelled at him. "This exchange means nothing. You're fucking dead."

I kicked his fucking son's butt, propelling him to his damn father, and they released David, who walked slowly, limping but smiling through a grimace of pain, towards me.

I embraced him. "Glad to see you, brother."

They didn't say a word, just retreated into the cars and left.

As soon as they were gone, I called to have Salvatore's security detail released from the house. Since they hadn't done anything wrong, none was hurt, and they left in a fairly good shape.

I hugged David again. "Later, dude, don't tell me anything now. Very glad to see you. Let's get you fixed up first." I turned to Arthur. "Ask the paramedic to attend to David immediately. The way he looks, he might need to go to a hospital. I just hope his body is in better shape than his face. And let's wrap it up fast. I have a feeling it'll be dangerous to stay in the castle now. Don't ask me what it is. Just a hunch."

We were on the choppers within minutes. The castle was still visible behind us, when someone noticed a salvo of short-range Grad-type rockets over the castle, followed immediately by explosions and smoke. And then another flight, and another. I doubted anything remained intact.

Holy shit! I didn't think they would have enough chutzpah to fire rockets in the center of Europe. That was something that would be investigated at a very high level, but they must've felt invincible when dealing with European authorities.

As most of our troops engaged in the operation were from the Lug battalion—a volunteer unit consisting of former special ops soldiers—and financed from my private funds, we needed to return them to the Luhansk area where they were quartered and engaged in defending against Russian and separatist's troops.

Arthur had a plan to disperse them so as not to attract attention to a large group of suspicious-looking Slavs rambling about. I let him handle that. Soon, two choppers split away from our group.

As soon as I received a report that David wouldn't need a hospital for he mostly had scars and bruises, I signaled Arthur to land, since I wanted to have a chat with David and offer him some refreshments.

The Black Forest in south Germany was an ideal place for a little friendly talk. We landed somewhere very close to Europa Park; I could see the gigantic roller coasters against the skyline.

Until one of Arthur's men could return with take-out from a local restaurant (and I specifically asked him to bring me a long, saucy German sausage hot-dog with a large beer), I offered David a sip from my flask of whiskey, the only thing I had on the chopper, which he rejected. We walked a short distance away from the others and sat on the grass on the hillside, overlooking a small river at the bottom of the slope.

I gave David my cell phone. "Here. Call Jessica."

He moved a little further away so I wouldn't hear their conversation. I had a feeling he was much more afraid of her than the Italian Mafia.

Indeed, after what seemed like a heated exchange, he returned to where I sat, puzzled.

"She yelled at me. Give me the flask, man. Now I really need a slug. She says I should disassociate from you." He was probably still too shocked, because in other circumstances, I was sure he wouldn't have mentioned it.

"Well, maybe she's right, mate. Now you look like a war hero with all the scars. About time to retire and claim your live combat veteran's pension. If before you attracted women with your handsomeness and charm, now it will be by your 'tough guy' look." I was really glad David was in better condition than he first appeared, so I felt comfortable enough to kid around.

But then I recalled that he might not know about Boris. "Some sad things happened after they got you, man. Boris—"

"I know, the fuckers told me. So sad. Was there a funeral already?"

"Yep, you just missed it. He saved a boy, protected him with his body, Tanya's son."

David looked like he was going to shed a tear. I felt the same. Maybe we should both retire, as Jessica had suggested.

"So, how did it happen?" I wanted to know what they'd done to David.

"Eh, leave it, man. Some other time. Don't wanna go back to that even mentally. I didn't tell them anything sensitive—I think, but they didn't put too much pressure on me, since, as I understand, they mostly held me as a bargaining chip. I did stress your ubiquitous and plenipotentiary reach to any of them though. Got them concerned, I hope."

"Yeah, they told me that much. How did you come up with the idea to rip the veil off of this clandestine organization?"

"Intuitively. I've noticed that illicitness is their prime concern. You know, if people would know what they do, nobody's gonna buy their products, take loans from them, invite them as seed investors."

"That's so true, Dave. Exactly my line of thought." That was a good course of revenge. I couldn't wipe out the seven dynasties, and I wasn't sure I wanted

163

to, as not all of them were hostile to me, but I could expose them to the world! It would require careful planning.

When I was excited, I needed to act. I couldn't just sit on the grass and enjoy the tranquil sight of the river. In the meantime, I had an idea for another tactical move.

"Hey, Arthur." I waved him over. "You need to find the best cyber experts or hackers, desirably former military, who can crack and take over a well-protected, sophisticated computer system. Maybe bring some guys that developed the Stuxnet—or whatever it's called— virus in Iran's nuclear reactors from the Israeli army."

"No, those were Americans."

"You sure?"

"No, I'm not. Nobody knows. But I get the idea. What are you up to?"

"After the castle, I'm in an invading mood. I have a bank or two in mind that I'd like to control for some time."

"I don't know, it's a criminal offense. I'm not sure I can convince legit cyber experts to take part in this. They wouldn't want to risk prison."

"Listen, Arthur, if the right people were put in prison, we would've rotted there a long time ago. White-collar crime interception rates are very low."

"But you're not white-collar."

"Yeah, you're right. I don't have a collar. Get to it. I'm serious. This is our next operation. I want those damn banks."

Before the banks, though, I had an Amsterdam detour waiting.

Chapter 19 - Unexpected allies

I decided that only Arthur and three of his men would come with me to Amsterdam. David would return home for further treatment and to his angry, beloved wife. He wanted to come with me, and I'd have loved that, but having someone looking that scary with all the bandages and scars coming on a 'blind date' of sorts, seemed like overkill to me.

We passed the coffee shop on Leidseplein, and I noted that it would be nice to come back to after the meeting to see if they had any new type of marijuana available.

***

It was time. I let Arthur dial Patrick from my phone in the hope that Arthur's English would be sufficient to understand where the meeting would take place. I didn't hear Arthur talking, but he killed the connection after a very short spell and led us towards the city center.

Two blocks away from Leidseplein, Arthur apparently found what he was looking for. He made eye contact with his men that followed behind us and made sure they saw where we went. We entered what appeared to be a Greek restaurant with only a few patrons. Arthur told the hostess that we needed a table booked by Richard.

We were led to a separate room, where Arthur followed the hostess inside, leaving me behind for a few seconds. Everything must have looked safe, because Arthur called, "Come, Misha."

A tall man in his mid-thirties with curly red hair stood to greet me. The only one in the room, he wore a formal business suit with a red tie and looked a bit strained. I regretted that the blonde who passed me the note wasn't present, too. At the funeral, her face had been covered with a black veil, but her body was still in my memory. She'd given me the impression of a fabulous gazelle.

"Richard Avenue." He shook my hand firmly.

His name sounded familiar. "Michael."

Arthur didn't bother introducing himself, so I had to do it. "That's Arthur. If you don't mind."

He didn't.

"Michael, thank you very much for agreeing to meet me. I'm sorry for all the secrecy. I see you don't know who the hell I am." He smiled, noticeably more relaxed. "So I'll tell you in a few words about myself and, of course, why I asked for the meeting. I'm the chairman of Pear Communications."

It took me a second to find the correct file in my memory, as there were quite a few apples, oranges, and other fruits in the telecom industry.

"Ah, but of course. You're really big in Latin America in cellular systems; have few operations in Eastern Europe and some hardware business in

China, right? You are in Fortune 500, if I'm not mistaken."

"Exactly. Very precise description of our business and position, I have to admit. You have an excellent memory, sir."

"Thanks, I used to, not any more, though. Becoming a bit old, I guess. We are not in direct competition in any arena, I think. How can I help?"

"It's not about business, Michael. It's more about survival. Our company is listed on three stock exchanges with considerable stock being traded. Aside from Pear, I, as an individual, like to toy with securities and I have an analytic team working for me. Something like a couple of weeks ago, when many securities started to collapse against the backdrop of the recent surge in Russian aggression, I was advised by my analysts that they'd spotted some strange behavior on the part of some traders. Their impression was that someone was buying considerable quantities of shares of Pear as well as those of a few other telecoms. We kept watching and analyzing. At some point I realized that there was a full-blown, hostile takeover taking place. I summoned an immediate board meeting, but I didn't have a chance to chair it, as my car was blown up just as I was approaching it to drive to the meeting and right after that I received a call from a blocked number, advising me that I'd better get lost. You know I'm in telecommunications, so we quickly traced the call, but it led only to someone in Somalia. I intended to just ignore the fuckers and hired some security, but the next day, when my driver picked me up to go to the office, I noticed we were followed by two jeeps with tinted windows. I know—how banal. They came alongside our car, a window in one of them rolled down, and they sprayed the wheels of our car with an M-16 and then disappeared. They obviously didn't mean to kill us, because if they did, nothing would really have prevented them from doing so. But they showed they could. I mean, hearing some threats from Somalia is one thing, but to have a car blown up and then being sprayed by a machine gun right near my house is a totally different story! I advised my deputy that I'd be skipping the meeting and lying low for a while."

"Welcome to the club, Richard. It's nothing to be proud of, but I also experience similar traumatic events every few years it seems, and they are not for intimidation, but for the real thing. Anyway, no matter how disastrous it all sounds and with all the compassion I feel, what do I have to do with all this?"

"Nothing much, except recently we've found out who was behind the takeover. It's Greenberg's Investment bank." He leaned forward to see my reaction better when he delivered the punch line.

"Okay, then. Now we're talking. Let's order something. I'm starving." I wanted to buy some time.

So there might be few of us, huh? I should've anticipated it, since several dozen companies were being targeted and their managers and major shareholders might've noticed and been approached by now. If we have our own Magnificent, or Shitty, Seven— or Ten or Twenty— we can maybe form a formidable counter-force!

Arthur beckoned and a Greek waiter came in. "Kalispera, sirs, what would you like to order?"

"Ah, kalispera, a little bit of bankruptcy and a write-off of debts for me," I couldn't help being a bit sarcastic about Greece's financial troubles.

"Huh?" Richard laughed loudly, but the waiter looked confused.

"Nothing, just a Greek salad and souvlaki, please, and here — this bottle of wine," I showed the menu entry to him.

Richard and Arthur also gave their orders and I had some more time to reflect about the situation. But first things first. I excused myself to the bathroom and sent a Whatsapp message to my secretary in Tel Aviv, as she was the quickest of all those I retained. *Find on the net, and send me all the pictures of Chairmen of Argentinean mobile operators.* I didn't want to mention him specifically.

I'd just finished pissing and was washing my hands, when I heard the familiar sound of pictures arriving on my cell phone via Whatsapp.

There he was. All right, I recognized him. At least I was most likely talking to the guy he claimed to be. With all the hush-hush surrounding the meeting, I had to make sure. But I still needed to be cautious.

I was more-or-less decided, though.

"Okay, Richard, you've invited me to a meeting. You must have some plan to offer. What is it?" We still had some time before the waiters would serve the meal.

"You know, I should have a plan, but I'm very new to anything like this, so I have only a remote idea of how to handle this situation. You, on the other hand, and I've done my homework on you, are a seasoned wolf, who seems to know what to do. So, I was really intending to offer my services and hoping you would know how to use them best to save us both. I don't know much, but from what I was told, you too have a major problem with the Greenbergs."

No matter how helpless he sounded, he was sincere and he scored few more points with me. On top of that, he didn't look like a chicken shit.

"Okay, I appreciate your sincerity. I have my own war already going, but having you around and, who knows—maybe some more guys—may give us a new edge over our opposition. The Greenbergs are not alone either; they have some really scary people watching their backs."

I outlined in general what I wanted from him: as much as possible, supportive international media and his analytical team to try to spot who else, beside him and me, might be under an ongoing, provable attack. I gave him specific advice to look into high-tech and telecom industries, writing down most of thirty-two corporations that I'd memorized. And generally to lie low, but to stay put when I had particular missions for him.

At the end, I couldn't help asking matter-of-factly, not really showing more than business interest, "Instead of Patrick, I would prefer if you appointed someone else to handle a contact between us. Maybe that lady that passed me a note?"

"Ah? Yeah, no problem. Her name is Suzy, and despite her tender looks, she's ex-French foreign legion. Fought for some time in Africa. That's why I wasn't afraid to send her to Ukraine. Here's her number."

Hmm, sounded like she was an Amazon of sorts—a woman warrior. Arthur looked attentive all of a sudden.

Before we parted, he told me where he'd be hiding and how to reach him, when necessary. I felt some sort of relief. Now we were a pack, not lone wolves, each fighting his battle. I had some confidence in this man. He'd made a good impression on me. And he was sharp. I was pleased I'd taken this Amsterdam trip, and I had a good reason to celebrate in the coffee shop. There were only a few places on Earth where weed was legal, and I couldn't resist the nostalgic call of my youth.

I was relaxed and confused as the marijuana crept into my system and started to spread its mild influence into my brain, when a TV report from the corner of the coffee shop attracted my attention. "A business-class passenger aboard an Amsterdam to Frankfurt flight was found dead upon landing. The details of the incident are being investigated by the Frankfurt police department with the assistance of their Dutch colleagues."

They didn't need to say who the victim was.

Chapter 20 - Cyber Fun

Poor Richard. We'd just met and I'd started to like him. Since he'd told me his next destination, I had no doubt that it was him. Fucking shit! Those blyads managed to block each of my next moves. He was right, they must've followed him. How else could they reach him so fast and whack him on the plane, or inject something before the flight? I figured no one on board would be allowed to disembark until the questioning ceased.

Feeling a bit stoned and having doubts whether it was real, since the news so contrasted with the cozy and relaxed atmosphere of the coffee shop, I turned to my silent bodyguard.

"Arthur, it's about the guy we just met."

He turned around, clearly suspecting that I was high, but when he turned back to me after watching the TV for a few seconds, he was damn alert. He understood what the score was and deduced that if Richard was followed, his followers might have spotted *us*. Seeing nothing suspicious in the cellar of the coffee shop, he went upstairs to forewarn his crew.

Richard was dead, but the information he'd shared gave me a whole new perspective. I needed my own analysts to check for others in the same loop. I remembered the companies on the list circulated at Seven's rally in Switzerland, but if there were no moves against their companies, contacting them would be useless. If I approached them with something that unbelievable, they would think I was delirious. I could, however, contact those that I could prove were under attack, or the possibility of attack.

In the meantime, I was eager to see what my opponents would do with my next little surprise. My thoughts wandered, and the good weed was getting the better of me when Arthur pulled me to my feet.

"Come, we must leave now."

Every time I heard something like that from him, I'd ended up under rocket, torpedo, or some other very lethal attack.

Now, for a change, as we popped up on the street's surface, nothing immediate happened, except for an autumn-like cold rain, which looked like it would last for hours, as the sky was covered by heavy, grey clouds.

Arthur didn't want to take the risk of having the people who were after Richard on our tail. He decided to abandon our rented cars and had two cabs, along with our security detail, waiting at the entrance. They took off at Arthur's signal once we were inside. But the next second, I spotted two motorcycles in the rearview mirror following closely behind.

I elbowed Arthur, but he shrugged me off in irritation, gesturing that he had noticed them much earlier.

They lingered for a few minutes, but as soon as we left the city and embarked upon the highway, they suddenly rushed forward and closed the distance. Maybe they were not just *following*. It might be a hit! I didn't even have time to think how to react before Arthur forced open his passenger door abruptly, a millisecond before the motorcyclist passed the car.

The rider had no time to dodge, so he hit the open door, which triggered a myriad of immediate reactions. The door got torn apart by the collision. The rider flew high into the air and landed ahead of us, motionless. The gun I hadn't seen him holding during his approach was thrown several meters away from him. Our driver felt the impact and turned sharply to the left, which caused the car to hit the second bike on the other side, and our driver to lose control of the car. The car swirled, the tires screeched. The smell of burnt rubber assailed my nostrils. The second biker kept on rolling. I heard his screams as his blazing bike flipped up and landed on his legs.

Our second car barely managed to steer clear and avoided the bits and pieces now scattered all about. From peaceful Dutch scenery, the surroundings changed to a collision scene, with burning, smoking pieces everywhere.

Thanks to God, we hadn't overturned. Arthur was out in seconds. He pushed our driver out and told him to get lost, producing a pistol hidden somewhere in his belt.

I must've still been stoned, for I couldn't find the seatbelt buckle to free myself from the car. It looked like a major road accident and cars started to stop on the sidelines and people gathered. Unless we wanted to get stuck for hours with local police, we needed to move.

Arthur checked the first biker and verified that he was dead, then approached the second, released him from under his own bike, put out the fire, and dragged him towards the taxi, which except for the lost door was otherwise unscathed.

"This man needs help; we'll take him to the hospital. Please, call the ambulance for the one lying over there," Arthur yelled to the strangers who had stopped to help.

He ordered me to move to the front seat, pulled the hurt biker inside, and drove cautiously through the thickening crowd, followed by our second car.

We seemed to elude any immediate pursuit by both Richard's assassins and the Dutch police by the time we boarded the chopper and were southbound. We landed near Nancy in France, where Arthur dumped the unconscious biker by the highway. When Arthur found a similar badge to the one given to me by Millingeri in his wallet, he decided he didn't need to question him.

It was a close call, but we'd managed to escape.

"Everything's prepared as ordered, Misha," Arthur said after he figured that I'd returned to normal after the potent marijuana.

"What do you mean?"

"You wanted the banks, no?"

***

I tagged the operation 'Night Encroachment'. We finally reached the bunker that Arthur had arranged for me some time ago in the outskirts of Kiev. From the outside, it resembled a buried military fortification; rather small above the surface, but inside — a huge bomb shelter. It didn't have the luxurious amenities my usual homes around the world provided, but Arthur vouched for its safety, and that was the most important thing.

Eager to inspect my new headquarters, I walked through its rooms and spaces.

Well, not only was it not luxurious, "shabby" would be a better descriptor, judging by all the moisture stains and lack of elementary finishing on the walls. But with so little time, Arthur probably deserved applause for installing elevators, bringing in two powerful electric generators, having brand-new utilities, and two hidden and unmarked fiber-optic lines connected to a broadband landline, thus ensuring fast and uninterrupted internet access. He also installed repeaters to provide mobile coverage in that deep, underground facility.

David also joined us, probably to be close by, if needed. He looked much better, having somehow reacquired a smug look on his damaged face. If he, like Emil, was sort of a playboy before, now he looked like a seasoned, self-confident warrior. I could only hope he stayed that way when confronted by Jessica.

Arthur introduced me to the people he'd recruited for the mission. Two were Sabres—Itzik and Ron, native Israelis in their twenties, freshly released from the Israeli army. After exhausting my scarce Hebrew vocabulary and realizing they had much more in common with David, who was also an army veteran, I left him to make sure they were taken care of, and took my laptop to the side of a large, open room with the intention of being left alone until we started the operation.

I looked at the stock markets that were still undecided, with more reds than greens despite a lull in the Russian advance.

Finally, after being on the run for weeks, I felt sort of at home, prepared to counter the recent threats and maybe to pose some of my own. My people were around, protected, and I was finally on my native turf in a kind of shelter.

Arthur told the 'hackers' to get started. I peered over their shoulders, but couldn't understand anything, seeing only symbols on the computer screens. Maybe it was extremely exciting for an IT specialist, but my undiscerning eye saw only five programmers playing with some enigmatic characters. I wondered whether Arthur understood the intricacies. Cyber warfare was more recent than his time as a special ops trainee.

After a while, realizing that I didn't understand anything and nobody cared to explain, I returned to my corner to browse the net.

Even if the computer geeks were engaged in a severe battle, overcoming fierce defenses, introducing malware, or otherwise struggling with various bank security firewalls, only a barely discernible humming of the computer fans and the click of keys could be heard.

After a couple of hours when I was about to leave for the living quarters, Arthur came by very excited.

"We are in."

"Where, exactly?"

"We've penetrated the bank's systems. Now our worms can override the systems. If we manage to accomplish that, we'll become the bank, not just be able to copy information, but basically to affect any transaction as if the bank's manager himself initiated it."

"That's what I need."

Arthur returned to the screens, and after a while, gave a thumbs up. His guys scrambled to their feet, hugging and congratulating each other. Whatever it meant, it looked good.

They might have had their small victory. Now I wanted mine.

"Congratulations, guys, well done. I want twenty billion dollars from each bank's correspondent accounts wired to these accounts now." I showed them several sheets of paper held together by a paper-clip with bank account details. Several jaws dropped. They didn't really expect to pry into the bank just for the fun of it, did they? It must've been the amount.

"And another twenty tomorrow."

Chapter 21 - Pole Position

Forty billion was the amount of the banks' own reserves. I'd done my homework. I wanted the banks' funds, not those of their clients.

The silence was deafening with everyone frozen in place.

"Cheer up, everyone. Don't be sissies, now. Jewish wisdom says: 'Stealing from a thief is legit'." I'd changed and abridged it slightly for my own needs.

"Don't worry, it's my responsibility and as long as your involvement isn't revealed, you'll be safe. Even if someone manages to crack our multi-layer IP addresses, it won't lead to you. You don't have much to worry about."

But they worried anyway. I could see that.

"I want it done in relatively small amounts of one to two million, sent to different accounts that I have ready here." I waved the sheaf of papers. "You'll have about ten to twenty thousand transactions. So get to it, guys. Your reward will be well worth the risk."

I had a plan for dispersing the amounts further. I thought that the Financial Action Task Force on Money Laundering or any anti-laundering agency wouldn't be able to monitor and stop that many transactions done in such a short period of time. The initial destinations for the money were just buffer accounts. From there, the money, partly converted into other currencies, would move further in smaller amounts, from that second buffer to the third.

Within a week, these initial funds would make a virtual electronic circle around the globe through two offshore tax haven locations and would land safely, I hoped, at other offshore accounts. From the final destinations, I intended to quickly invest some of it into legitimate projects, like Belarus' highway, for example.

Here in Ukraine, I could even fend off NATO's rapid deployment forces, if my enemies could manipulate them to go after me. While in the bunker, I wasn't afraid of retaliation.

I'd noticed the hackers' hands were trembling noticeably. Only Arthur remained cool. Knowing me, he probably suspected I was into something grandiose, meaning something involving seriously big money.

I called him aside.

"Pay attention, man. I want your people, and I mean security, not hackers, here the whole night. Now it's fear that dominates their feelings, which should pass after a couple of hours. After that it will be temptation. They'll say to themselves, 'Damn, why is this Russian or Ukrainian cunt taking all the money? Who would notice if I wire some funds to myself or my fiancé or credit my gambling account?' That's what I want you to monitor. I don't care if they put a little in their pockets, but I don't want to be busted because of some electronic theft, since their unprepared improvisation would be easily traced, understood?"

Arthur nodded. Now the sounds of the computers humming transformed, in my mind, into the swishing sound of money counting machines. I was improving my position against the fucking M7.

But then a scream shattered my happiness.

"Look at this. They're fighting back." Ron pointed at something on his monitor while all the others gathered around him.

"Shit, they've spotted us too early. You must regain control and hold it until we're done." I realized it would be a sleepless night for these guys.

I asked the staff who had been relocated from my regular office to this fortified bunker to take care of the guys by the computers and make sure they didn't need to leave the monitors for anything.

The entire atmosphere reminded me, for some reason, of Hitler's bombproof command center that he had been building near Vinnitsa in Ukraine until the Soviets threw the Nazis out of the country. If the hostile media campaign continued to accuse me of all the current evil in the world, soon I would be perceived as worse than Hitler. I had hoped to get ahead in my confrontation with the Seven before the damage to my reputation became irreversible.

Depleting their banks of funds was supposed to put me in the pole position.

I didn't understand any of their moves, counter-moves, or overall results. The monitors didn't seem to be exploding no matter how fierce their battle for control of the banks was. Bored but agitated, I left the 'war room' for the cozy apartment that Arthur had set up for me with my assistant's desk just next to its entrance.

I called Masha first to report that I was safe and protected in an adapted bomb shelter that was forty-five meters below the ground. My enemies would need one of those bunker-buster bombs to hurt me here.

"Wanna come join me, Masha, sharing with your husband the atrocities of war?"

She laughed. "Thank you for that. I've shared enough in the past. The last time I had to cater to your needs was while you were asleep in your coma. You handle it alone this time. Call me when you are in trouble."

I was glad to end the conversation on a playful note, but that 'alone' thing wasn't quite on my book. I recalled that blonde that had worked for the late Richard.

Wouldn't she need some sympathy over her boss's death?

I didn't like to overthink something like this, so I found her number, punched in the number, and pressed the green 'call' button.

"Hello." Her voice was plain; I couldn't discern whether she was sad or felt any other emotion.

"Hello, this is Michael speaking. Is this Suzanna, Suzy? I got your phone number from Richard."

"Yes, it's me." Now I heard some sadness after mentioning Richard's name. "Do we know each other?"

"You saw me in Ukraine under rather tragic circumstances." I hoped she would understand who I was without the need for a long explanation.

"I see.... I think I know who you are."

"My condolences, Suzy."

"Yeah, it's so sad. What is it that you are calling for?"

"It's not really for the telephone. It's something connected with Richard. I know you've been to Ukraine before. How about you pay me a short visit, so we can discuss it more privately? You'd be my guest and I'll cover all the expenses."

"You don't need to worry about that. The matter sounds important enough, so I'll be checking the flights right after we finish."

"No need, I can send a jet to pick you up." I wanted her to be impressed.

"Oh no, sir, thank you. That won't be necessary."

"Okay then, I'll look forward to receiving your itinerary to come meet you at the airport."

I fell asleep dreaming of what was under that veil she had worn at Boris's funeral.

186

When I woke up, Arthur reported that twelve billion had already been wired, although cyberspace was still red hot from the heavy battle.

The second thing I saw was a text message from an unidentified number, which I attributed to the mysterious blonde. "Landing at Kiev at 16:43, KLM flight 2371."

Chapter 22 - More Allies

I didn't go to the airport to meet her, both for security reasons and because I had more urgent stuff to handle.

Arthur sent someone to pick her up and gave the driver the contact details, since we didn't know what she really looked like.

Now that I was set up in this bunker, I could really attend to all the issues at hand. Our cyber attack continued, although we were trailing behind schedule. We were able to siphon eighteen billion dollars from Greenberg's before they, being unable to force us out, disconnected the bank from SWIFT and the other wire transfer systems.

This move must've cost them some serious losses, hee-hee, I thought with satisfaction.

That was it for now, but my guys had installed some Trojan malware or something similar (they tried to explain, but that was too much for me), so that when Greenberg's bank renewed the connection—and they would, since they needed to process client instructions — we'd have a chance to continue plundering.

With Millingeri's bank, we were less successful. Our recurrent attempts to break in were repeatedly blocked or thwarted.

Damn! We weren't' inflicting enough damage, though the eighteen billion could cause some real short-term troubles with Greenberg's cash flow. But the operation would go on.

I had David working to regroup our own assets in case our public companies were taken over. The risk was high and I hoped we weren't late with our moves. I'd been shocked to discover that some unknown purchasers had acquired a considerable amount of stock in some of them. Unknown to others, that is, but *I* knew who they were.

And finally, I already had some preliminary indications from my analysts about other possible takeover targets pursued by my enemies. I'd ordered my Singapore securities division to allocate the necessary manpower and to hire more if necessary, just for that mission. Here also, our delayed reaction might've been tardy. Some of the target companies had already switched control, and without doubt were already governed by the Magnificent Seven. Some others were still in the process and their shares were being accumulated for takeover or buyout. I wasn't sure the controlling shareholders were aware what was going on, as the accumulation of the shares was done gradually through different channels and intermediaries, so the price wouldn't peak.

That was where I could get involved. I'd asked to arrange meetings with as many chairmen of these companies as possible, telling their secretaries that it was about an urgent matter. I hoped my name was known well enough by now to make any businessman curious as to what I wanted.

On the other hand, I had enough negatives surrounding my name in both the Western and Eastern worlds, that some disqualified me because they didn't want to take the risk that meeting me would leak to the press. Well, the loss was all theirs. Unaware of the danger, they would soon find themselves stripped of their assets and positions, since the M7 was just as ruthless as I was.

With the few who agreed to meet, it was hard to arrange a suitable venue. I didn't want to travel to the States, as the Feds had started a probe into my possible involvement in the atrocities surrounding Eastern Ukraine. My 'friends' from the CIA were mysteriously silent about that, even though I'd tried to contact them a number of times. And my invitees didn't want to travel to Ukraine or other remote places.

In the end, I had only one who agreed to meet me in Kiev, and I planned for him to be brought to my bunker. Another one agreed to come to Kazakhstan, and three more to Singapore.

For the rest, I hoped I could use a delegate to speak on my behalf. Maybe this mysterious Suzy would fit the task?

⁂

She appeared at my apartment door much earlier than expected. Her plane had landed ahead of schedule, and Arthur's men were able to smuggle her in through a VIP route, bypassing regular procedures.

Damn, she was pretty! She had already been questioned by Arthur, and maybe even frisked. Arthur gave her a clean bill, but for some reason was reluctant to leave. That was odd. I shook Suzy's hand, offered my condolences, had her seated in the armchair with her long legs carefully crossed but still very visible under a relatively short-for-a-business-meeting skirt. I offered her refreshments and took Arthur aside.

Was I hallucinating or did I just see Arthur turning red?

"I, ... err, ... I kinda like that girl, Misha." It was probably an awkward thing for his tongue to say.

"Wow, is my bodyguard suffering a crush? Maybe you have a multilayered personality after all. I know a killer and a muscle. Let me read some poems you write during your downtime."

"I don't write any poems, Misha, and don't sing serenades."

"Do your feelings towards the chick evoke some humor in you?" I still couldn't believe this metamorphosis.

"I understand your unspoken request though. If you have a crush on her, I'll let her be for now, so you'll have your chance, but if you fail, I'm gonna try, because such a fabulous bird shouldn't leave this place unentertained. It would be rude."

I was annoyed, since *I* wanted to bed her, but our rules were that if someone had feelings, the other stepped aside. Arthur was my friend more than he was my bodyguard. I cherished this and a few more principles from my childhood.

I returned to the main room where we'd left her. If she wore a wire or other eavesdropping devices, she could've used this opportunity to plant whatever she wanted. To my further annoyance, Arthur seemed forgetful and oblivious to that possibility, so I'd need to remind him to scan the place afterwards.

"Suzy, I'm very grateful, that you came over so quickly. I'll allow you to have some rest after the trip, but first I wanted to discuss with you some things that I thought were important."

"I don't need any rest, Mr. Vorotavich. We can talk as much as is needed." She was quick to correct me. No wonder Arthur liked her. It wasn't because of her looks, for sure.

"All right, young lady. Then straight to business. I didn't get to know Richard for long, as these tragic events cut short our possible friendship. By the way, I was probably the last person to see him alive before he boarded that damn plane." I poured myself some water and offered some to Suzy while I arranged my thoughts. "I won't go into all the details that we discussed with Richard, but I'll give you the bottom line of what it was about. It so happened that Richard and I came under attack from the same group, which calls itself the Magnificent Seven. Just before Richard was killed, we agreed to join forces and to look for others suffering from the same encroachment, as well as to coordinate our efforts in fending off this Bullshit Seven organization."

"I'll help you kill those fuckers and avenge Richard, if that's what you need."

"Not quite. Well, maybe with that I would need help too, but first I need you to assist me with something else. You see, since Richard's death, I've continued alone in a quest for other potential allies and I have a list of them. I'll be meeting some of them personally, but I won't be able to meet them all. I need a representative, an emissary of a sort, who I can trust, someone who can protect him, or her, self, someone who won't be subverted by big money, and finally— someone having a personal reason to hate those Seven motherfuckers. I thought of you as my delegate. Richard assured me that I could trust you completely. What do you say?"

"I think that I'm better in combat, but I can perform liaison missions. I want the score evened with these people that killed Richard, so if we share a common purpose and this helps to bring it closer, count me in." Her comments were plain, emotionless, and to the point.

" I hoped you would agree. If you take the job, let me figure out the logistics and the schedule in the meantime. I'll call Arthur to show you your room. We'll have dinner served soon."

Arthur was more than eager to accompany her. After they left, I couldn't help imagining Arthur and her trying to strangle each other as a sort of foreplay before kinky sex.

Fuck that! I shook the distraction from my mind. I lost a bed bunny, but I might've acquired another Arthur-esque woman in addition to the one I'd appointed as Luhansk's governor.

Speaking of which .... Now that I had the entire plan formulated, I needed to call a meeting of my chiefs-of-staff to assign everyone his tasks. After a certain bit of hesitation, I decided that Andriana should be present. If I'd put her in Luhansk' electric chair, I might as well let her in on some strategic decisions.

Chapter 23 - Military Conference

As with any plan, things often go awry.

Andriana couldn't make it, and I respected her for that. The Russian/separatist troops had embarked on a new offensive, and she preferred to stay close to the theater of war. Arthur knew how to choose real Amazons.

I tried to gauge Arthur's progress with Suzy during dinner. His new passion looked somewhat tamed, judging by the blush spreading over her white skin when looking in Arthur's direction, and there was something barely noticeable in Arthur's behavior as well. Normally I wouldn't pay attention to anything like that, but now I was curious as to whether he'd bedded her, so I paid close attention to their actions. It was about the care Arthur showed her, offering her dishes, eyeing her from under his eyebrows, and things like that.

I hoped I didn't lose my head of security now that his priorities seemed to change. Bodyguard and love didn't sound like a foolproof combination.

Anyway, I didn't have too many close people left, so it was David, Arthur, and me who made up my military council that we held right after dinner — without Suzy, who could be a delegate and suck Arthur's dick, but couldn't be trusted yet with more sensitive plans.

When the service staff cleared the table, David joined Arthur and me, and we summarized our cyber blitz.

"Arthur, what's our progress with the banks?"

As he was much less wordy than me, I preferred using him to fill David in on the results.

"Twenty-seven billion dollars from both banks." He said it plainly, as if it was some average employee's salary. However, David understood the magnitude and his eyes grew wide in surprise. That was a tremendous amount of money on any scale!

I felt rather proud. "Ha-ha, at moments like this, I'd rephrase the idiom to 'Shut up and count the money'!"

Arthur continued nonchalantly, "At the moment, we are pretty much thrown out of their system and I was thinking of dismissing the crew and spiriting them safely away, because it seems that the whole cyber community is after us at the moment."

"Thanks, Arthur. It's below my target, but it's sufficiently big to make an impact and put us in a better bargaining position. I hope you have dummy hackers for a decoy, so that the theft won't be traced to us directly?"

Arthur nodded.

"Good. The guys in the banks know it's me, but there's a big difference between knowing and being able to prove it."

Having this handled, we had few more topics to cover.

"David, were you able to deplete the assets of our vulnerable public companies and to siphon off what I need?"

"Yes, Misha. Most of the valuable assets changed hands and your public corporations are more like a balloon now without any value. That's another major criminal offense we're committing, as we've embezzled funds of public companies without even reporting the reduction in their balance sheet asset entries to the stock exchanges."

"Thanks for that, Mr. Lawyer. Isn't there something like theft in self-defense or anything else that could be used to our benefit?"

"Nope, not really."

"Well, as long as we don't hear police sirens around, we can worry a little less about that. If it works out well, we'll put whatever is out, back into the companies and nobody would even notice."

"And what if it doesn't?"

"In that case, we are all doomed and have even less reasons to worry about anything. Criminal prosecution would probably be the mildest punishment we'd be facing." I knew it didn't sound that reassuring, but I always preferred truth to illusions. "Lastly, what's with the Russian offensive?"

Arthur handled that, unfolding a map and drawing arrows as he explained. "The direction of Russian strikes clearly shows that they mean to create, solidify and broaden a land corridor to Crimea and further on to Transnistria, an unrecognized republic. You see, the Russians are stuck here in Eastern Ukraine, and further Southwest they have unconnected enclaves of Crimea and Transnistria. Looks like they want to connect the dots now. Doesn't look like all-out war, though."

"Shit, but that's worrisome enough. If they accomplish that, they'll chop off almost half of the country!"

"That's gonna happen. The Ukrainians won't be able to stop them and the NATO suckers won't intervene."

"Thanks for the optimistic assessment. I should probably be moving, selling, blowing up, or donating my assets in the Southern regions, Odessa, and everywhere to the south of Kirovohrad. But who would buy them now for a decent price? Too bad I can't just uproot the entire factory and move it elsewhere. David, you must do something. Maybe we can sell at least some of the assets to Russian businessmen? Russians shouldn't be afraid of Russians coming, should they? It's only that they'd prefer to take them for free rather than pay me. Fuckers!"

I was really upset by the prospect of losing those properties because of a Russian political agenda coupled with the unhealthy ambitions of few perverted aristocrats.

All of a sudden, we felt a very distant humming, and the compound vibrated weakly but noticeably.

"It's a fucking earthquake. We gotta get out of here." I jumped to my feet. Arthur and David followed suit.

We were on the way up to evacuate the place, when one of Arthur's men intercepted us and reported to Arthur.

"Sir, our reconnaissance sighted a huge tunneling machine working about a kilometer away from our position. It might be aimed in our direction. It's guarded by a platoon of unidentified, heavily-armed troops. We lost contact with the scout who relayed the report."

I looked the tunnel-boring machines up on the web. *Holly fuck*, the monsters could drill through anything! They were used for cutting the La Manche tunnel and similar jobs. I showed them to Arthur.

"Our bunker won't hold out against it. We need to prepare to retreat," was all he said.

So much for an impenetrable fortress, huh?

But the retreat wasn't that easy. Arthur's guards reported that all our exits were covered by unknown snipers and soldiers with shoulder-launch rockets.

After making all those plans, and just when the situation started to look as if it was under control, I was blockaded in my own underground bunker!

Chapter 24 - Run, Misha, Run 2

"Arthur, how fast is the drilling rig moving?" I must've been in a bit of panic to ask. Arthur was not a road engineer; he couldn't give me an intelligent answer. "Forget I asked."

I searched the Internet for the answer. I finally found it.

They could go as fast as seventy meters, let's assume the worst, — eighty meters per day, and maybe faster if the soil was soft. Okay, so I had ten to thirteen days until they would be here.

They couldn't react *that* fast after my bank robbery. Each machine had to be purchased some time in advance, at a cost of dozens of millions of U.S. dollars, and needed time and surveys before launching. Even if it was done with lightning speed, it was impossible to stage something like this in days. That meant my adversaries had it ready in advance, or had prepared for a need to use it against my bunker pretty close to when Arthur had found it. We had a serious intelligence breach in both directions.

First: my rivals had had an early warning about my bunker, and second: I didn't know shit about their counter. Their preparations couldn't have passed unnoticed. The info must've been monitored by every fucking intelligence agency and I usually got my share of intel from our informers, especially about anything which concerned me personally.

It didn't take me long to figure this out, and all the links seemed sound.

"Arthur, we haven't been getting info from SBU and military counter intelligence."

"What makes you think that?"

"Because we didn't know about this drilling fucker and they must've known and didn't share it with us."

"I'm not sure. Here, this is what I've found." He showed me an Internet article on his phone. I ran through it quickly.

" .... American-British Joint Venture was granted a concession to build and operate a tunnel for freight traffic around Kiev. ... would use a tunnel-boring machine .... Few analogues in the world.... The boring to start in September..."

I perused the route of the tunnel and its position on the map. "Arthur, it's about a totally different area. It shouldn't be anywhere near here."

"Exactly, they turned this driller against us without anyone noticing it."

"I don't get it, why would they bother with the driller: it's so slow and complex. Why not just try to storm this facility?"

"They probably have some smart commanders. I can defend this bunker with as few as ten men for weeks, months, years even, if I have enough food and water. They understand that. Attacking this head-on is suicide. And nobody would let them bomb the place, as an alternative."

Who the fuck would authorize such thing here in Ukraine? Especially against me??

I called the President's mobile phone. Long beeps and no answer. I called his Chief of Staff. No answer. I called his public number and a girl there promised to pass on the message that I needed to speak urgently with the President.

Since no one replied, I thought I might know the answer as to 'who'.

Now, I didn't believe Yaremchuk, the President, would actively support anyone attacking me personally, but it might be that he didn't have any choice but to step aside. After all, Ukraine now relied heavily on Western support and financing, so maybe someone from the U.S. or Europe called him, and this someone was at a high enough level that he couldn't refuse. That was my educated guess, and these were usually correct. *Okay, so the establishment won't interfere in my favor. Wankers.* For a moment, I wanted to order Lug to disband, if that was the 'gratitude' I received from the political echelon. But then I decided against it. I was financing the battalion for Ukraine, not for the authorities.

The naked truth was that I had to rely on my own forces to free me from this impromptu blockade, or die trying.

All my meetings had to be rescheduled, since I didn't see myself fleeing that soon.

These fuckers were probably also intercepting my cell and data traffic, so I restricted contact with the outside world.

After weighing my limited options, I hatched an idea and invited Arthur and his new girlfriend for a short consultation. I had the blueprints of the compound spread on the table.

"Arthur, Suzy, take a look at the plan, I wanted to consult with you about my new and, as always, suicidal idea. We've got two exits from the compound, which are both watched and I'm sure covered with enough firepower to annihilate anyone sticking his head out." They shifted their gazes from the blueprints, to me, and back to the prints again.

"Now, we don't have time or manpower to open a third escape route, unless you think otherwise."

They shook their heads.

"So my idea is this: The tunneling machine, or whatever it's called, approaches us from the south and should hit our southern wall approximately here." I showed them the probable place of collision. "Now, what do you think they plan to do, once they pry our wall open?"

They didn't answer.

"Right, I don't know either, but we could safely assume that they would either use some explosives to make sure we all die in an explosion or would use

203

some kind of gas, in case they want to try to capture me alive to make me return their money. Do you think these are plausible assumptions?"

They nodded.

"Fine. They're gonna know when they approach and penetrate the wall, right?" They nodded again. "So we need to dig in their direction!"

They looked startled.

"We'll meet them farther from the wall! They won't be prepared to meet us fifty meters away from their anticipated breakthrough! The driller would move into an already dug tunnel, they won't have the gas handy and maybe even the assault squad won't be in position yet—and we'll be prepared to attack first." I drew small crosses to show our path towards the enemy's path and the projected new place of encounter, and marked it with a big, black dot.

Now my plan began to dawn on them. Seeing their concerned but business-like faces, I assumed they at least thought it was worth considering.

"Hey, that could be actually a good idea. But we can't dig that long a tunnel. Not without instruments or personnel. But maybe we can have our cyber experts adjust, untraceably, the machine's course a little, so we'll just need to make a small opening and surprise them from behind." Eagerly, Arthur marked their anticipated trajectory so it missed our underground facility, and an arrow crossing it to show where he thought we could intercept them.

"We need to figure out how to open a short passage into their tunnel, since we don't have a driller, but we can maybe blow our way through. I have enough arms and explosives stashed." Arthur loved everything that had a kamikaze touch to it.

"And we'll stage a decoy breakthrough from one of the exits at the time of the collision, so those guarding the exits will be busy and won't leave their positions to help their friends in the tunnel," Suzy added.

"Sounds like a plan to me." I stretched. "Now work out the details and see to the implementation. We need to get out of here. Preferably alive. I'm hounded in my own fucking bunker. I can't believe it." I was still pissed at how fast my retreat into this fortified compound, which had cost not a small sum to build, turned into a disadvantage and possible death trap.

Chapter 25 - Breakout

We went for it on the eleventh day.

Before we did, an emissary, sent by my dear "friends", waving a white flag, brought us a message which read, "Send out Vorotavich, and no one else gets hurt." They deduced that we knew they were very close.

I read the note aloud and looked at the people surrounding me. "What do you say, guys? Sounds like a fair proposal." I was teasing them in the hope they'd spurn this ultimatum, but I couldn't be one hundred percent sure. Millingeri's son's security had surrendered. These guys shouldn't have any special sympathy towards me.

"No, we stay and fight."

"Misha, throw that away. It's not an option. Hey, get back to work." Arthur prompted the people around.

We scheduled the breakthrough to start at twilight, so it'd be more difficult for our opponents to discern how many were involved in each breakout; the fake one at the exit, and the real one behind the tunnel-boring machine.

Just before the start, I had a real argument with Arthur, who wanted Suzy by his side, while I suggested she'd be leading a decoy breakthrough.

"Misha, the moment they sense a breakthrough, they're gonna pound the exit with rockets. It's too dangerous a mission for a girl." Arthur looked clearly concerned—the first time ever.

"But she's a fighter, it was her idea." I was too surprised to come up with something more persuasive. "I wish you had more fighters with the brains to act independently up there by the entrance and make sure the opponents treat the breakthrough as real."

Suzy saved the situation by insisting she, and no one else, would head the false maneuver.

We sent her to the main entrance together with five fighters, whom Arthur likely ordered to protect her with their own lives, if necessary. She was to engage in an exchange of gunfire, imitating the preparations of a getaway, but not leave the armored entrance block, so as to minimize losses.

In the meantime, we were prepared for an assault on the drilling machine and whoever guarded it. For this operation, I had Arthur and another fifteen men. I counted David and me as half a fighter.

Not as many as I wanted, but it was kinda hard to recruit volunteers in the depths of the earth.

At 7:30 p.m., Suzy reported that she was opening the main door. We asked her to leave communications open, and shortly after heard three consecutive enormous blasts.

"What is it, Suzy, are you OK?" Arthur yelled.

"We are fine. Good thing that we've retreated far back."

The sound of Suzy's voice was a relief. "They're using shoulder-fired rockets with powerful, delayed, explosive charges. We've spotted the sources and we'll be targeting them." She cut the connection.

It was our turn now. If enemy combatants were called for reinforcement to the main entrance, we had to act now.

***

We'd been lucky that the soil behind the wall was soft, rather than rocky. We were able to make a ten-meter long tunnel, wide enough for us to trickle through in pairs with bullet proof vests, arms, and a few laptops that I couldn't risk leaving behind

The drilling machine had made over a thousand meters and judging from its geo-location, missed our bunker just by a few meters, thanks to our programmers' efforts to compromise its GPS, which reported to its operators that they hadn't reached the compound yet.

When we'd started digging our own tunnel, we didn't care much about noise, so we'd blasted a hole of about two and a half meters in diameter behind the outer wall, while making sure the entire structure didn't collapse. Most of the work was done with explosives, but as our enemy progressed towards us and came closer, we switched to silent digging. We left a meter of soil separating the dead end of our tunnel from theirs, to be blasted just before the breakaway.

Arthur arranged the line of paired fighters in front of our tunnel's entrance, placing the best six at the front, and took the bag with the plastic explosives inside with him. Everything was prepared precisely for this moment. Arthur reappeared from the tunnel within seconds, and counted "Five, four, three, two, one....."

We heard the blast.

It was time, and they all waited for my command. I wiped some sweat away, prayed silently in my head, *God help us,* and yelled "Go!" trying to project confidence to the others as well as myself.

Arthur disappeared into the tunnel first, followed by the paired fighters.

David and I were the sixth pair. The passage was very narrow, and although its walls were slightly cemented with the remains of recent renovations, it gave me the feeling it could collapse at any moment.

I was still in our tunnel when I heard one explosion followed by another, and then the chatter of automatic fire. Arthur instructed us to stay put until the shooting died down. We stopped in complete darkness, bumping into each other. The wait wasn't long. The shooting stopped, and almost immediately we heard Arthur's voice. "Move, it's clear!"

For those going first, Arthur didn't allow flashlights, but sent them off with night vision goggles.

Our tunnel ended abruptly, and when my leg didn't meet the floor where it should have, I fell forward. After getting to my feet, I looked left, where I saw the flashlights searching in all directions, and had a good glimpse of a huge machine, probably three times bigger in diameter than a railway train, slightly damaged by grenades, with sparkles of electrical shorts dancing over torn wires and few bodies of dead or wounded enemies. Seeing how few of them there were, it was clear they hadn't expected us to show up.

"Come, they are all dead. We need to run and get through this tunnel as fast as we can." Arthur wanted us fully mobilized.

He ordered the vanguard to move first and the rest to stay close behind him and his men, who held two flashlights.

We had only one kilometer left to breakout!

Arthur advised Suzy that we were in the tunnel and she was to leave her position in five minutes, get down, and follow us.

It would take time before the enemy realized that whoever had fired from the main entrance had left.

We'd probably covered half the tunnel when we heard a massive fire fight, apparently between our reconnaissance unit and the enemy. A few bullets hissed by.

Arthur yelled, "Down!" then put out the lights and rushed forward with five more men.

David and I were left with only four bodyguards.

As this was the only route, the outcome of the fighting ahead didn't matter, so we crawled forward towards the exit. After a few minutes, the shooting died down again, and Arthur *(thank God!)* yelled, "It's all clear, get here fast."

Arthur and his crew waited by the exit. I spotted only six people standing. I assumed we'd lost four or five men.

After donning infrared goggles, Arthur saw at least a dozen heat signatures approaching.

"Misha, you take David and five of my men and run. There's a highway two kilometers from here. Drop your vests here so they won't hinder you. You highjack a couple of cars there and go southwards to Smela. Now that we are out, I'll try to contact Andriana to send fifty men from Lug battalion to meet you and keep you safe."

"What about you, man? I'd rather wait to make sure you have enough time to reach the highway and to see that Suzy is out of danger."

"Misha, you don't wait for me or anyone else. You go out of here, as far and fast as you can."

The conversation was over. Arthur told five of his men to follow, and after seeing us off, started to arrange his remaining crew some distance from the exit.

We hadn't come close to the highway before we heard a renewal of fighting.

Later, I learned my men had wiped out those who rushed into the tunnel, but that was pretty much the only success. The enemy's reinforcement was a super-proficient unit; they outnumbered Arthur and his men and had superior firepower.

As soon as Suzy and the rest were out, Arthur ordered a retreat, leaving four more dead comrades behind.

They didn't make it as a group. The Italian assassins, Arthur later told me, had closed the distance between them in remarkably short time, and it all turned into close-quarter combat.

Two men near Arthur went down immediately—one from a knife through the nape of his neck, and the other by a gunshot. Arthur barely dodged another knife thrown at him by moving away, instinctively, from a hissing sound.

Someone was on him before he even had a chance to uncoil.

As soon as Arthur felt someone grab him from behind, he rolled, which saved him from two bullets fired into the darkness where he had just stood. With a sweeping, low kick Arthur knocked someone down and leaped to finish him with his knife. But the opponent was on his feet before Arthur managed to stab him.

They'd been facing each other in the darkness, when Arthur saw three more silhouettes approaching. He didn't know whether they were friends or enemies since his fighters were scattered around in the dark.

No time for a fist fight, so he'd reached for a hidden gun behind his back and fired into the man standing in front of him.

Shot at close range, he went down immediately, but before Arthur could assess the damage, the three on approach opened fire.

One bullet struck Arthur's shoulder. He'd yelped in pain, leaped behind a broad tree, and returned fire. He must've hit someone, as he heard a muffled scream.

Alone against an unknown number of assailants, he had to run. Almost every leap from one tree to another was accompanied by fire while the pursuit closed in on him.

The pounding footsteps approached from two directions. Arthur sat on his knees and popped out low to the ground, firing at the first assailant he saw. Another one was quick enough to kick the gun out of Arthur's hands. It was one-on-one again, with Arthur down to one arm because of the shoulder wound.

Dodging a one–two combination to the head followed by a kick aimed at his side, Arthur rammed into the opponent and pinned him to the ground. With one functional hand to keep his balance while lying on the other man, he sank his teeth in his throat and hung on against a torrent of blows, not letting go until the man died.

I shuddered when Arthur recounted this particular part, and even looked at Arthur's mouth to check whether he'd grown fangs.

Arthur had ripped the bloody neck chain off the corpse and staggered towards the highway.

***

We'd escaped by the skin of our teeth and met up with the Lug reinforcements. Arthur and his accomplices had suffered heavy losses. Only Arthur, Suzy (who had run fast enough to escape the pursuit), and another man, also wounded, made it out alive. The rest remained in the forest.

Our opponents' losses weren't clear. The news reported later that a total of fifty-five bodies were recovered from "the place of a mysterious and severe fight, involving shoulder-fired missiles and automatic fire, which erupted between unknown troops seventy kilometers south of Kiev."

With our losses at nineteen, we could assume that other thirty-six belonged to the Italians. We knew it was the Italians because the chain Arthur had grabbed bore the sign of the Sicilian assassins.

I grieved our losses, especially the hackers. Unlike Arthur's men, the hackers were just kids who'd come to work the heist, not die for me.

Following the TV report, Kiev was in panic. They didn't know and could never imagine Italians in the

Kiev forests. Everyone was sure that covert Russian GRU troops were approaching Kiev. The panic died down a bit after the TV news clarified that the gunfight apparently hadn't been connected to the anti-terrorist operation in Eastern Ukraine, and that the parties involved were supposedly Sicilian mafia and the security forces of a businessman—Mikhail Vorotavich. They showed a similar chain to the one Arthur brought on TV and identified a few of my guards. The reason for the gunfight was still reported as unknown. The most important question of how the Sicilian mafia had penetrated Ukraine in such numbers without being noticed, and what it was doing there, wasn't even raised. What lousy journalism!

The public relaxed, but I became more worried when Arthur commented, "They say there are only fifty-five dead on both sides, and I know for sure that we were fighting at least one hundred men in the forest."

After doing the math, even fifty Lug soldiers protecting me no longer made me feel safe.

Chapter 26 - Cancun Rally

I'd barely escaped from the trap I'd put myself into, and the toll was heavy. Any wall has a ram that can pierce it. So far, most of my plans had been thwarted, and my attempt to deplete their banks of some cash was only partially successful, as I'd managed to siphon off only a bit over half of what I originally planned.

I needed to move faster. Whenever I gave them time while procrastinating my own plans, they were hatching theirs. They'd come close to finishing me off three times, while I was nowhere near posing any serious threat to them. My luck might've been running out.

The best option seemed to be to replicate. If there were ten Mishas instead of one, it would be much harder to deal with all of us. That could be my 'soft power'.

I began rescheduling the meetings with those who might be under attack from the Magnificent Seven. I wanted all those meetings crammed into only a few days. To accomplish everything swiftly, I needed to be closer to places that were comfortable for the companies' managers and chairmen, at least for those who were curious enough to agree to a meeting. Most were in the States, but I didn't want to risk traveling there for the same reasons as before: The FBI probe might be underway; and what appeared like severed contact on the part of my CIA friends.

We agreed with Arthur that Cancun, which was close enough to the U.S., would be a good choice.

It was impossible to coordinate a joint meeting, so I scheduled ten, spread over three days. If I could accomplish everything in those three days and come out with at least few allies, I would call it a success.

I landed near the time of the first meeting. I'd never been to Cancun before. It was surprisingly beautiful and well-developed, maybe a bit too Americanized. Five-star clubs and hotels competing with each other via architecture and luxury, neatly decorated the bustling tourist area, which offered pristine stretches of sand that embraced the magnificent, emerald-green Caribbean.

I didn't have that much leeway before the first meeting, so I let Arthur, his arm still in a sling, thoroughly check the conference hall in the hotel, which I had booked for three days, for any eavesdropping gadgetry and station a guard there. As we were low on our own security personnel, Arthur hired a local security outfit to supplement our scarce resources.

Although I had it all thought out, I was nervous before the meeting. I didn't need to sell myself, as these guys were under attack—which they might've noticed or not—so I hoped their recruitment wouldn't require much convincing. On the other hand, allowing for my demonization, some wouldn't want to be associated with me. That was why only a portion of those I approached had agreed to meet.

I'd made an arrangement with the hotel to have one maid dedicated solely to serving my guests and me. None had arrived yet, so I drank coffee in an attempt to overcome jetlag and talked to "Priscilla", as our maid's badge read.

She was probably just a local girl, but her tiny figure and dark complexion attracted me. Strained before the important meeting, I tried to relax by flirting.

"Tell me, honey, how about I cancel all these boring meetings and we spend some time together? You're assigned to the conference room for the entire day anyway, so how about we have a couple of drinks together?"

Her smile was cordial and sincere, and her English was decent. "Come on, sir. Are you trying to seduce a working girl?"

"Sure, exactly. I'm glad those damn meetings gave me an opportunity to meet a rare thing such as you on this fabulous coast. I insist on having a drink together during or after your shift. What do you say?"

"I don't know, sir. We are not allowed to associate with our guests."

"Hey, Priscilla, you can call me Michael, or what would be its Spanish equivalent?"

"Miguel." She burst out laughing.

"Oh, Miguel, that sounds conquistador-ish enough to me. I like that. So how about Priscilla and Miguel meet for a drink tonight at nine or ten?"

"You are a guest. I'm not allowed. What if after drinks you invite me to your room? What would my fellow maids say?" She giggled heartily.

"Good point. I —"

Arthur entered and advised me that Felix Ohio, Chairman of Fomalhaut Space Industries was here.

"Damn! How about you meet with him and I'll continue my serious discussion with Priscilla here? You know that girls are more important than business."

Arthur was used to my fooling around, so he didn't bother to answer, while Priscilla kept giggling and suggested, "You meet your appointment, Mr. Miguel."

"Fine, Arthur, bring him in."

As he entered, I rose and walked over to greet a short, well-built and elegantly-dressed gentleman who exuded a scent of exotic tobacco, almost overlaying an expensive au-de-cologne.

"Hi. Thanks for coming over. Mikhail Vorotavich." I enjoyed a rather firm handshake from him.

"Felix Ohio. Please, call me Felix."

"Nice name. Do you know who Iron Felix was?"

"What? I've no idea." He looked confused.

"It was Felix Dzerzhinsky, the founder of CheKa — the KGB's predecessor."

"Well, I don't know whether it's that flattering a comparison." He smiled. "But Iron Felix sounds formidable indeed."

"Yep, just an association." I offered him some refreshments and once I had him sitting with an ice water, we got down to business.

"Felix, jokes aside, but it might well be that you will have to be 'Iron' soon. Did you happen to notice that somebody's buying your shares at the stock exchange and privately?"

"Yeah, I did. Is it you?" I noticed how he'd become worried.

"No, I'm quite certain it's the guys from Millingeri's bank. You know, the owner of Subliminal Investments?"

Felix nodded.

"I have checked, and they are also the biggest creditors of your company. Do you have a debt convertible into equity option in your arrangement with them?"

"I might, I'm not sure, but if it's not you, why do you care?" I felt that he didn't want to discuss sensitive information with me.

"I'll explain, because we are in the same boat. I'm also under the attack from those very rich people, united into a so-called Magnificent Seven. You wouldn't believe me, but they control over a half of the global economy and are keen to expand their empire through your and my companies as well as many more by taking advantage of the current stock exchange meltdown."

"Wow, wow! That's a grandiose plot you're talking about here."

I recounted for him some of the events that I had uncovered and some of my conclusions.

He was virtually knocked of his feet.

"I know, it's hard to believe, and hey, it might not all be accurate, especially the parts that concern their plans. But don't take my word for it. Make your own inquiries and check. I want you to know for yourself what's going on around your company. It's so obvious that my analysts didn't have a problem selecting you out of many corporations traded on NASDAQ."

"I'll surely check. Thanks for the heads-up. What were you thinking of doing? The bank that provides me financing turns on me, who would believe that?" He was still in shock, confused and lost.

"That's greed, my friend. Money is the only belief they have. These people just want to keep ruling the world and maybe other worlds in the future if your space industries are part of their interest."

"Shit! We're just approaching our first commercial launch. I hope the company will still be under my control when it happens." Felix could barely control his emotions.

"Wow, really? Do you have tickets on you? Because I'd buy a trip right now for me and Arthur here, my bodyguard. Not sure he'd be able to protect me against aliens or drunken Russian cosmonauts though."

I'd started to lose focus, so I returned to the main issue.

"Listen, Felix, how it goes would largely depend on what you do. Now that you know who you're facing, you can make your choice from the following options. First, you don't do shit and they swallow you. You'd still be able to sell your stock for a half-decent price in the turmoil market conditions. Second, you enter into a race with them. You buy shares, search for alternative financing and stuff like that. Alone. But who would loan you money in the midst of such a crisis? No one. Lastly, you can join my group which I'm trying to form to fight these guys, maybe even defeat them."

"Sounds like an ultimatum to me, and I don't like ultimatums." He was not a sissy and that was good.

"Not at all. Just a pragmatic assessment. You don't need to give me an answer now. Go, think it over and tell me when you decide. Believe me, even if you don't join my little opposition association, I wouldn't do anything against you, as you have the same enemies, and I would appreciate your efforts to fight them, whether with me or on your own. Now, in case you do decide to join, I want to share with you a few rules that I was thinking of implementing. These guys are using the availability of endless funds from their investment banks and the favorable market conditions, so we need to counter with our own money and try to revive the stock exchanges. If you join, I'll share with you a much more detailed plan. Now though, I'll tell you only that as an organization, we would have our own security fund, designated to rescue the members when the final stage comes and these guys want to leverage either debt or stock."

"So what do you mean? If I need to close my line of credit with Millingeris, I'll have an alternative source?"

"Something like that. But it's not for commerce, Felix. I want to make that clear. It's for survival. We are not gonna compete to give you better financing terms, but we're gonna extend you a helping hand, if and when you're drowning under Millingeris attempt to push you under. You understand the difference?"

He nodded.

"Now, one more thing. My war with these guys is really dirty, including very physical. These guys do what they want, so you can't be sure they wouldn't attack you personally, even if you don't attack them. It doesn't work that way. But if they learn that we are together, your chances of being involved in something violent become higher."

"That's a huge risk."

"It is, but you are into space exploration, after all. Get over it, sir." I was much less polite at this point.

"I see." He took some time to contemplate what he'd just heard. "Listen, what you said makes a lot of sense. Maybe it's a no-brainer, but let me sleep on it anyway, so I won't make a hasty decision. I'll get back to you."

I gave him my business card, equipped with new cell numbers and designed especially for the new organization I was trying to establish—New Millennium Alliance, as I called it.

Felix was about to exit the conference room, when he suddenly turned around. "Hey, Michael, I just recalled something. You're from Ukraine, right?"

I nodded.

"You know, a couple of months ago some ... err, I don't know whether I can disclose his name." Felix looked uncertain. "Let's call him 'intermediary'. Anyway, he suggested that I buy a huge factory for rocket propulsion engines in your country. Ukraine actually boasts a fairly advanced space industry. My lawyers checked and found this enterprise was on the list of those that are not supposed to be privatized, so I dropped the idea. But now that I've met you, I'm thinking maybe you know how to make this happen. Their engines are a bit outdated, but superb, it could be a sweet deal. What do you say?"

I didn't know who the 'intermediary' was, but I knew exactly what plant he was talking about, and tried to recall the latest developments regarding it. Unable to remember anything extraordinary, I decided to share what I thought about the entire idea.

"Felix, in Ukraine everything's possible. They have all those 'NOT' lists, so that someone pays to make some of the 'No's' a 'Yes'. Thus, if something is not subject for privatization, it's just a matter of time and for whom it goes private. It's possible, and I can help you with that, but think first whether you want to do business there. They just wait for seasoned businessmen like you, which think they know everything, but arrive very naive in local terms. It's a thieves' place. Your driver would steal the gasoline from your car and sell it on the side, your manager would inflate contracts to get some fat kickbacks, your nineteen-year-old secretary or assistant would surprise you with a divine blowjob and would manipulate you into spending lots of money on her. And you know what's the worst part?"

I obviously caught Felix by surprise. He stood with his mouth open throughout my rant. Nevertheless, he regained control soon enough.

"Well, what could possibly be worse than what you've already described?"

"Ha, it's just the beginning. What's worse, after a few years spent there, you'd start to understand that they steal from you, and how and when they do it. You are a smart guy. But then—without even noticing—you'd become one of them! You'd be fed up with being a sucker, trying to live by the book while everybody else abuses rules. You know how many Western businessmen I've met, who complained about corruption and lawlessness and black markets and all the righteous blah-blah? Dozens. And guess what? A few years later, I discovered many of them have started to bribe officials just as any native son would. Only even more cynically. Once you cross the line to the other side, you go to the extreme very quickly. And by the way, you need to upgrade your watch, if you want to be treated seriously there. Primitive as it may sound, nobody's gonna respect you unless you have at least a one hundred-thousand-dollar watch on your wrist."

"What about the mafia, does it still 'protect' businesses there?"

"Mafia? The state is the mafia now. Everybody's mafia. Firemen there don't serve to extinguish fires! Their task is to extort bribes. Doesn't matter what a great fire extinguisher you have in your office; they would claim it deficient to make you pay them some baksheesh. The tax authority doesn't collect taxes; it's there for enrichment of its bosses who charge high personal fees for allowing you not to pay taxes. That's mafia. The more organized state mafia superseded and subdued less organized street gangsters."

"Is Russia also like this?"

I couldn't easily switch to his question, as I was pouring out all the filth sitting on my conscience.

"That's what happens when the only God you worship is the dollar sign. Of course, officially, they are all good Christians. The rich clowns there build churches, thinking that God would be indebted to them and should work for them now. That's why they have those uprisings all the time, when the people come and throw out each new thieving, pilfering, and plundering pack of rats. Good people, by the way—really. Don't get me wrong."

I returned to his question.

"Russia? Much the same, but there they also have an ideology. A perverted Russian patriotism that says: 'We are an empire, one sixth of the fucking world, we are great.' But it's only a facade for their insecurity and sense of inferiority, which results in aggression as an attempt to cope with those feelings."

Felix was obviously aghast. "Wow, I didn't think it was that different in Eastern Europe."

"It's not that different, if you think about it. It's just much more crass and unrefined. In Ukraine everyone steals from everyone. The driver knows that his boss is a big thief, paying no taxes or giving anything back, so he steals too. His boss doesn't pay taxes, because he knows that whatever taxes he pays, the fucking politicians or functionaries will steal from the budget for their own pockets and so on—a vicious circle. In the West, it's so subtle and institutionalized that those at the top enjoy every benefit of the capitalist world, while the rest, common people, are trained and brainwashed to believe everything's 'democratic', 'pure', 'for the greater good', et cetera. That's why on a lower level, you have less street cops or firemen taking bribes. But only until you go higher. Instead of outright corruption, you have lobbying. Instead of bribes, non-direct benefits, support for election campaigns, and so on. The schemes are so delicate, it's hard to discern what's wrong and which of the rich guys exerts what influence on what politician or government official. Those who get caught or have their schemes revealed are rare, but they exist and you know it. The big game is how to trick a sucker to part with his money and to protect yours, and it's everywhere. That's our world in a nutshell."

Felix sighed and nodded. He knew how his world worked. He shook my hand again and left shocked.

***

After a three-day marathon, I had eight out of ten enrolled, and two more likely to follow. It wasn't that I was articulate or persuasive. They didn't really have a choice.

The most interesting part of the Mexican visit, as sometimes happens, had nothing to do with business.

Chapter 27 - Chill out

It was about Priscilla. She didn't join my emerging business community, of course. The complexities were a few parsecs away from her IQ, but she did go out with me and made me stay for another day. When it came to chicks, I frequently acted like an infantile idiot.

Since she was assigned to us for the entire three days, we got to know each other a little bit better during the lulls.

She was a bright and funny girl, underestimated by her current bosses. If I ever decided to enter the hotel business, I wouldn't hesitate to appoint Priscilla as CEO. And this had nothing to do with her sex appeal.

We went out after the conclusion of the 'Cancun Founding Conference', as I ceremoniously called it. I insisted that her contribution to its overall success had been decisive, and I paid her and the hotel a huge tip, praising her service specifically, and made sure she got a day off afterwards. She had no choice but to celebrate with me.

To alleviate her concerns, I took her out to Playa del Carmen, a small town further South on Riviera Maya, so there would be fewer chances of rumors of our romantic meeting getting back to her hometown. Another concern was to distance myself from Cancun, as my meetings most likely hadn't gone unnoticed, and my ever-agile enemies might've been closing in.

I picked her up at a hut—at least that how it looked to me. I rented a Cadillac and convinced Arthur to wear something less militaristic and more elegant for the occasion.

"I arranged Suzy for you, remember? You owe me one, Rambo."

Her appearance was simply mind-blowing. All of a sudden, I saw a miniature angel flowing gracefully on the lawn in front of shabby surroundings. Her pristine white dress (*I hoped she didn't count on a wedding*) and a chain of artificial pearls gave perfect contrast with her tanned skin and black, curly hair. Reinforced by the angelic self-humorous smile, her entire appearance was so enchanting that she rendered me speechless for a few seconds.

After I regained my composure, I hurried to express my appreciation. "Darling, I fell in love when I saw you wearing a hotel uniform, but now, baby, you've really brought about a tsunami of affection, a Mexican hurricane of emotions. Don't know how best to describe it. With the lust you've managed to evoke, I would take you straight to the bushes on the other side of the road to taste and feel whether this goddess image is real."

In the few days we'd been hanging out in the hotel, she'd become used to my somewhat vulgar and savage sense of humor. She might even have liked it.

230

"Miguel, flattered as I am, I'm just going to return straight back home, if you're going to drool over me the entire evening." She giggled and turned around playfully.

"Arthur, tie her up and put her at the back seat."

Thankfully, Arthur understood that I was joking.

She retreated a few steps towards her home, but I grabbed her from behind, swept her from the ground, and carried her to the Cadillac.

"Hey, Señorita, you can't seduce an elderly gentleman like this and then run away. My Viagra is about to kick in, and what would I do then? There are only Arthur and some jaguars around, right?"

She burst out laughing, maybe featuring me screwing a jaguar, while Arthur put the Cadillac into motion.

I was in an especially good mood, as my negotiations seemed to have succeeded. If I had a coalition of the high-tech heavy hitters that I'd started to put together over the last few days, we could challenge the old-school motherfuckers.

Having Priscilla around made me feel twenty-something again, not much older than her twenty-three years.

When we reached the place, we joked while devouring delicious dishes served non-stop at my order, and downing Margaritas, mojitos, and mezcal with a worm floating at the bottom, which was supposedly the local specialty.

Drunk and horny towards the end of dinner, I suggested we move to a more private location, since I had a "President's lodge" booked.

But she flatly said she was going home. I hadn't experienced disappointment like that for a very, very long time.

"What is it, baby? Just when I wanted to propose to you, you turn your back on me?"

"I've checked you out on the internet, Miguel. You're a married man, you can't propose." She was teasing me, God damn it.

"I was just thinking of converting to Islam, under which polygamy is still allowed."

"Michael, you don't need to go that far, and it wouldn't help anyway. It may sound a bit old-fashioned, but I'm not sleeping with anyone after the first date. I'm a modest girl." She looked down shyly, but I could tell it was artificial and playful.

"I see, Madam. How could I be so wrong? I'll tell you what, I'm so wasted that I don't wanna go back to Cancun, I'll book another room for you in a beautiful, local hotel and let you be for the night. What do you say?"

"You promise to restrain yourself and not to try anything funny? Do oligarchs keep their word?"

"Never, but I do." I knew I was lying, because I wasn't going to bed without at least a sensual kiss from this gorgeous Mexican superstar.

"Okay then, but remember your promise. Somehow I doubt that you can become a billionaire being an honest man."

"How many billionaires do you know?"

"None. You are the first. But my women's intuition tells me that much."

"Then, it's just stereotypes, baby. The way we are portrayed in the movies. In reality we are much worse." I smiled, as if it was a joke, but for me, the words reflected what I thought.

I did get a long, lasting kiss, but then she pushed me away, entered her room, and locked the door.

***

A bit hungover after mixing many different kinds of drinks the evening before, I ordered breakfast sent to her room and knocked on her door at 10 a.m.

She opened it wearing the same gorgeous dress from yesterday, without anything underneath, as I found out few seconds later. I greeted her with a kiss—a runner-up of the one from the previous night. Encountering no resistance, and then wholehearted cooperation, I was on her in less than a minute. Or maybe it was her who rushed the whole thing. She was no less passionate than I.

Engaged in a festival of wild sex, we didn't want to open to room service when they knocked on the door — for too long to my exasperation — and had to reorder everything an hour later as we lay on the bed, exhausted, with happy smiles.

Damn! Maybe her behavior was conservative, but as far as sexual pleasure went, she was front line. I was still excited over her. I would have taken her with me and offered her some kind of position, salary, and maintenance if it wasn't something that would prevent from her meeting someone worthy enough for a serious relationship. I wasn't selfish enough to have an exclusive harem of young ladies, although I probably could have.

I would definitely stay in touch though, as long as she remained available, since she was hot, exotic, easygoing, and extremely sexual. We spent the entire day together, never leaving her room. I didn't even expect that I'd still be up for some of the things we did that day.

I took her home that evening and, rejuvenated, returned to my much less rosy reality. I had a war to fight.

Chapter 28 - Chechens

To Arthur's credit, he didn't bother me throughout the day I spent with Priscilla, and even did me the favor of answering all telephone calls, explaining that my meetings with Western oligarchs exceeded the three-day schedule, and I was very busy closing last-minute details.

However, the next morning, when we were on the way back to Europe, Arthur catapulted straight back into business with some surprising information that he'd just received.

"I found the Chechens."

I thought he meant the squad that had killed Boris, but he clarified "Sanayev."

That was the Chechen who'd sent two assassins to finish me off in the hospital while I was still in a coma.

"All right, where is he, how do we get him?"

"No need. He'll be waiting for us upon arrival."

"Huh? He asked for a meeting? That's something extraordinary. I won't be surprised if he plans the same trick as I did with the Puppet Master and he would try to kill me when we meet."

"Could be, but let me worry about it."

I was still too much under Priscilla's charms to tackle the upcoming encounter seriously.

"Fine. By the way, it would be best to meet him at the International Space Station, so the absence of gravity would make it more difficult for him to do something nasty, but I'm not sure our jet would be able to reach escape velocity. Therefore, you should instruct the pilot where exactly you plan to hold those meetings and where in general we can hang out safely until my new organization accumulates enough muscle for a counterattack."

"I already did. We are returning to the Balkans. We'll stay at Opatija—a small recreation town in Croatia."

"Doesn't ring any bells, but OK."

***

Sanayev wasn't waiting for us in Opatija, but he got there the next day. The last time I saw him was probably fifteen years ago, and I would rather never see him again. The years had left their stamp on him.

Arthur frisked him, told me he was clean, and stayed in the front room of my suite with Sanayev's bodyguard, who looked even more frightening than Arthur.

I hoped I was safe, but was still a bit wary.

No handshakes. We just sat opposite each other and I tried to contain my hatred. This guy tried to kill me!

I couldn't know whether he tried to contain any feelings, because he just rubbed his terrorist beard and spoke up.

"Vorotavich, you stole my money, you've inflicted damage to my reputation, but you didn't hurt me, my pride or my family. I'd prefer you were dead, but it's not mandatory. I don't like you, or Jews in general, but we might have one thing in common."

I interrupted him for he was clearly mental.

"Listen, Sanayev. If you want to 'forgive' me and issue an amnesty, you are misperceiving the entire situation." I wasn't sure he understood complex words, but I didn't care to clarify. "You don't kill because of business conflicts. You lost in court. Even if you think you are right, it's not a reason to order a hit on me. Money and life are not on the same scale, however some of your countrymen probably don't have that much respect for human life."

He smiled through his beard, confirming my assumption.

"If I was younger, you would already have a bullet in your skull, just like I have in mine." I pointed to my head. "But now, I don't care. Vendettas don't interest me anymore, although you do deserve death for what you did. But let's hear first what this "common thing" is."

"Some of my unruly compatriots are said to have killed your friend in Severodonetsk. I want you to know that the members of this gang are my personal enemies. I can't align with a Jew, and I don't want to, but if you happen to catch any of them alive, I want the honor of cutting their throats and separating their infamous souls from their bodies. In return, I can forget about the financial loss that you've inflicted on me."

I chose not to ask what the reasons behind his hatred were. It was his business. After all, I was glad to hear that I was not alone in wanting these fuckers dead. Hell, taking into account their savage and ruthless behavior, they must've had a lot of enemies. But who was likely to deal with them?

"Wow, it sounds like you are enrolling me into ISIS with this throat-cutting and stuff." I couldn't help joking. "But fine, if I do capture some of them, I'd let you even your personal score."

He stood up to leave.

"But on one condition—I don't want to look behind my back, if and when I assisted with your revenge."

He nodded. "You have my word."

We didn't shake hands when he left, and frankly, I didn't trust his promise that much. I thought I'd heard they were allowed to lie to "infidel" non-Muslims.

I looked at myself in the mirror to check for signs of age. *Am I losing it? I just let the guy who ordered a hit on me leave alive.*

Chapter 29 - (Mis)Alliance

This Sanayev must've had more faith in me than I had in myself, because I didn't have the slightest idea how to put my hands on this cruel Chechen troop which operated from occupied Ukrainian territory.

Arthur relayed several different orders, advice, and intelligence regarding their movement and whereabouts to Andriana and the Lug commanders, but so far, none were swift enough to put together an operation, based on this changing input.

In the meantime, the New Millennium Alliance came into existence and started to operate—first as a sort of liaison office between us, but in few more days we had two more offices allocated by the members from their own office space, a functional bureau, staff, budgets, and an agenda. I pushed everyone to give the Alliance top priority and to act promptly. We were in a state of war. Not only I, but everyone else must've felt safer now.

We could, to some degree, confront the Seven economically, but militarily, only I had some experience and abilities. For now, I couldn't call it a new NATO, but I did intend to give it some kind of security and a fast deployment capability.

Yet, maybe it was too late. Every now and then, there was an announcement of this or that company losing, switching, or selling control. The Russians continued to create tensions, thus bringing more and more uncertainty into the markets.

I was more than confident that my opponents had accumulated enough shares of my own publicly-traded companies to make some moves, and they had probably made progress in tracing the money I'd stolen, despite endless layers of hackers and dark-net resources.

The apparent lull was no less menacing than a direct assault, because I knew they were preparing their next moves. I wanted to beat them to it this time around.

All the time, I thought "how". There wasn't a simple recipe. Institutionally, they were much stronger than my young high-tech sidekicks and me. I didn't have former U.S. presidents or vice presidents working for me or any of my partners. I didn't have the CIA's services at my beck and call.

Militarily, I estimated that even with Arthur's depleted security ring, Lug battalion, and a few stray combatants, I wasn't the underdog. But only if we took the Russian army, which seemed too obedient to my opponents' requests, out of the equation.

And finally, in the media, it was a clear mismatch in their favor. I had an advantage only in Ukraine, while they controlled many of the major TV channels, internet media, newspapers, etc.

Having analyzed the layout, I could figure where their weak spots were. It seemed there were...none.

Too bad I didn't have Boris to consult with. His impudent, experienced and cynical assessment was always of value.

I didn't have a multidisciplinary friend to confide in, so I decided to present my political/media plan to David and my elder brother, and the combat plan to Arthur and the two Amazons: Suzy and Andriana. I wondered whether I should bring them together, as the former was Arthur's current passion while the latter his ex-wife. If not, then Suzy was out. Arthur could fill her in on the details if necessary. I made my choice in the governor's favor. A weird thought of having the two fight each other in the mud to see who would come out the winner crossed my mind. Hee-hee, I should share with Arthur the idea.

***

First, I held a 'civil' consultation. David and Sasha came together.

"Why the Balkans? Not again, Misha. I was held captive here for long enough," David complained.

"Listen, mate. It's not because of your imprisonment; it's because of your fucking marriage. You seem to complain about anything these days. Minsk—not good; Balkans—not good; I bet if I held this meeting in paradise, there would be something wrong about that, too." I couldn't help giving him a verbal slap in the face to get him focused.

Then, turning on the charm, I turned to my brother, who never complained about anything. "Hey, Sasha, thanks for coming over. I really need your advice and opinion."

Sasha hugged me and sat quietly on a chair.

I'd arranged everything on the terrace of a rather old hotel, but it offered such a magnificent view of the Adriatic Sea that it outweighed all the drawbacks. I updated them on my meetings in Cancun, omitting Priscilla's part. Maybe later I would share it with David to make him a bit envious of the romantic adventures he'd been missing lately.

"Dave, some things that you've told me about your incarceration made me think. Was it your impression that they were sincere in their fears of being exposed to the world?"

"I'm pretty damn sure. That's their way. They control everything illicitly. They recoil from anything public. But how can you expose them? I mean, you can write and publish whatever, but if you don't provide proof, they would sue you, or anyone alleging anything like that, for libel,and having all the press on their side, everybody would soon make a joke of it. You know these conspiracy theories are hard to sell these days."

"David, my man, don't you know that when acting in concert with Arthur, I'm not that bad in procuring evidence? I understand what you're saying. Let's formulate it more precisely. If I have irrefutable proof about their informal union, their goals, their global reach, and some of the atrocities they've instigated, do you think disclosing it would cripple them? Do you think their institutions would be boycotted, some dealings investigated?"

"Hard to say. For anyone else, the answer would be a clear "yes". But these guys hold everyone by the balls and much of the media is theirs. But I'll tell you what; if you have strong factual backing, then definitely you stand a chance. Not one hundred percent, but a decent chance."

"Fine. Sasha, do you agree?"

"Yeah, that makes sense." He didn't say much, but I knew that if something sounded flawed to him, he wouldn't let it pass.

"Okay, then, good. I'll figure out how to procure evidence and disseminate it afterwards." This gave me some confidence that I was thinking along plausible lines.

"Now, I want to intimidate them economically."

Seeing both of them shake their heads, I conceded, "Yeah, yeah I know. Their consolidated wealth is far beyond mine and my new partners'. But! I have about twenty-five billion of my own funds, borrowed from our adversaries' banks, and maybe another twenty-five from my Alliance, ready for action. I want to intimidate them, to show them they have real opposition now. Snatching one or two landmark companies from their grip might do the job. What do you think?"

"Sounds like a waste of time and money to me." Sasha was the first to react. He didn't show much emotion and continued to recline in his chair. "That's too expensive for a bluff. And why even to engage in an economic showdown, if you don't have a chance to win? You'd just invoke a disproportional reaction."

"To demoralize them. They've started the whole thing for money, and I want to show them that they may lose more than they would gain. Hopefully, there will be no reaction, as it would be perfectly synchronized with my media and military coup." I stated it confidently and matter-of-factly, but I wasn't all that sure what I said was achievable.

"My opinion—it's chancy and superfluous, brother."

"It would require a profound planning, precision, and instantaneous implementation," David chimed in.

"I'm glad that you're raising this issue, because that would be your job. Your sick leave because of your beatings is over. You need now to choose two flagship companies that these motherfuckers own or just wrestled out from somebody and prepare a detailed plan of how we can take them over. You know the budget, but, of course, you don't need to spend it all, eh?" I didn't give David a chance to reply. "Okay, guys, thanks, stay put. Let me have a word with our Admiral Nelson and our Joan of Arc here about the

244

military part and then we'll dine together. Take a break.

"Ah, and another thing that I almost forgot."

"What is it?" They turned around.

"I've agreed with Felix Ohio, the chairman of Fomalhaut, who has ties with RosKosmos- a Russian NASA, that he would try through those contacts to have a meeting with Russia's President, or at least Premier. He's an important enough figure to meet with and has a clean reputation in Russia. Now in the view of sanctions, any such meeting would be seen as a victory for Russian propaganda, while it might have an adversary effect on Felix, but he's willing to take the risk. I'm not so naive to think that he'll be able to stop the offensive, but maybe he'll be able to show a different angle on what is happening and what motivation the so-called 'Western friends of Russia' have."

They nodded appreciatively, but having nothing to add, left the terrace and then the room, to be replaced by a different pair.

***

Andriana, whom I'd referred to as "Joan of Arc", looked somewhat dissatisfied when she entered. Arthur, as usual, didn't reflect any emotions.

I hoped it wasn't about Suzy or unrelated shit like that, and was tactless enough to ask, "What is it, Andriana?"

Thankfully, it wasn't about petty stuff. It was about strategic concerns and she was sincerely worried.

"Misha, the Russians recently beefed up their troops in what they call Donetsk and Luhansk People's Republics from fifty to seventy-five thousand, consisting of regular army and insurgents trained and commanded by Russian instructors along the new line of separation. If they proceed with the offensive, nothing can stop them."

"It's been like this for over a year now, Andriana, that's why they capture towns and heights at will, but I'll tell you what could stop them." I knew I had them intrigued.

"The threat that some of their officials might lose their money hidden for them abroad by our dear blackmailing Magnificent Seven."

"But how are you going to achieve that? The Seven would never pull the rug from under Russia's feet." Arthur was all ears, though, probably already drooling over the prospect of some major fight or conflagration.

"Ha, that's precisely what I want to consult with you about, and ask you to prepare an operation to implement it. Who controls the access to their money and thus is able to extort these bizarre actions from

Russian militants?" It was a rhetorical question, which I didn't expect them to answer.

"First, Emil, because I heard him doing so on the phone. Then maybe his mother and this Italian fucker Millingeri. So best thing—bring me this Emil, failing which, any of the other two."

I knew I was giving them a tough task, more to Arthur than Andriana, because I was not really going to exempt her from her duties as governor.

Arthur just shrugged. "I'm on it." He was my man!

"You and Andriana must deal with those Chechens. I don't know, maybe assign a rapid deployment unit from Lug battalion to mirror their moves. These fascists killed Boris and many more innocent people."

"I know. It took some time, but I've made some progress. I have infiltrators that work with the Chechens behind the lines. Whenever there is an opportunity, believe me, we are not gonna miss it."

As if prophesied by Andriana, the opportunity soon presented itself.

Chapter 30 - Chechen Squad No More

Andriana received a tip from her informer that the Chechen troop was crossing over the armistice line into the territories controlled by the Ukrainian army for some kind of mission. It wasn't hard to figure out that the mission wouldn't include milking cows or planting vegetables, but rather seeding mayhem and fear, and killing as many soldiers and civilians alike as they might bump into on their way.

I thought the best way would be to somehow set the Chechens loose upon the Sicilians and vice versa, but I wasn't sophisticated enough to come up with a doable plan of that complexity. We had to deal with them on our own.

***

Arthur woke me at 3:00 a.m. to advise he was leaving, but that he would keep five bodyguards in place and that I should stay put and not abandon my security entourage until he returned. He meant *if* he returned, but I didn't see a need to make a point out of it. I didn't want to jinx anything.

The encounter between Lug, reinforced by additional forces tasked for that mission, and the Chechens happened at dawn. Arthur was still on the way when it started, but was able to arrive towards the end, and who knows, maybe his last-minute appearance made the difference.

I didn't know whether they also had infiltrators on our side. I guessed not, since we *did* manage to surprise them.

The Lug group deployed by the bridge, the Chechens needed to cross over the Vovcha River in order to get to wherever they were heading. Bushy hillside surroundings, together with the pre-dawn twilight that was just beginning to force the night out, helped to mask Lug's presence. No mobile phones were allowed, so that no unintended sound would betray the ambush.

Three rocket launchers went into action almost simultaneously. The bridge exploded as two rockets hit it, while some enemy troops were already on it. Another one missed, but in the circumstances, it was a reasonable result. Having no way forward, those who didn't fall off the blown-up bridge into the river didn't have any choice but to retreat—where our troops were waiting with machine gun fire.

The Chechens quickly disembarked from their armored vehicles, probably fearing further rocket fire, spread out, dove to the ground, and returned fire.

With the initial rocket attack, we must've wiped out about a third of their platoon, but there our luck petered out.

Lug's commander, Pavel, was killed by Chechen sniper. His sudden death caused disarray in the chain of command. Andriana wasn't there to assume command, and maybe that was for the best, as I couldn't know whether the Lug troops would've accepted her authority. Despite the loss of their commander, nothing implied possible deterioration. It seemed our troops were clearly superior in firepower, and one of their units waved a white flag of surrender. Our boys rejoiced in anticipation of a swift victory. But as soon as they encircled the first Chechen who walked toward them with his arms raised, he detonated an explosive device attached to his body. Ten of my men were killed on the spot. Those who followed the bomber quickly produced weapons and started spraying our soldiers, who were still in shock from being blown off their feet by the explosion.

The Chechens managed to find a clear breakaway route, and were about to escape except that Arthur, heading to the battlefield in a car, steered right into their midst, jumped out, rolled, and hid behind a huge stone. I didn't know how many grenades he'd had, but he'd been able to throw an anti-infantry grenade without peering over the stone every seven to ten seconds, thus preventing the Chechens from getting closer. The grenades didn't hit many, if at all, but they kept the Chechens at bay until the Lug survivors managed to regroup and come to Arthur's rescue. Arthur was still sitting behind the stone, protected from bullets, throwing grenades backwards, until he heard gunfire that wasn't directed at him.

Burned by their first attempt to take the Chechens captive, the Lug soldiers didn't approach until they verified the enemy troops were either dead or sufficiently injured. Even then, they approached with great care so as not to step into the same trap again. And they were right! One of the seemingly dead terrorists suddenly opened up with automatic fire. Fortunately, Arthur was near enough to finish him off with one precise shot to the head.

My boys did it! The worst Chechen squad of all was annihilated, but at a very heavy toll—we lost thirty-seven people and eleven more with various injuries.

Arthur called to report once all the dead bodies were counted and collected, and all the injured cared for. Hearing his account, I was glad I hadn't received a real-time report. I would've exploded from anxiety over each twist of the battle.

"We have seven captive terrorists. All of them injured. What do you want me to do with them?"

"Thank God, I'm glad to hear your voice. You're alive! Well, let me think. Ha, maybe we can manufacture some women's purses from their skin? Pity, they are injured. We can't wait 'till their skin heals. Give them to Sanayev then. Although I don't feel particularly happy about helping that fucker. He's just as cruel and repulsive as they are, but then it'll save you from charge of executing prisoners of war and the result would probably be similar." I chuckled a bit.

Arthur was indifferent to my humor, so he hung up and maybe even regretted that I didn't allow him to torture or kill a couple of them.

I was especially disgusted over the suicide bomber thing. They were so eager to sacrifice themselves in return for the expectation of scores of virgins waiting for martyrs in paradise. How could anyone convince those naive Muslims that it was a heroic or blessed thing to do? Never, wrong on both counts, no matter what purpose, under any religion!

Was Boris avenged? Not really. There were those that had given the orders or pointed out targets. I hoped that someday I would be able to give them what they deserved as well.

Boris died to save my beloved Ukraine, and it was still in danger. I hoped that my new Alliance, which gained momentum, would shift the balance into Ukraine's favor.

Chapter 31 - Wrestling Back

I made an appointment with Felix. It was important to see him before he traveled to Russia.

I prepared a rather large file of direct and circumstantial evidence that I'd garnered about the Magnificent Seven and its peculiar influence on Russian army maneuvers. I also tried to cover, at least to some degree, the roots of such influence—the enormous number of Russian officials kept in Greenberg's and Millingeri's pockets.

"It's not conclusive yet, Felix, but I'm working on procuring something first class, more direct. Please, leave a channel open for sending them further info. If they want to make serious inquiries, it won't be hard to trace the calls and find out who called whom on the dates I gave you."

Felix looked distracted, enjoying the view from my terrace, while I'd already grown annoyed by it. I couldn't stand the same scenery for more than a few days. I might ask Arthur to have dolphins jump by the pier or some birds that I could shoot at.

"I'm taking the file with me, but I'm not sure how much opportunity I'll be given to talk about it, as the meeting is supposedly about space exploration—"

"You must, Felix. You don't need to end up in a Russian jail for coercion to make someone listen, but other than that, all means are valid. They need to know that they are just part of somebody's grand plan and its outcome doesn't promise anything good, neither to them personally nor to Russia as a state. When the dust settles, they will end up with a war-exhausted country and a bunch of worthless territories that nobody needs, because they need to be supported financially, and which the world would never recognize. That's the fucking truth and all the rest is just daydreaming. They are being used as secondary players in somebody else's game."

Felix nodded. I saw that he was a bit afraid, and I was sure his fear would go up a notch at crunch time, but we needed to utilize any opening.

"Hey, Felix, relax, we'll make sure some celestial body, soon to be discovered, will bear your name. Good luck, man!"

During the trip to the airport, I showed him the contents of the file and explained the nuances of each item.

We also discussed the details of our attempt to steal the Seven's corporations. After some hesitation and arguments, I'd managed to convince my New Millennium Alliance to give it a try. As an Alliance's contributor, Felix was also privy to our mutual plan to wrestle control of a business social network the Greenberg's had recently acquired and a telecom from Millingeri's that had been theirs for two decades. If we succeeded, it wouldn't have any global significance to Seven's business, but it would be a resounding slap in their faces.

Our cumulative efforts in the States also seemed to bear fruit, as an anti-trust probe was initiated into Seven's food-related industries. That too could result in a bite out of their influence.

Right after Felix disappeared behind the VIP passengers' area gate, I called Hugo, who had been appointed by the majority of the Alliance to manage the organization's funds. That had made him a first signatory of a handful of our accounts, which now contained funds equaling the annual budget of a few African countries put together. Hugo—a young man who just turned thirty, was the owner of a huge internet gambling network worth a few billion dollars. He struck me as a decent guy, and was probably perceived as one by others, since everybody voted for him. I didn't insist on being a signatory on purpose, so the others wouldn't be afraid to include their funds because of my reputation of a swindler.

"Hugo speaking." Young, yet very confident, voice.

"Hey Hugo, it's Michael. When's the countdown, what's the benchmark?"

"It's not a telephone conversation, you know, but supposedly within a few days, and above fifty percent on each count respectively." That was the share we hoped to achieve in each of the two companies.

"Will be looking forward to some good news, Hugo, and I've got my fingers crossed."

I felt satisfied. Finally, I had some serious forces engaged in the battle and doing some important work without my direct involvement. If we succeeded, it would mean that my impromptu Alliance was ready for some global tasks.

And also, if we had a track record, I had no doubts that other tycoons would be knocking on our door, and that might just result in a snowball effect.

Now it was a waiting game for me, which I hated the most. At least Masha came over with the kids to lighten my nervous solitude. I really missed them, with all the jet hopping and mortal danger I'd been exposed to. I owed my family more of my time, but I couldn't have them by my side with all the crap I was going through. My adultery was nothing more than a mix of mischief with self-destructive motives.

Hours passed, but news didn't arrive. I'd agreed with Felix that I wouldn't call him while he was in Russia. His calls would definitely be monitored and we didn't want our connection to become obvious. He was supposed to ring me once he'd left.

A full day passed, and the guy had ... disappeared.

I called Hugo a couple of times during the wait, but he pointedly refused to give away any bits of concrete information.

Nobody cared to spare me from bad news, though. Within a three-hour interval, I received notifications that unknown buyers had accumulated sufficient stock in two of my companies and had called extraordinary shareholder meetings to change the management.

I'd already become upset and dejected when somebody knocked on my door. Since the knocker had obviously been admitted by my security, I opened the door to watch a drunk-out-of-his mind Felix stagger into my suite and fall on the floor. Almost immediately, he started snoring.

"Hey, hey," I called the security guys in. "Take this piece of shit outta here. Grab a room for him and see that he's not choking on his puke while he's out. When he comes to his senses, bring him in."

That was an unexpected, disgusting show, but he was alive, and that was something.

***

He reappeared, still looking terrible, in five hours, leaning heavily on the security guard, with a green face and trembling hands. His eyes showed recognition, though, when he looked at me. *Is it Felix or a zombie?* I wondered.

"Hey, Felix, you had a helluva time in Moscow, huh? Want a beer or a shot of vodka?"

I thought he would throw up into my face. My words triggered some sort of convulsion in his body.

"All right, all right. Here, take these. They should help." I gave him some pills that were usually good for fighting a hangover. In his case, I wasn't sure how much they would help, as it didn't seem like a hangover; more like alcohol poisoning. Seeing that his lips were moving and he was trying to talk, I gave him some tonic. "Okay, man, the intensive care unit is closed. Tell me now what's happened to you. I put you on the plane in one piece and you return a day and half later, completely shattered."

"Wow, M...Michael," he started to stutter. "Thanks. I feel a little better. You Russians—are totally out of your mind with your—drinking traditions." He paused for a deep breath every few words.

"I'm not Russian. Actually Jewish-Ukrainian, but that's not important."

"Whatever. These guys fucking pumped me full of vodka. We had a two-hour meeting—and what felt like a two-day drinking binge. They took me to a—dacha', I think they called it, and we ate and drank—and used a sauna, and returned to the table, and on and on—" He stumbled mid-sentence, turning noticeably bluer.

"M...M...Michael...I think that I told them about you." He looked puzzled and ashamed.

"You what?"

"Uh-ah, I'm beginning to remember it now... Shit." All of Felix's emotions were clearly visible on his face. "I might've told them some of our plans—"

"You did *what*, you stupid fuck?" I couldn't hold back. "You piece of shit. If you don't know how to drink, you don't fucking drink. You know the saying, 'what's on a sober man's mind is on a drunken one's tongue'? No? I thought not. You're an imbecile. You gave away our moves. Did you do anything I asked you to?" I didn't care really that he wasn't my subordinate or anything similar, but a high-level businessman and a peer.

He looked frightened for a second. "But ... but, of course! I did. I gave them the file. I explained the situation. They were very attentive. Listen, they promised that if their inquiries corroborate my intel, they might stop the bloodshed." He looked sincere, even convinced.

"You are a fool. They tricked you and then got you drunk to get more info." I was sure he'd been played. *Yeah, right, seeing your drunken ass, they would stop all hostilities.*

But in a few days, I had to take my words back and apologize, when the Russian foreign ministry announced they were going to force a ceasefire on the rebels and cut their military support and Andriana confirmed Russian troops were leaving the arena. True, there were announcements like this all along, but this time it was real. All the bombardments stopped instantaneously after the Ministry's announcement had been aired. That would never happen unless there was a direct, unequivocal order from Moscow. I had to eat my hat. Did my plan really work, and Felix succeeded in his mission? It seemed so, but it was too early to jump to conclusions. On the other hand, it could've worked, as Russians, like

Arabs, valued pride and respect, and if they thought they were being used, there was a good chance they would reconsider playing along.

***

In the meantime, Hugo pissed me off by not telling me how the takeover attempt was going, so I asked David to pay him a visit without Arthur's men as back-up, so as not to scare him. But depending on the visit's results, my next emissary might well be Arthur and his conquistadors.

I didn't like failures, especially when I had a lot of money at risk.

David flew to Paris, where Hugo operated, and came back with reports the day after.

I was so impatient I didn't even ask him whether he wanted anything before barraging him with questions as soon as he entered.

"David, do we have those companies or not?"

"Hello to you too, what's the temperature of the water in the Adriatic?" Seeing me so impatient, he was deliberately teasing me.

"Hey, David, stop clowning around. I've invested a lot of money into that bunch of impotents, and I wanna know what they've managed to do."

David finally became serious. "Listen, they are on it. They don't want to attract attention, so they are buying relatively insignificant stocks on the exchange.

Also they don't buy on peaks that resulted from announcement of the ceasefire. Instead, they wait some time for a lower point in the share's price fluctuation. They struck me as professionals; it looks like they know what they're doing. We had four percent of the network and seven of the telecom when I left."

"Disappointing." I stood and paced the room. "Is the money still there?"

"What money?"

"The money that I wired to these 'professionals' to use for the acquisitions."

"I think it is, but I don't wanna vouch like I did once for Johnny. He ended up stealing from you." David was all caution.

"Ah, you *do* learn from your mistakes, huh? You know what, I'll show you another valuable lesson. These guys, Hugo and his staff are going by the book. I know that the market is going up and it's not like it was a week ago, but still they don't have enough vision for these operations and act too slowly to succeed. I didn't ask them to invest money wisely into a telecom stock. It's a fucking hostile takeover! I'll show you how it's done. Something that I'm starting to learn from our adversaries."

David was intrigued. I got excited as I switched from passive waiting into a proactive approach.

"The shares that they target are traded at the London stock exchange, right?"

David nodded.

"Call Martin now—the Chairman of CAFO and tell him to issue an announcement that our cross-Atlantic cable was damaged, we investigate the circumstances, and had to cut off all the Internet providers' and telecoms' traffic routed through the cable. You can add that Russian military vessels were seen at the location of the possible rupture during or before the incident, or a killer whale, or whatever the fuck you want, to make it juicy." I was the major shareholder of CAFO (that's how we called Cross Atlantic Fiber-Optics Ltd) and controlled its activities closely.

"You know, it's a serious felony, securities fraud, to make a false announcement on the exchange and to mislead the investors. Misha, he would never do it. He's American."

"No? Fine. Then take your ass to the Atlantics and cut the cable yourself, because we are going with this announcement whether with Martin or without him. If he refuses, fire him. I don't need gutless managers. There is zero risk that someone will find out, as we will cut the traffic and no one will know what's really going on with the cable. I'll have Arthur and our legal team verifying that the technicians keep their mouths shut whether because of physical or legal fear."

"What do you want to achieve?"

"You'll see. Get to it now, and tell Martin to really cut off all the internet and cell providers from the data traffic. He's fired if he doesn't cooperate."

Reluctantly, David left my room, probably clueless as to how to present my bizarre idea to Martin.

I'd monitored the LSE announcements, and two hours later, there it was. I went to David's room and knocked on his door to ask how he'd managed it, but it was locked. He was probably taking a nap, which I hadn't allowed after his return.

So, alone, I followed the chain of events that the announcement triggered. Our shares plunged, followed by the shares of the internet and cellular providers affected by the disruption of the data traffic, and then - by the entire telecommunication sector, since the shares of the same industry followed the tendency.

However, I saw occasional greens on Millingeri's telecom share's fluctuation chart.

Hugo called me the next morning, all excited. "Misha, we've got a controlling interest in the telecom—and cheaply! Just yesterday, I bought over forty percent of their shares, using the price drop of the telecoms at the LSE!"

I knew it would happen exactly that way, but I played along. "Hugo, you are a genius, well done! You are my man."

David, sitting beside me and a having a joint breakfast, was awestruck during this brief exchange.

When I hung up, he couldn't resist. "Misha, you fucker, you created this artificial crisis just to accomplish the takeover for peanuts?"

"Yep, I have. Now, please, issue an announcement that the cable is fixed and the problem was swiftly taken care of. I want CAFO shares to regain their value soonest. And reconnect the telecoms, of course. Tell Martin his small favor won't go unnoticed when his annual bonus is considered."

David choked and coughed a bit from my cynical performance, but nonetheless dialed Martin to advise him about the miraculous 'repair'.

"Misha, it's disgusting. So much dirty dealing. Maybe some British pensioners lost some money from investing in the Internet sector yesterday." David admired and despised my trick at the same time.

"Maybe. But imagine how much they lost from Magnificent Seven's few months of crisis? That's a trick I've learnt from them. I'm the one who's trying to return some stability into the market, and eventually the pensioners will recoup their losses. Don't blame me, route your anger in the right direction."

"You have a point," David conceded.

I was finishing my second cup of espresso, which usually concluded my breakfast, when Arthur interrupted my chat with David. "I have an important meeting for you. Come, we'll be leaving Opatija."

Chapter 32 - Prison

"Where are we going, man? What's the rush?" I asked, already on the move.

"It's a prison on a private island, not far from Guernsey." Arthur was forthcoming as ever.

David also joined us, complaining that it'd be a third flight for him during last two days, and that as a forty-something family man, he was in no shape for these breakneck adventures any more.

"Arthur, we need to stop by some facility for elderly people on the way and leave this moaning cunt there." I pointed at David, having gotten tired of his complaints. "Or better yet, if they have a free cell in this castle or prison or wherever we are going, I want to book one for David, as he already deserves incarceration. On top of the loss of freedom that his wife provides, that is."

Despite David's annoying behavior, I felt elated, sensing an adventure in the works. Arthur was never impulsive or spontaneous, and if he urged us to go, it was probably important.

Once we boarded the plane and figured out where the closest airfield was, as the island didn't have one, Arthur finally elaborated.

"We're gonna meet the guy who was one of the richest people on the globe, probably even before *Forbes* started to publish its billionaires list. From what I was told, he would've topped the list, as he was a very sharp businessman, until he crossed Seven's path. He's been shut away for many years, and his mental health might be somewhat impaired, but we may benefit from hearing his story. He waged a war with the Seven for over five years."

Arthur paused to answer a call. He listened to something and killed the connection without saying a word.

"The boat is ready." He commented and continued the story. "His name is Theodor. The entire story is hidden so well that almost nothing can be found in the public sources and very few pieces can be found in the archives of the intelligence community. Knowing the story of his defeat, may help us come out victorious in this round."

"Holly shit, Arthur, where do you find these dinosaurs? I wonder whether you can find Ms. Greenberg's first lover, or something. It's like you are taking us on a time machine trip some forty years back."

***

My expectation of going back in time was fairly close. After a two-hour journey on a speedboat, we reached a shabby, half-ruined quay, which was erected at least a few decades ago. There was a relatively new "Private property" sign positioned by the pier, underneath which someone had added

"Fuck off" in handwriting with red paint. We disembarked and proceeded on foot into a forest, which concealed any sign of inhabitants on the island.

The isle was small, so I didn't expect a long a walk, and indeed, just beyond a curve in the path, we had a view of a two-story, black stone building with a partially patched roof and rusted metal bars on the windows. Near it was a small, hunter-like hut.

When we approached, a double-barreled shotgun popped out the window of the hut, and someone yelled, "What the hell do you want?"

"Not nice people," I observed.

One of Arthur's men approached from the forest side, crawled under the window, then pulled the barrels forward forcefully. Whoever held the shotgun must've hit something with his head, as we heard a flood of strong swearing while Arthur's man pulled the weapon through the window. He sprayed gas into the opening, eliciting louder cursing, then entered the hut and pulled out a young, dirty man, whose foul tongue we'd already been honored to hear.

The entire episode was rather comical, so I couldn't help making a smart-ass comment.

"Hey, Arthur, I thought you'd made an appointment for us, and instead we come barging onto somebody's private island. Where are your manners, man?"

"They don't have a phone here for appointments," Arthur snarled.

"I see. Then use a pigeon or a bottle with a letter inside, thrown into the sea. There is always a way to be polite, if somebody wants."

"I don't," Arthur snapped.

"Well, tie up the host and let's ring the castle's door bell."

Instead (and maybe because there *was* no bell), Arthur broke the door with a kick and pried it open, swinging and squeaking.

"Not an armored one, huh?"

We entered and stopped in the darkness, unable to find a light switch.

Arthur lit a lantern and examined the wall. There were no switches.

"I can't believe it. They went off the grid." I joked, as obviously the building was never electrified.

It was gloomy inside, despite light cast through the windows. At night it was doubtlessly one hundred percent dark, like being in a black hole.

Most of the doors on the first floor were broken, so, after a quick look around, we climbed the stairs to the upper one.

We immediately spotted an occupied cell, since there was only one closed door on the entire floor. A ring with two keys hung near it on the wall.

Arthur grabbed the keys with his right hand, readied his knife in the left, put a massive old key into the lock, and turned it counterclockwise.

The lock squeaked, as if grudgingly letting us in, and the door creaked backward slightly.

Arthur waited for a couple of seconds, but since no one rushed out, he pushed the door with one hand without lowering the knife.

Through the opening, we saw a slender figure sitting with his back to us in a lotus pose, probably oblivious to our intrusion. He looked either craftily mummified, or deeply meditating.

Arthur went forward and cautiously put his palm on the man's shoulder. The man shuddered, jumped to his feet, and quickly retreated to the farthest corner of the cell. His window faced west, and the setting sun was directly on us, making all the metal parts of our gear and ammunition sparkle, like Arthur's knife and David's fancy watch. We must've looked like aliens to the man, who stood in the corner with his eyes wide open.

"We came to free you. Theodor, right? You have nothing to fear," I took the lead in negotiations.

"I am free." The man answered in a strong and steady voice.

"Well, then we came to imprison you in the outer world." I liked grotesque and nonsensical conversations.

To my surprise, he understood the joke, but took it seriously.

"You are right. The outer world *is* the prison, for you are not free there, and it seems to me you know it." He stared defiantly, straight into my eyes.

Interesting chap. The guy struck me as rather shrewd. I took a more attentive look at him. The closest comparison was that of Robinson Crusoe, mostly because of his white untidy hair and a beard that hadn't met a razor for decades.

"Okay, you know what, we'll stay in your free world for a little while. Would you mind telling us your story? My friend Arthur here told me you are my prototype of a sort in a sense that you tried to become the richest and most influential businessman at the time. Is it so?" If this guy was mentally impaired, so far it wasn't evident.

"Arthur, please send someone to find a box or a wood log or something to sit on."

It looked like Theodor was somewhat hesitant to answer. His cell was bare, except for a small heap of straw, which probably doubled as a bed.

"I see you are a rich man. You come with bodyguards and an entourage. But you should realize that it's all a fallacy, a misguided purpose, worthless material goods."

I nodded, because to a degree, I truly concurred.

"If you want to know, I was there myself. On top of the world. I was controlling industries rather than corporations; my word was a commandment. There were many envious bastards that wanted to dethrone me, but I defended myself well, never giving them the chance...until at some point, I lost my motivation, and they took over. But then I found new motivation. I just needed some solitude, it seems." He was half-delirious, sharing afterthoughts and consequences of the events that were clear to him, but meant nothing to me.

"Theodor, sorry for interrupting you, but what you say are generalizations. I don't understand sh... much. Please, tell me what happened *first* and your attitude towards that after. I'd like to know the factual side."

"I thought everybody knew." He looked puzzled. "I was controlling global, ferrous metallurgy and some heavy machinery industries in the US in the eighties. And I was only in my thirties then."

I detected a tone of nostalgia.

"I was the leader of the Magnificent Seven. At some stage, it became a Magnificent Six plus one, as I figured my dynasty was far ahead of the others. The rest didn't like this turnabout though, but I cared less, because I felt I was the emperor, invincible."

That had a familiar ring. He didn't finish his thoughts, as he probably wasn't accustomed to conversations after all these years.

"They tried a putsch, but they were afraid, so they didn't throw me out of the council. Although young Millingeri assumed the chairman's position instead of me. They are bankers. They started to choke industries through the credit they controlled. They choked me, but I endured. I went into banking too, to generate independent sources of financing. That's how they did it for centuries: they give you money, playing with the conditions all the time. When they want to be cooperative, the interest is low and re-financing is easy, but at their whim, they can change all that to put on some pressure, and squeeze and squeeze until you give up. They are subtle. They've refined their methods for centuries, servicing financial needs and the appetites of the most liberal presidents to the extremely cruel despots and monarchs. They are everywhere. They own stock, but most of all they own credit. To be king's, chairman's, god's creditor is better than to be a king, a chairman of corporation, a god." Theodor was reliving all the events again. He was in his own world now, telling the story to himself primarily with little attention to his audience.

I was fascinated by his tale and started to better understand his style of delivery and expressions.

"But then my brother Emil switched sides. He sided with—"

"What? Emil is your brother? Emil Greenberg?" I became uneasy for some reason over this revelation.

"Half-brother. We have different fathers, and therefore a different surname."

A kaleidoscope of thoughts ran through my brain. "Arthur, where is the guy you sent to look for something to sit on?" I got nervous for some reason.

Arthur shrugged.

And then it dawned on me. "Arthur, it might be a trap! These Greenberg guys are Jewish, and their family ties are stronger than competition. Cain and Abel's story is only the first murder thriller. Pure fiction. This is a set up. I have a strong feeling."

They must've bugged the place and listened to the conversation all along, as immediately after my words, a loudspeaker blared, "Very well deduced, Misha." It was Emil's voice. "Theodor, this guy came really close to where you've been. Maybe you can lend him your residence for a while?" I heard the chuckle through the loudspeaker.

Mobile phones didn't work, as the isle had no coverage. I looked at the satellite phone, but it wasn't connected. They'd probably jammed the communication.

Arthur stalked towards the window to check the layout, peeping from behind the window wall.

"Let's tie him up and put a gag in his mouth, we don't want him to reveal what we do from the inside." Arthur pointed at Theodor, who didn't protest.

"Dear Arthur, the resistance is pointless." Emil was obviously enjoying himself. "I saw you counting, but you shouldn't have bothered. We have seventy men here, their armament ranges from sniper rifles with full coverage for any place in the building to manual rocket launchers, capable of razing the whole building to the ground. I give you twenty minutes to take a quick dump and to dry your pants of the piss you've spilled from fear. After that, we come to get you, but don't entertain the thought that we need you alive."

Good, my watch is mechanic and not digital, as it could've been jammed too. It was a random thought as I looked at it and calculated a twenty-minute interval.

"Hey, Michael, there is a mutual friend who wants to say a few words."

I heard someone clearing his throat. "Michael, it's Felix Ohio."

How could that be? I thought Felix was 'mine'.

As if reading my thoughts, he clarified. "They were persuasive. They offered better terms. The resistance is pointless. It doesn't have to be the violent way. You can come out alive and well and spare your people. Whatever you attempt, the Seven is simply superior and they come with a constructive approach. Think about it."

If my Alliance was already penetrated, it was another major blow. Whom could I trust? They had me completely cornered.

I looked around. David was on the verge of fainting, but kept it under control so far. Arthur was calm. Three of his men looked indifferent. The fourth, which Arthur had sent out for the improvised "chair", was probably in Emil's hands. Theodor lay quietly on the floor with his eyes closed, but I was confident he wasn't slumbering.

I didn't want to say it out loud, but I had no intention of surrendering. I didn't have any intention of dying, either. I beckoned Arthur into the corridor. I hoped he could help figure out how to combine both goals.

Chapter 33 - Attempt to Escape

We stepped out into the corridor and walked a distance from Theodor's cell.

"Who told you about this Theodor, Arthur?" I asked, preoccupied with the 'trust' issue, as if it mattered at the moment. Never before had Arthur led me into such a trap, and I wanted to watch his face and hear his answer to sense whether he was implicated.

"My intelligence guy, whom I'd tasked to provide intel on M7." Arthur looked genuinely puzzled.

Taking a pause for a second to listen to my intuition, I decided that I believed him. If he betrayed me, then I had no chance anyway. "You realize, he's a traitor, right?"

"Aye. I wish he was here so I could finish him off right away." Arthur gritted his teeth.

If we left this place alive, I didn't envy the prospective fate of his informer. But how to escape? I didn't see even the slightest chance, nor did I count on Arthur and his men to prevail against a dozen to one ratio of trained opponents.

"I'm not gonna surrender," I whispered, adrenaline pumping.

He nodded and leaned over. "We need to hold on for approximately an hour. Communications are down, but I left instructions to send over a chopper with a team if they don't hear from us by 18:00."

"Will your people fight against a much superior opponent?"

Arthur frowned. "Of course, their destiny is to fight. That's what they live and die for. Now, there is no time for hesitation. If they wait twenty minutes, like Emil said, they will then fire gas into the building. We don't have enough masks, so only my men should use them, while you and David will be without them. If you faint, you faint, we'll pick you up later. Or not."

I understood what he meant. Before I could comment he continued, "Now, if the chopper comes, they can easily shoot it down with a rocket. We need a hostage by then that would 'protect' the chopper."

"I'm not sure Theodor would qualify.... Although that's what we have."

"I know. We must look for a better option."

I started to suspect Arthur might not have a good grip on the gravity of the situation. I, on the other hand, realized it fully. It was most likely the end, but I didn't feel fear, just tension and even relief that today was the day.

We returned to the cell, and Arthur gestured to his men to put gas masks on and prepare for battle. He helped David and me retreat to the corridor and pulled Theodor with us.

Emil's people probably saw the preparations and got the gist. Moreover, I was sure Emil didn't believe for a second that I would come out with my hands raised. He knew me too well. For whatever reason, they started firing long before the twenty-minute limit's expiry.

As Arthur expected, they threw gas grenades through almost all the windows of the second floor, and then sent an assault team in. One or two grenades hit the bars on the windows and didn't get through, but those that did were enough to render me, David, and probably Theodor unconscious. I conked out with the hope that it would be Arthur who'd update me on how it went and with unspoken goodbyes to my kids and Masha.

***

We were dealing with professionals as good as Arthur's men. Arthur had gotten to know Emil's chief of security, who was a retired commander of the British SAS special ops, experienced and professional, on a par with Arthur.

First, they tried to storm the building. Arthur and his men were hidden behind the corridor walls, not even attempting to shoot from the windows. Instead, they concentrated on guarding the stairwell.

In such a small space, the overwhelming number of attackers wasn't much of a disadvantage. Arthur and his team held out for a quarter of an hour, suffering a few hits, which were deflected by their bulletproof vests, and one of his men lost a pinkie from shrapnel. The attackers must've lost a couple of fighters, since there were at least two bodies visible from the second floor.

After the second unsuccessful attempt resulting in losing two more fighters, they probably decided that capturing us alive would take too heavy a toll. They retreated, abandoning their attempts to breech Arthur's defenses. Arthur assumed that something was cooking, and it was still at least twenty minutes before the chopper's arrival.

He acted swiftly, but was almost too late. His men had just started to throw hand grenades from the back windows to soften up the opposition for a break-out, when the building shuddered and started to crumble from two rockets which hit the second floor. More followed. Obviously, Theodor's presence didn't represent that much of a shield.

The hand grenades, thrown by Arthur's men, gave them a moment of relief, long enough for them to grab those of us who were unconscious, jump from the windows, and roll behind the trees of the forest which was just behind the building.

Emil probably received information that our crew was out of the compound, because the rockets stopped pounding it. He must've sent reinforcement to the rear of the building. Here, they didn't have enough open space to fire rockets, so the conflict devolved into a gunfight, which Arthur chose to avoid.

He left me, David, and Theodor lying unconscious, sent two of his men to dash away from the building, which immediately attracted all the enemy fire, and resulted in a hot pursuit. Arthur crawled back into the prison with another fighter. He'd counted on at least a few minutes before the assailants would figure out the diversion.

They changed into the uniforms of two of the fallen enemy soldiers. The uniforms bore a distinct insignia resembling a Maltese flag with some sort of cross in its white part. They put their gas masks back on, then dressed the dead bodies in their clothes, and placed them on the stairs. They lay low for a minute to make sure their move went unnoticed, and then crawled back out into the open to mix with their new team. Coming close, as if from the direction of the forest, to our unconscious bodies, Arthur waved boisterously to other assailants and mimed that his communication was broken. Then he pointed to our fake "bodies".

The soldiers rushed to Arthur, assuming he was one of theirs, to check his findings. Someone must've reported that some others and I had been found. The shots near the building died completely, while at the farther end of the isle, where Arthur's two other men had dug in, the sound of gunfire was still heard.

Fifteen camouflaged fighters, almost identical, with the same insignia and gas masks grouped around our bodies, awaiting their bosses, anticipating praise for a job well done. Emil and his security chief approached.

Before anyone could understand what was going on, two figures, Arthur and his sidekick, darted from the group. Arthur jammed his handgun against Emil's temple, and his subordinate did the same with the Emil's security chief. It all happened in a split second, before anyone had a chance to move. Caught by surprise, no one reacted at first. Only after seeing their chiefs under threat did their men raise their guns.

It wasn't an even standoff, since Arthur had their chief at gunpoint. With a gun jammed against his temple, Emil's legs failed and Arthur had to hold him up to save him from falling. Emil must've realized that if he wanted to win, he'd have to sacrifice his own life. He wasn't a kamikaze, he ordered his men to lower their weapons.

"Order your men, pursuing mine, to retreat," Arthur took charge. "Drop all your weapons into one pile and back off. I won't tolerate any abrupt movement. Anything funny, and these fuckers are bidding this world goodbye."

Arthur couldn't be sure that they dropped all their armament. They might have had hidden weapons, so he didn't lower his gun from Emil's temple even for a second.

When his other two men returned, he ordered them to frisk and tie Emil and the commander, and to revive David and me.

I came around in synch with the chopper rotor's annoying "whopping" right beside us. The noise immediately triggered small explosions of pain in my aching brain.

When Arthur retold what happened after we'd conked out, I was appalled that he'd used me as bait again, but had to give him credit for finding a way out under impossible circumstances.

Despite the acute pain, it was a blissful sight to see, my once dearest friend, Emil, securely tied and being loaded into the chopper. There was not enough room, so we just took him and Alan, his security chief, and left Theodor, still happily asleep, in the company of few dozen angry faces which appeared from under gas masks, still visible for some time as the chopper flew away.

Felix was nowhere around. He must've left even before the fight began.

I missed my friend Emil so much, I couldn't wait for the opportunity to catch up.

Chapter 34 - Catching up

I hoped that the major setback caused by our escape from their trap, plus taking Emil captive, would derail the Seven for some time, so I would have at least few days of peace to chat at my leisure with my new prisoners.

The question was 'where', but apparently Arthur had an answer, because he never asked me, and instead took us all to my jet, and from there to Kiev. If he felt secure there, I felt likewise. After all, Arthur had proven again that he could still extract me unscathed from a hopeless situation.

During the flight, I didn't talk much to Emil. To express my hatred was pointless; he knew that much, and besides, I didn't have a clear understanding yet of where I wanted to take the conversation. He too didn't try to initiate contact.

Only after we settled at Boris' now empty dacha in Koncha-Zaspa—a prestigious recreation district near Kiev—and designated his billiard and wine cellar as a torture chamber, did I finalize in my mind what I wanted from Emil.

In the cellar, the lights were dim and only those hung above the billiard tables, of which Boris had two—one for Russian billiards, and another for pool—were bright. Arthur tied Emil to a chair, which was placed with its back to the billiard table, and stuffed a rag in his mouth. The pool table was right in front of him, but some distance away.

When everything was ready for a chat, I came in with David in a pretty good mood.

"You know, everything here just so Borisish: the cigarette stench, those tasteless naked models posters, the billiard tables that he loved so much. Here I feel it so acutely, and his absence is so striking, because this entire atmosphere is hollow without its owner." I addressed both David and Arthur, but only David would pick up on what I was up to.

"Yeah, this is a palace without a king. A pearl that has no one to host or entertain. I can't really accept that he's dead, and I didn't even have a chance to say my goodbyes when he was buried."

The nostalgia was real and overwhelming. Emil was not important at that moment, and his presence here was alien. To alleviate the sudden change of mood, I had an idea.

"Hey, let's play some pool to Boris's memory! I'm sure he would want us to."

David sighed, but started to arrange the balls on the pool table.

"Listen, Dave, we'll play it a bit differently. Take a look." I hit the white ball too hard, making it ricochet from the triangle of the other balls and hurl over the edge of the table in Emil's direction. Emil recoiled and the ball passed few centimeters from his face, falling to the floor.

"The one who hits this fucker's face wins a point."

"You should play against Arthur, then. He'd love it," David half-joked, but extended the stick to Arthur.

He didn't have to offer it twice. Arthur took the stick, aimed, and hit the ball straight into Emil's face, never bothering to hit another ball on its way. Emil's recoil was futile this time, and he got hit above the eyebrow.

"One to Arthur," I cheered. "But whoever hits the nose gets two."

I aimed and hit Emil's face too, pretty much on the same spot.

"One-one."

The fucker wiggled like a whore on his chair. *This little exercise should prepare him well for later*, I thought. He'd realize that we were not kidding or haggling.

At one point, I really got into it, trying to beat Arthur, who held a seven to five lead.

"You really want to hurt this guy, huh?" David commented, maybe a bit disgusted with the entire enterprise. Emil's face didn't look that handsome after twelve direct hits, but the gag still worked.

"You know, David, for me it's like placebo effect— the ball hits him, but I really feel the pain. This guy symbolizes pretty much what I am. He's my copycat. We are the same, but on different sides of the front line. By torturing him, I mean to torture myself to let my self-loathing vent."

"Ah, I didn't know there was a philosophical side to it. And I don't know how much pain *you've* absorbed, but Emil's face already looks like a bloody mess." David couldn't help being sarcastic.

"He deserves it. And me too, for he and I are just arrogant, naughty, cynical, sons-of-bitches who don't care shit about anything. What we long for is power and dominance, and money as the instrument that brings them."

The dialogue didn't interfere with the game, but Arthur took advantage of the distraction. He led twelve to eight, and I was getting pissed, hitting the ball more and more viciously. If I missed, it landed on the Russian billiard table, but if I hit, it caused a fracture to Emil's facial bones.

"You see, this guy is a devil," I explained to David. "And I'm a very similar devil. The only difference, maybe, is that he has a pedigree, while I'm a slum dog, but other than that, we are like twins. Ah, and this fucker actually helped me to find another distinctive feature."

"Which one is that?"

"That, unlike him, there are prices that I'm not willing to pay and that may be my weakness."

"Hmm." David might've not liked my deeds, but he seemed interested in hearing my ravings.

"Now, we know that we are devils, no doubts there, but you know what our motivation is?"

"What?"

"To be the first devil, the richest devil, the most bad-ass, motherfucking devil. Ken?"

"I see." David didn't argue. He knew my character better than anyone.

"But there is a last mile problem."

"What is that? Isn't it something from telecommunications?"

"Exactly. You know you can bring an awesome network or telecom line through the ocean, pass the hills, the woods, the cities, all the hardships and you are almost there. But then to bring a small piece of a fucking rod representing maybe the tiniest fraction of the distance that you've already covered into the condominium or public building would be harder than what you did covering thousands of miles of laying a cable. And that's because the old networks are so old in the residential buildings, and you can't just replace them, if not all of the end-users want it. On the other hand, it's not economic to lay a separate line to each end-user. And sometimes, even if you want, you can't because other residents object."

"Yeah, I heard that much, but what does it have to do with you and Emil?"

"Ah, I thought you understood the analogy. I'm already richer than seven or eight—or how many there are?—billion people on Earth. It wasn't easy, but I've done it. I'm now at my last mile, man, trying to elbow my way through these cunts who've sat on top of Olympus for decades, if not centuries. And you see how hard it is, how I'm bleeding to get there."

"Wow, Misha, you are a poet. Are you striving to become the most devilish devil of them all?"

"I'm afraid I am, my friend. But to do so, it's not like surpassing billions of unaware laymen, who didn't pose an opposition. Now I'm in the league of these sharks." I nodded in Emil's direction. "And I need to push through those who know how to defend it."

When the score became fifteen to eleven in Arthur's favor, and Emil had stopped trying to dodge the balls, probably because he fainted, David pleaded for us to stop.

"Didn't you want to talk to this guy? He's already missing a few teeth. If you continue, he'll be unable to communicate. What would lovely Ms. Greenberg say when she finds out what you did to her son?" David assumed a comical look of awe and loathing.

"I know, I know." I sighed melodramatically. "That's such a misfortune. I'll tell her he started it. Besides, in comparison to what they did to you, I'm giving him almost a spa treat. And by the way, don't look so smug, David, for you are a devil, too. An accomplice and instigator may even be worse than the main executioner. Why didn't you convince me to live like honest people do back then when we were students? We could've been gardeners or shoemakers now."

"Yeah, right. Get outtahere."

"As for this fella, I'm not sure this blyad will live long enough to see his mother again. But you are right, I wanted to have a word with him."

I shook Arthur's hand to congratulate him on his victory and put the billiard stick away. Now—the main dish.

***

It took few minutes to shake Emil back to reality. Being unconscious must've been better, as he was very unhappy to wake up to the role of target for the billiard balls.

I asked Arthur to take the gag out. As soon as he did, Emil spat on the floor, expelling blood, saliva, and maybe a few teeth.

"That was gross, Emil, couldn't you swallow?"

Emil just murmured something, probably unfriendly.

He didn't like my competition with Arthur, huh? I congratulated myself for that idea.

I wanted to stun him right away before he fully recovered mentally.

"Listen, Emil, you look like piece of shit, and that was just the beginning. You know it wouldn't be a problem to finish you off, and I will if you play stubborn. What I want are the records of your conversations, meetings of the Seven, and others, and then I might let you go free." Seeing doubt on his face, I added, "Yeah, yeah, that's right. Although you or your friends tried to kill me, I don't care much for vengeance. Plus, Ms. Greenberg would be upset, I suppose, as David here said." I made it sound like a joke. "I don't want to kill anymore, as long as I have a better idea, which is to kill your entire organization, but I will if I have to. You may believe me or not, I don't care."

"I don't have any records; I don't know what you are talking about."

I was bluffing, of course. I didn't know about any records, but that was my educated guess, and I was intuitively certain about it. The way he'd recorded a telephone conversation between us made it clear it wasn't his first time doing so.

He'd barely finished his words before I grabbed a billiard stick, broke it over my knee, and brought the sharp end of the splinter to his throat.

"Listen, fucker, I understand very well your psychological type and how you operate. You fucking have materials on everyone, including your friends, that you can use to blackmail them if the need arises. Sure, you do. You keep denying, blyad, you are dead, but not until after Arthur gets to try all his arsenal on you to squeeze every bit of info that I need."

I pressed the sharp end hard enough to raise blood.

His eyes bulged, full of fear. "I mii...ight have a few things."

"Of course, you do. That's my boy. You will now tell me where all of them are hidden and after Arthur brings them to me, I might actually let you go, unless you prefer to stay for my next billiard challenge against Arthur." I laughed in anticipation.

"Sorry, please don't get upset, but you can't get them." He shrank in anticipation of a blow. "They are in our family bank's underground vaults in Bern, and the vault is fingerprint sensitive. If anyone tries to open it other than me, everything inside will be immediately incinerated."

My gut feeling told me that he might not be bullshitting. I started to consider different options of how to bypass the trap.

"Let's seize the bank and bring this son-of-a-bitch with us, or I'll chop off all his fucking fingers and take them with me," Arthur cut in with the most obvious and blatant approach.

"Thanks, Arthur, but maybe we can think of something more subtle than that, and by the way, I'm not sure we can move that freely in Switzerland, after our last visit. I'm sure the personnel working for Millingeri that we released have already updated the authorities."

Arthur quieted, and David chimed in. "Let's bring the vault here."

"What do you mean? It's *built into* the bank." I frowned.

"Well, someone brought it in some time ago, installed it. Whatever's installed, can be uninstalled," Arthur jumped on the idea. "It would be safer than taking Emil there."

Noticing that Arthur was still contemplating different violent operations, I reined him in a bit. "Relax, man, we haven't robbed a bank yet." Recalling, though, that we'd done just that, and recently, I added, "Well, not in a traditional way anyway, so I hope we can deal with it somehow without guns and your cutthroats."

"Here, Emil, call your mother, your bank's chairman, or whoever you want and tell them to deliver the vault to Ukraine. If they need to dismantle the building to do it, you have my permission. I'll make sure it makes it through the border." I gave him my cell phone, then took it back again after a second thought. "Hey, Arthur, do we have a spare Russian or Belarusian SIM card that we haven't used?" I thought using my regular Ukrainian cell number would give away too much information about our location.

Once Arthur assembled a phone with a new number, I gave it to Emil. "Don't spit your blood on it. If you say or hint where you are, you won't live five seconds. Understood?"

He nodded.

"Make the call."

And he did.

His family must've valued the lousy snob a little more than Theodor, because the vault arrived. I had an undercover observer dispatched to Bern to supervise the entire procedure from afar, and he reported that the bank went through a lot of trouble extracting the vault, putting it into a container, and having it hauled by truck from Switzerland to Ukraine, but they did it, meticulously and diligently, with German efficiency. We were all eager to see what was in it.

Chapter 35 - The Vault and The Revolt

Along with the vault came a note from her Excellency, Viscountess Greenberg, which read, "Misha, please, let my boy go."

What a smart lady she was, to understand that threats wouldn't do any good. Her polite manner would play much better on the strings of my heart. Maybe she, as opposed to her colleagues and offspring, saw some hidden kindness in my soul. I always suspected I had one, but never thought anyone would notice.

I was inclined to satisfy her request, but it depended on her son's behavior. If he gave me what I wanted, I just might release the clown.

***

Since I was busy with arrangements for my final clash with the Seven, I didn't see Emil for several days. I made sure that Arthur understood not to hurt him too much, but on the other hand, not to let him feel like he was at a recreation resort. I probably needed to be more specific, because Arthur had already shot Emil's chief of security twice in each arm, claiming that by doing so, he prevented him from reaching for the guard's gun, swearing that he saw Alan's arm moving towards the holster. I didn't buy that, but rather attributed it to Arthur's overzealous approach. I allowed him to beat Emil up, but not too much, since we'd already battered him with the billiard balls.

"This is your moment of glory," I told Emil when they brought the vault into Boris' dacha, and finally left it in the main hall after few unsuccessful attempts to squeeze it down the stairs to the cellar. Emil didn't look too good. I didn't think Arthur had beaten him much, rather our billiard spree was still showing on his face.

He didn't say shit, so I reiterated, "You open this vault, fucker, otherwise that's it, finito. Give me some good stuff, and I'll call it Emileaks in your honor or Emilgate. Which one sounds better?"

He eyed me angrily, still silent.

"Are you upset, Emil? Because I don't want you to deal with the vault when you are upset." I made to kick him in the groin, but stopped my leg a millimeter short of hitting him. He doubled over, trying to save his balls.

"Want a real one?"

He shook his head.

"Listen, Emil, here's your chance. You open the fucking vault, I don't like to repeat myself, and if what I need is inside, I let you live. You have the word of a barbarian mobster, or whatever you think of me, but that's what you got. Anything goes wrong, I'm not gonna ask why, I just shoot your fucking brains out.

Now, say: 'Misha, I'm gonna open the fucking vault.'
Say it!"

I took the gun that Arthur gave me and played with it, waiting for Emil's reaction.

"I'll open the vault."

"Good, let him approach," I ordered Arthur's guys.

I'd already made up my mind about his fate.

The vault was a fairly large cube: about two-by-two-by-two meters, and I could probably place Emil in it and send it back to his mommy after we were done.

Emil approached and put his entire palm into the special cavity on the right side of the vault's front door. After a few seconds, the digital screen came alive flashing a green light. Emil entered a code, we heard a *click*, and he opened the door. It looked smooth and simple.

"Get in first," I instructed, just in case there was some sort of trap, and then followed in his steps.

It was more like a small storage room with shelves on both sides and the back wall. It was pretty well-organized except for a few items that must've fallen during transportation. The shelves were three-quarters full. Some contained boxes with documents, two were filled with DVD and audio discs, and another had three cardboard boxes of video and audio cassettes. Obviously Emil's recordings went a long way back. We also found smaller boxes with exquisite jewelry and precious stones, which I examined casually. For me, the really precious items were the documents and records.

Looking at the boxes and piles of discs, records, tapes, cassettes, and flash memory sticks, I understood that it would take me weeks to hear or watch everything myself. I didn't have that much time. I wasn't sure who was getting the upper hand in my contest with M7, so I needed to strike a powerful and decisive blow right away.

I'd ordered someone to take Emil back to the room where we held him, only to call him back a minute or two after he left.

"Err... Emil, you didn't keep a catalog or something, eh?"

Emil pointed to his head with his finger. *Good boy!* He wanted to believe that I would let him go, and had decided to do anything to speed up the process.

"You must show me where Millingeri is shagging a sheep first."

I didn't believe it, but he started to rummage through the videotapes.

"Really, you have something like this?" I was utterly surprised—it was just a joke.

"No."

"So why the fuck are you wasting your time and mine, blyad?" I was getting angry again.

"You told me to look, so I thought I'd at least make an effort."

"You're a moron, you know that? You need to show me the records that contain cartel arrangements, planning, your organization's meetings, bribes to politicians and functionaries." I assumed a business-like tone.

"If I were you, I wouldn't touch the latter, because you would have a huge number, much larger than you can even imagine, of politicians against you."

Emil was right of course, but the decisions were mine to make, not his.

"I want to see those too and then decide!"

"Fine." Emil went among the boxes here and there, occasionally taking out different media, looking at the abbreviations and putting some stuff aside. Some bore dates as early as the seventies. The records probably even preceded Emil's time and must've been recorded by someone else.

After making a few piles, Emil formed a much smaller one. "That should be enough for now."

"Add what you have on me there," I ordered.

He leaned over and extracted another small box from one of the lower shelves.

"Thanks, my man, you've made my task much easier. You've done a great service to mankind. Do you wanna switch sides and publish all this stuff yourself?" I was curious whether Emil felt any kind of remorse.

He laughed angrily and answered with an evil smile. "I'm not sure you would want this published after you watch and hear what you've got."

My curiosity rose a notch. I ordered him out and asked Arthur to send someone to bring the matching equipment for the variety of tapes, discs, cassettes, and files. Arthur didn't disappoint. He had almost every antique that we needed at hand.

***

The arrangements didn't take long because Arthur had set up an impromptu video salon when customs advised him that the truck had crossed into Ukraine. I asked David to step out for a second, and inserted a flash stick with an "MV", my initials, sticker on it. I wanted to be alone while watching it.

Motherfucker! Of course the entire orgy scene at his yacht had been recorded. I suspected as much. Other than that, there were three or four telephone conversations that didn't contain anything too incriminating, except for the one already aired. That seemed to be it. It was a good thing we'd only known each other for only for a few months.

I called David back in and we eagerly immersed ourselves into the other records.

Shocked and aghast at first, we eventually settled into our task to the point that we simply couldn't stop. We watched and heard and shared thoughts, spending the entire night rummaging through Emil's stuff.

The overall picture we pieced together was sensational, overwhelming, and unheard of. Some records connected directly to top news events as well as economic happenings, and encompassed almost fifty years. Invading countries based on false intelligence, financing guerilla fighters turning against their masters, coups, political blackmail, misspending of public funds and outright corruption—there was plenty of everything. In most cases, we didn't even need to search the web to recall the situation to which these conversations related. The evidence collected, although some related to legitimate business transactions, was sufficient to indict many of the incumbents involved in bribery, election rigging, cartelization, fraud, election bribery, misconduct in election financing, revealing state secrets and classified information to persons having no clearance, and much more than that. Some seemingly neutral lines, I was almost certain, were disguises and stood for more grave felonies, involving murder and theft. But these were in coded language.

And who were involved? That was the most interesting part. I didn't have much doubt about the Seven, as its members were the superstars, but I was surprised again and again how high their influence went, and often in equal degree to seemingly implacable political, national, and military rivals.

These guys controlled everything, every fucking thing that was important to them! At first, I didn't even get it right. It wasn't that their connections went so high, it was that they appointed or procured appointments to the highest positions in many of the superpowers and their satellites. *Is this world corrupted or what!* I felt somewhat mollified over the small, innocent corruption that I created back home. Mine was kindergarten, theirs was super league.

The magnitude of their network was so enormous that any piece revealed and brought to light by a nosy journalist was never attributed as belonging to anything much larger than that particular episode. Many saw this or that part of the picture, but no one saw THE WHOLE PICTURE.

When we finally finished at 7:00 a.m., I refused another coffee and suggested we take a quick nap. I needed some time to digest it all.

***

I opened my eyes at 10:00 a.m., still groggy after the sleepless night.

I asked for some coffee and barely managed to wake David up.

"Hey, Dave, no time to sleep, wake the fuck up, man."

He turned his back to me. Only when I was about to spill the boiling coffee pot on him to augment my futile verbal attempts, did he finally make an effort to sit up.

I didn't know whether it was true or false, but I had a sense of urgency. My, or more correctly, *our* — along with my new colleagues — stand-off with the Seven was at a fragile equilibrium, and besides that, the vault's trip to Ukraine might've become known to a wider range of interested folks. They might not know what was inside (and I doubted whether Emil's mother even knew), but they could guess, and might well try to prevent any negative consequence from its opening.

When David came to his senses, and after we had a third cup of coffee with apple strudel baked by Boris' cook, who was happy to have someone to cater to, I wanted to hear David's opinion.

"We can't possibly disclose all this, Misha," David said wearily. "I'm not talking even about the danger, because it'll probably be your death warrant. But there is a huge opportunity. Imagine, you'd be holding the entire world by the balls. You can't blow that. That's your dream, bro. You can supersede all those fuckers and call the shots from now on. That's the highest peak, the Everest, the ultimate number one position, something you've craved all your life. And you're gonna blow it for what? For some insubstantial ideals, for the greater good? Come on, Michael."

"You, of all men, David? Or should I call you, Brutus? I thought you would support me in my righteous quest." I was truly surprised that he had backed out. Usually we thought in unison and our motives coincided. "If I just replace them and leave the entire system as it is, then I don't change shit, man. How don't you see that? It'll just be a constant struggle for who sits on top of the pyramid. I'll hold out for a while, but then someone else will replace me and it'll be the same all over again. If we think this shit is flawed, we might as well dismantle it for good. It's no good to have that much power in the same hands for long periods. It brings stagnation, perverted self-preservation instinct. Why do you think they sometimes limit the number of terms that one can hold the position of president, for example? To avoid the possible usurpation of power, because power is addictive and destructive in the long run. Whoever has it, wants more."

"Funny that you say that, because that's exactly what my sister wrote in her book," David commented gleefully.

That was another surprise.

"Huh? But you told me she writes erotica. Sorry, I haven't yet read the book you gave me. I even thought it was modeled on real life: a gigolo brother and a smut-writing sister."

"Yeah, but it's political erotica. Not like a poor secretary or assistant sucking some president's dick, but like leaders fucking their people in the ass, virtually and literally."

"Sounds like a good book, educational. I wonder why nobody wanted to publish it. Anyway, let's disseminate this shit, David. I hope your resistance is not entirely sincere. We used to be decent people once." I wanted him convinced.

"Never, don't deceive yourself, Mr. Scammer." David was right, of course, but you could always change for the better, couldn't you?

"So, you are against it, right? And you call me a scammer? You know well that business always has the element of deceit in it, of selling an illusion. The deceit is in everything concerning moneymaking to greater or lesser degree. If you look for investors or partners, you sell them the idea of a profitable business and your conviction that it'll work. But do you know that it will? You don't know shit, but if you say that, nobody's gonna give you money. But once you receive it, you'll do everything to make the idea work. Now, if I sell a product, I'll try to have the best possible promotion for it to get people to pay that extra dollar or so above the cost to make my profit. It doesn't matter whether my product is good and worth the money. What matters is its image, how it's perceived. Take the shaving industry or that of perfumes. They pay dozens of millions to superstars to convince you to pay ten, twenty times more for their product, to make mega profits. You're right, I've excelled in deceit, fraud, raiding, abusing, and manipulating the system, but we now have a chance to redeem all of that, man." I didn't know why I was so passionate about it myself.

"Since when did you start to worry about redemption? Are you gonna run for president now, or what?" David, in his turn, still hoped to dissuade me. "Instead, you should think about the following: if you release this info and the Seven survive, not as an organization, but as individuals, you'll have an endless war on your hands. The materials we have are enough to implicate many politicians as well as some of the Seven members, but I'm sure not all of them. Those who don't get prosecuted and incarcerated will never let you be. Now you have so much dirt on each and every one of them that you can actually demand what you want and I doubt they would disobey."

David sincerely believed in what he was saying. I saw it in his face.

"You know what, you might have a point, and I might change my initial plan a bit, but let's release just a little bit at first. I want those fuckers to understand that I'm serious, and I wanna see what happens." A plan began to hatch in my mind.

"Do what you think. You are stubborn like a mule anyway," David relented. "Are you letting Emil go?"

"Hmmm... I'm not going to execute him, but... I might keep him just a little longer. I have an idea that

I want to chew on a bit more. I might need Emil handy."

We finished breakfast quickly. I wanted to launch the first portion of the "Emileaks."

Using the advice of a new computer geek recruited by Arthur who wasn't involved in our attack on the banks, we registered a few unidentified email accounts, uploaded two episodes that I'd chosen to the cloud, and selected five investigative reporters that I'd handpicked. One worked for a leading New York newspaper, another for its LA competitor, two more were UK journalists, and the last one — an Australian semi-star reporter.

The first episode involved informal conversations between a prime minister of one of the European countries and two members of the Seven, and clearly proved the prime minister had awarded sea shelf oil exploration licenses to a company belonging to the Seven through a rigged tender and few buffer layers.

Another episode contained a record of a senior U.S. official promising to extend his office's full influence and support in order to promote a huge armament shipment, in exchange for a specific amount donated to the election campaign of his party's presidential candidate.

Both episodes related to recent events, and were potent enough to stir quite a scandal.

Five emails were sent via the incognito emails to the reporters with short description of what it was about, and with a link to the info we'd placed in the cloud, along with access details.

I bit my nails, periodically checking the web for a trace of a news explosion.

I spotted it in just six hours. The Australian beat them all. Although unrelated to Australia, it went out on the front page under the title "Alleged Corruption in Awarding Recent Oil Exploration License." And further down the same page, "Questionable Donations to Candidates in Recent U.S. Presidential Campaign Might Require a Probe".

That's my boy! In Australia, they rarely had something of global importance, so he must've figured that it was his golden opportunity.

In a span of twenty-four hours, the news had been reproduced virtually around the globe, except where the editors-in-chief traced the connection to their shareholders and banned airing the story. It snowballed into interviews, accusations, explanations, and all the usual stuff. Corporations and officials directly involved kept a suspicious silence; their representatives announced only that they denied the content and authenticity of the produced materials, and would seek remedies against the media.

The sensation peaked, resulting in the onset of investigations into both affairs, and started to die down towards the fifth and sixth days after the initial release.

That was a satisfactory result. I consulted with David as we both watched the news and provided a TV to Emil, so he'd know we meant business. We figured there was a good chance that those involved would get what they deserved, unless some patrons or protégées jumped in to save their asses and keep everything hushed.

***

I prepared a calendar plan for further releases and asked that Emil be brought to me.

I handed him the schedule, starting from one week's time on and explained. "My dearest Emil, it's time for you to go. I can't host you any more, as you've got a mission to carry out. Remember what I told you about a cap on wealth accumulation, that I think should be appropriate?"

He nodded, surprised, recalling our conversation while on coke in Ibiza.

"Well... they say that one should always start with himself and serve as an example to others, so I decided to implement my theory on—" I paused deliberately, "You and your colleagues. You know how similar we are, you are almost my twin, so starting with you is like starting with myself, heh-heh."

Emil stood with his mouth open, unaware of what I meant.

"I've made a quick calculation and have come to the conclusion that one hundred million bucks is a sufficient amount beyond which it becomes ineffective to hold the wealth stashed away in bank accounts with no useful purpose. So you go back to your friends and tell them that I give them a week's time to go public and launch a program for donating their money to those in need and to sell assets that I will designate, and again donate the proceeds to the needy. And also to promote legislation in the U.S. and Europe on the wealth accumulation cap."

The look on Emil's face was such that, were he in charge, he would have called a psychiatrist for me right away.

I continued, nonchalantly, though.

"I have a pretty comprehensive list of your assets and I will form something like a private antitrust service for the bunch of ugly bastards that you've formed. You will have six months to wrap it all up. To anyone who disagrees—I won't hesitate to release all the info and resources which you've so helpfully provided."

He muttered something like, "You're crazy" and "No one would agree."

I didn't care. I wanted the entire plan explained properly.

"What you've mentioned might be their first reaction. The second will be anger that you've given me such explosive materials. I don't envy you when you have to explain what I've gotten with your help. But eventually, maybe after a few days or weeks, I hope they will appreciate my offer, as I let them go without paying the price for all the atrocities they are responsible for, and even allow them to keep that one hundred million. That's a very reasonable offer. They come out clean and wealthy for a modest price. They can find some comfort in that the billions they donate will probably boost the economy in general, because so much private money will be injected into it that it will have a positive, beneficial effect."

"You are an idiot. I've always suspected that, but if that's what you want, fine, let me go and I'll pass your message to the others." Emil's desire to escape was so great, he would agree to anything.

"Good boy. Here's the phone number where I want to hear Millingeri's voice in exactly one week." I gave him the note with my new Ukrainian cell phone on it. "If it doesn't happen, I go on with the publications in accordance with the schedule. As you can see, the first release is dedicated to Millingeri bribing the Bundestag deputy president. That's something small for an aperitif."

I beckoned Arthur's guy standing behind Emil's back and asked him to take the handcuffs off him.

After he did, Emil turned to leave.

"One more thing, Emil, that you should know. I have carefully copied everything you gave me and have a backup of ten very influential people holding the copies with clear instruction to disclose everything at once, if something happens to me. Just in case you were thinking of a violent resolution to our standoff."

He hesitated for a second, but decided to spit it out before leaving. "I'll tell you another thing that you are overlooking here, my dear, stupid friend. Let's assume you hold us by the balls and you are a fucking king, right, and we don't do anything to you. But imagine what happens when you go with this ludicrous idea to your fellow Ukrainian or Russian or Georgian oligarchs? You would say: 'Hey, guys, it's time to give up on what you've stolen all these years'. Ha-ha-ha. Do you think they'd applaud? I have a feeling you won't live beyond the second or third sentence of your little motivational speech. I believe you'll be hung on a pole at some central square one sunny day, Vorotavich." He forced an evil smile onto his battered face.

"Let me worry about that. Get the fuck outta here." He was pissing me off.

He left, and I felt some kind of void spreading in my stomach. He was right, of course. If a few in the West had the decency to think of donating most of their wealth, for my fellow gangster-oligarchs, it was unheard of.

I felt empty. That was my final move. Would it work?

As the days passed, I became progressively more nervous, sleepless, and irritated. David poured some oil on the fire by mocking me for releasing Emil and offering such a bizarre deal.

"Did you really think they'd go for it? You know those rich people. They're more likely to commit suicide than to give up on a penny. Come on, now."

"Shut the fuck up," I would yell at him, getting even more nervous. The call came earlier than the deadline, but I'd already lost my temper.

My Italian 'friend' didn't wait until the time expired. He called two days before the deadline.

He simply told me, "Misha, fuck you, *and* your deal," and hung up.

David was right. It was silly of me to look for idealistic solutions with ruthless magnates who cherished money above anything else.

That meant war.

I was disappointed, but when you give an ultimatum, you should be prepared to use the threat if it wasn't heeded.

Epilogue

I set things in motion, uploading a large amount of material to the cloud and selecting a wider list of recipients. Being meticulous about the timeline, I cast nervous glances at my watch, waiting for the time to expire while pouring David and myself another single malt.

Biting my nails in anger and disappointment, I counted the last ten seconds aloud. I still had a tiny hope that I would not have to do it, and they would reconsider their refusal. But nothing happened. Having no other choice, I pressed 'Send' and pushed myself away from the computer screen.

Only ten minutes had passed when my mobile rang. This time it was Ms. Greenberg.

"Oh, Michael, have you already published the materials?" For some reason, it sounded as if Juliette hoped I had.

"As I said, I would. Did you have doubts?"

"No, it's just these are such unfortunate times for all of us! Only this morning, Mr. Millingeri was found dead. He either committed suicide or had a heart attack. What a disaster!" Ms. Greenberg, as always, sounded *almost* sincere.

Yeah right.... Suicide, huh? I couldn't help thinking, nevertheless being surprised by the news.

Since the materials I'd just released related to Millingeri, I could understand now why Greenberg wasn't that upset about it.

She continued in the meantime. "You know, we here discussed again what you'd suggested and we find your solution pretty fair. You didn't happen to publish hmm... other parts of Emil's private collection yet, did you?"

"Other parts? No, ma'am, I haven't published them yet. I'm glad you found my approach reasonable. I thought it would be an amicable solution too. Once again, it's nice to do business with you, Ms. Greenberg." I doubted whether she'd personally done anything bad to me, so there was no reason to display enmity towards her. *Ha!* I thought I read her cards— she wanted to blame everything on Millingeri, comfortably dead, as once they'd wanted to blame everything on *me*. I would have bet anything that my assumption was correct.

"Err... Michael. There is a small question that I wanted cleared. The one hundred that you mentioned, it's personal, right? Not for the entire family?"

"Well, now that you mention it, I meant the entire family, of course, but, if you prefer, we can allow each family member to keep fifty percent of the limit, but I'd hate to find out that your family grew instantaneously in numbers, ma'am."

"Oh, how can you say something like that? It's very fair that you take that into consideration. You know our family—it has only seven members."

I didn't know the family that well, but I thought they had only *three* members. "Five."

"Only two hundred and fifty million for such a big family?" Ms. Greenberg attempted to sound upset. "I think I'll need to sell few mansions to finance our expenses."

I wanted to come back with something sarcastic, but there was no point. "That's the deal, dearest Ms. Greenberg. Do you accept?"

"You are a hard negotiator, Michael, but yes, we do. Please, keep the materials safe and let us work everything out."

***

Six months later, the Seven became insignificant. I'd made a difference! My organization eclipsed some of their power, but I didn't want us to become a cancerous cartel, choking the competition, so we played it clean. Moreover, most of the members agreed that a cap was not that bad of an idea, and we were brainstorming on how to implement it.

I became a deity of sorts. Not many knew, but those who did referred to me mostly as "The one who killed off the Magnificent Seven."

Once everything was arranged, I had a chance to enjoy some peace and quiet, spending more time with Masha and my family.

Ukraine fared poorly, but survived and retained sovereignty over most of its regions.

I felt my missions were accomplished. I could retire, if I had something interesting to do in retirement. Or maybe I could solve some other global problems.

David did ask me, "What's next? You keep neglecting the enjoyment part of being a mega-rich. Buy a new yacht maybe, take your family on around-the-world cruise and I might even convince Jessica that we join you."

"Hmm... Now that you mention Jessica, I'm not sure I'd prefer her company over risking my life again for something worthy. You are just not yourself around her."

I didn't know the answer then, but I was trying to figure it out. To enjoy life, indeed? David, as usually, was right. *Money is just the instrument for achievement of other things, thinks the guy who spent his entire life chasing after the dollars, heh-heh,* I mocked myself. It was never too late to realize that. Maybe I should really put my focus on other things that were available now?

It was nearing the end of the year when Arthur, very relaxed now, asked for some vacation time to spend on a honeymoon with his new love.

"Go for it, man. I hope I need less guarding now."

Arthur lived with his bride in my compound in London.

He'd distracted me from studying the London stock exchange numbers, so I barely paid attention to what he said. After few minutes, it struck me. *Honeymoon? Have I missed the wedding or something?*

I went to Arthur's quarters for clarification. Suzy came out of the side corridor, and with a quick and unexpected move, reached for my neck. I felt a prick, and immediately everything around became sort of unsteady. I staggered forward, towards Arthur's room. The door was open, and Arthur lay on his back, throat cut, blood gushing all over the floor.

Even while fainting into the puddle of blood, I felt surprised more than anything else, as Arthur had always seemed immortal to me.

No, not again, where is Aidan Snow or anyone to save me? I'm a deity now, who would dare?

I fell into the realm of delusion and lost touch with the reality.

Acknowledgements

Many thanks to Carlito Sofer for co-launching my writing career, to all the beta-readers, who provided an insightful feedback, to Al Kalar and Elle, aka L.T., for their editing, to Deranged Doctor Design for a marvelous cover design and to my family for their patience and support.